FATAL BLOW

To Bryan

Best wishes,

FATAL BLOW

BRIAN PRICE

This edition produced in Great Britain in 2023

by Hobeck Books Limited, 24 Brookside Business Park, Stone, Staffordshire ST15 0RZ

www.hobeck.net

ISBN 978-1-913-817-24-2 (pbk)

ISBN 978-1-913-793-23-5 (ebook)

Cover design by Jayne Mapp Design

Printed and bound in Great Britain

Are you a thriller seeker?

Hobeck Books is an independent publisher of crime, thrillers and suspense fiction and we have one aim – to bring you the books you want to read.

For more details about our books, our authors and our plans, plus the chance to download free novellas, sign up for our newsletter at **www.hobeck.net**.

You can also find us on Twitter **@hobeckbooks** or on Facebook **www.facebook.com/hobeckbooks10**.

To all those scientists, commentators, enlightened politicians and campaigners who are striving to convince the venal and wilfully ignorant that climate action is urgent and vital

Note from the Author

This novel is set in the imaginary southern English town of Mexton. It is set approximately nine months after the events described in *Fatal Dose* and refers back to some of them. It can, however, be enjoyed without reading the previous book.

As before, I have telescoped slightly the timescale for the return of DNA and other laboratory results. In real life, shortages of lab space and funds mean that these can take a long time. I have also omitted some of the more boring aspects of police procedure.

Within the text there are fourteen references to Sherlock Holmes stories. If you can find them all, consider yourself a sleuth! They will be published on the Hobeck website and in my newsletter in due course.

Prologue

Karel lifted the barrier and let the sandwich van into the police station car park, unaware that he had only moments to live. He started to wonder why the driver ran out of the car park, instead of ringing the bell for entry, but his musings were cut short by a thunderous roar as the van exploded. He barely had time to register the flash before the blast wave pulped his body, killing him instantly.

A column of orange-brown smoke rose swiftly into the air, quickly followed by black billows as the van's vaporised diesel ignited. Vehicles were overturned and those running on petrol added their fuel to the flames. The back wall of the police station began to collapse and windows were sucked out as the blast wind pulled debris back towards the site of the explosion. A brief, eerie silence was followed by screaming.

Two minutes earlier

On the other side of the building, the incident room was packed. DI Emma Thorpe's colleagues gathered round to wish her well as she began her maternity leave. Detective Superintendent Gorman presented her with an envelope of gift vouchers and made a slightly embarrassing speech, during which he attempted to say he hoped she would be producing another little constable. Unfortunately, he sneezed half way through the last word, which remained incomplete.

'You'll be next,' grinned DC Martin Rowse, nudging DC Mel Cotton, who had never publicly expressed any aspirations to maternity. 'Where's Tom, by the way? I thought he'd be here.'

'He's getting some flowers for the guv from the car. He'll just be a minute.'

The chuckles at Gorman's faux pas were cut off abruptly as the shock wave from the blast ripped through the station. Furniture shifted, glasses fell over and the coffee machine tumbled from the worktop. Light fittings fell from the false ceiling, which bulged ominously. Smoke alarms shrieked. Officers stumbled, windows rattled and acrid, choking smoke poured into the room. And a single thought crashed its way into Mel's brain. Where was Tom? Where the fuck was Tom?

Chapter One

Day 1, Four days later

WITH HALF the police station destroyed, and the remainder unsafe to work in, officers and civilian staff were relocated to whatever premises were available. Some were transferred to the County Police Headquarters, some worked from home, as they did during the pandemic, and DCI Farlowe's Major Crimes team found themselves in some old council offices in central Mexton.

It took two days to remove all the casualties, living and dead, from the ruins of the station. Nineteen people lost their lives, including thirteen police officers, three civilian staff and a prisoner who was en route to the cells when the blast occurred. Some were killed outright, by flying debris or the force of the explosion, while others succumbed later, to blast lung and other internal injuries. Many people suffered life changing damage, and PTSD would become common as the days went on. A solitary cyclist was blown into a concrete lamppost, crushing her torso to pulp, a passing pedestrian was also killed, and four more were injured.

DSup Gorman addressed the detectives assembled in a former council chamber, now converted into an incident room.

'Thank you all for returning to work so soon after this atrocity,' he began. 'I cannot begin to express how outraged I am, and I fully understand the difficulties you faced in coming back to work. Counselling will be available for anyone who wants it, and if you need to work shorter days or take time off, you are free to do so. You will, no doubt, mourn your lost colleagues in your own ways, but there will be a special, non-denominational, memorial service at St Stephen's on Sunday for anyone who would find it comforting. Individual services for those murdered will be held in due course. Before I hand you over to DCI Farlowe, is there any news of DC Ferris's condition? I gather he was quite close to the explosion.'

'DC Mel Cotton is by his bedside, constantly,' said DS Jack Vaughan. 'He's in a medically induced coma at the moment, but they're hoping to wake him up soon. They are still not sure about the extent of his injuries.'

'Thank you, Jack. Please keep me informed. Now get out there and catch these bastards.'

As DSup Gorman left the room, DCI Farlowe stepped forward and introduced a smartly dressed officer who was standing beside him.

'I think most of you know DI Steve Morton, from Counter Terrorism Command. He and some of his colleagues will be based here for the duration and will be supporting our efforts to track down the terrorists. Steve.'

He stepped back as the SO15 officer began to speak.

'First of all, please accept my deepest condolences for the loss of your colleagues. I have been in counter-terrorism for twelve years and this is the worst incident I've dealt with.' His voice trembled slightly. 'There has never been such a lethal attack on police officers in mainland Britain and we will find the perpetrators, whatever it takes. The Home Secretary has authorised extra resources, and we will be liaising with the Security Service and the National Crime Agency. So, to business.

'The bomb consisted of about 200 kilos of ANFO, a mixture of ammonium nitrate, used as fertiliser, and diesel oil. It would have been set off with a stick of gelignite or similar. There are restrictions on who can buy the nitrate, so we need to look at suspicious purchases and reports of thefts from farms and other premises. At the moment we have no intelligence about who's responsible, but...'

'We know fucking well who's behind it,' snarled Jack. 'It's those bastard Albanians we dealt with last year. They shot up the Environment Agency and now they've come for us.'

'You may be right, Jack, but let's not get ahead of ourselves,' said Farlowe. 'We need to keep an open mind and follow the evidence. Already social media is buzzing with theories about Al Qaeda, the IRA and God knows who else. We mustn't fall into a similar trap.'

Jack scowled.

'Anyway,' continued Farlowe, 'we need good, solid

police work and information-gathering. The operation's name is Fieldmouse. I'll be leading on this, and we are expecting a new DI, to provide maternity cover for DI Thorpe.

'Some of our colleagues from County Headquarters have been doing door-to-doors in the area, and signboards are up in the streets asking people who may have seen something to contact us. So, Jack, can you co-ordinate the tasks? We need ANPR and CCTV trawls of the area, focussing on the van. Forensics may be able to recover the VIN, so check with DVLA and trace it. Get people canvassing for witnesses who may have been in the street or nearby buildings at the time – build on the work County have already done. Talk to local informers – did anyone pick up rumours before or after the event? The Chief Constable has called a press conference for this afternoon, asking for the public's help. Anything to add, Steve?'

'A couple of points. The NCA is looking at possible OCG involvement. I share Jack's suspicions, but we have no evidence that Albanians are involved, as yet. We are also considering right-wing extremists, since you took down a group of them not so long ago, but that looks less likely. DS Angela Wilson and I will be working in an office just along the corridor. Please drop in and see us at any time. We will also be drafting in a couple of DCs to help with the foot-slogging. I'm sure you'll make them welcome. Thank you.'

'I know you don't need a pep talk,' said Farlowe, 'so I'll leave you to it. Don't hesitate to come to me if you have any problems. Oh, and get a decent coffee machine for the incident room. I'll pay for it.'

No-one joked or bantered while Jack allocated roles.

The atmosphere of grief, coupled with a ferocious determination to avenge their colleagues, left no room for levity as the team of grim-faced officers set about their tasks. And in an office, in another town, a devastated individual planned revenge.

Chapter Two

THE PRESS BRIEFING room quietened down when the Chief Constable, accompanied by DSup Gorman and the Chief Press Officer, entered. Journalists looked up from their phones, cameras began to hum and all eyes were on the platform, behind which the force's insignia had been draped with black cloth.

'Ladies and gentlemen,' began the Chief, 'it is with enormous sadness that I have to report that Friday's atrocity cost the lives of thirteen police officers, three of our civilian staff and three other civilians, one of whom was in our custody. In addition, several dozen people, inside and outside the police station, suffered injuries, some of them life-changing. Before I continue with this press conference, we will have a minute's silence in memory of those people so brutally murdered. Please stand.'

When the journalists had resumed their seats, the Chief Constable made a statement before taking questions.

'We need the public's help tracking down these evil

people, and we hope you will be able to assist us in getting the message across. Anyone who has any information should call the phone number on the screen behind me, or email us at the address below it. They should not, repeat not, approach anyone they suspect of being involved, and nor should they speculate on social media about specific individuals.'

Then the questioning began, and the usual biases of the journalists were evident.

'Is it Islamic terrorists?' asked a reporter from the *Daily Mail*.

'At the moment, we do not know who is behind the attack,' the Chief replied. 'Nobody has claimed responsibility. Obviously, we will be following all relevant lines of investigation, but it would be inappropriate to speculate.'

'Is it the gang you arrested last year?' asked Jenny Pike, from the *Mexton Messenger*.

'As I've said, Ms Pike, we are looking at many possibilities.'

'Is MI5 involved?' asked the *Guardian*.

'We are working with a number of other organisations, including the National Crime Agency and Counter Terrorism Command. But, as you should know, we do not comment on the activities of the security services.'

The questioning dwindled as it became clear that the police had little information to share.

'Thank you for coming, ladies and gentlemen,' said the Chief, winding the proceedings up. 'My office will provide you with details of a planned memorial service, but there is one thing I would urge. The bereaved families have suffered enough. Please leave them alone, to grieve in private, in the name of common decency. Thank you.'

Mel Cotton sat by her fiancé's bedside, her heart in pieces. She had barely left his side since he had been returned from the surgery that had amputated what was left of his hand. The doctors couldn't say whether his brain had been damaged, but as there was some swelling, they had put him in a medically induced coma in the hope that things would improve. His face, cut by flying glass, was bandaged and tubes supplied air and nourishment, while another drained away his urine. The muted beeps and hisses from medical equipment were the only sounds in the room, apart from Mel's frequent bursts of sobbing. Was it worth it? she asked herself. Was this bloody job fucking worth it?

She knew she needed sleep and food, other than the half-eaten sandwiches that found their way in to the rubbish bin, moments after being opened. But sleep had been a stranger for some time, and recurrent nightmares involving sharp blades drained what sleep she had of proper rest. Perhaps she should get back to work and go after the bastards who had done this. She was no use to Tom here, after all. So, she stood up, stretched her cramped spine and gathered her things. She kissed Tom on his one exposed cheek and whispered to him, 'We'll get them, my love. We'll get them.'

Chapter Three

Day 2

'ABSOLUTELY FUCK ALL. That's what we've got,' raged Jack at the morning briefing, ignoring the DCI's aversion to swearing. 'The van belonged to a sandwich delivery firm and was hijacked after it left their premises. The driver had his throat cut and was dumped in a ditch. No-one saw it happen. The person who left it in the car park was picked up by our CCTV and appears to be a fit, stocky male. His face was obscured and we've no idea where he went. Obviously, there were no forensics on the wreckage, and we haven't been able to trace the ammonium nitrate. Local grasses have been unusually co-operative but have heard nothing. Has anybody got any good news? Anything?'

'Radio Mexton did a phone in on crime, last night,' said Martin. 'The DJ contacted us this morning. Apparently, a caller tried to say that "the police deserved it for poking their noses in", but he was clearly very drunk so they didn't let him on air. Someone in the background told him to shut up, apparently, and cut the call. The station didn't record him either.'

'How does that help us?' asked Farlowe.

'It doesn't, much, apart from the fact that he had an eastern European accent. The station gave us the number he called from, but it's a burner.'

'OK. Ask them to record him if he calls again. We may get something from voice analysis.'

'Already done, guv.'

The briefing was interrupted as Mel entered the room, looking as though she hadn't slept in years.

'Mel!' called Jack. 'You don't have to be here, you know. You're on compassionate leave.'

Mel shrugged. 'I'd rather be working than moping.'

'How's Tom?' asked DC Trevor Blake, his arm in a sling.

'He's recovering from the surgery. They couldn't save his hand. A flying piece of metal from a window frame smashed it to bits. He'll have a few scars on his face and may be permanently deaf. We'll see. They're keeping him in a medically induced coma for a while, to protect his brain.'

Mel's efforts to hold back the tears were obvious.

'Anyway, the wedding's postponed. Again. No idea when we can reschedule. And I know he'll be desperate to keep his job.'

'As long as he can pass the fitness test, he'll be OK,' reassured Farlowe. 'Give him all our best wishes. We've had a whip round, so think about what we can get him.'

'Thanks. Will do. But I need to be doing something useful, here. What have you got for me?'

Farlowe thought for a moment.

'I'll keep you off the bomb investigation for the moment. You're too personally involved. 'I'd like you to...'

'We're all personally involved,' interrupted Mel. 'I need to help catch these shits. It's all I want to do.'

'I appreciate that, Mel. But I want you to do something else. We've had reports in from the pathologist and the forensic anthropologist on those remains found in your garden. They took ages as more urgent cases pushed them to the back of the queue and Dr Fox, the forensic anthropologist, has been on extended leave. Take a look at them and see if we should open an investigation. If the bones are more than seventy years old, we're not interested.'

'OK, guv,' said Mel, seething inside but avoiding a public row with her boss. 'I'll get on to it right away.'

Stefan Paweski was nervous. Since being attacked by protection racketeers and nearly having his shop burned down, he had been on full alert for threats. Much like an experienced police officer, he could tell when something wasn't quite right. And the white van that had cruised past his shop four times in the past hour looked definitely wrong. He waited until it was stopped by the traffic lights, sprinted after it and yanked open the door. Two men, with baseball caps pulled down over their eyes, stared at him in shock.

'What the fuck do you think you're doing?' Stefan shouted. 'Are you planning to rob me?'

There was no answer, but a fist caught him in the face, breaking his nose. He stumbled back as the van accelerated away, leaving the smell of burning rubber behind it. Holding a paper towel against his face, he cursed and walked slowly back to his shop, thankful that he had noted down the vehicle's registration number the last time it cruised past. He pulled out a crumpled business card from a pile beside the till and dialled the phone number on it.

'DC Cotton speaking. How can I help?' the familiar voice said.

'It's Stefan, DC Cotton. Stefan Paweski,' he mumbled, the damage to his nose making it hard for him to speak. 'Something odd has been happening.'

'What do you mean?'

'The same van has been driving past my shop all afternoon. When I caught up with it and challenged the men inside, one of them broke my nose. I'm scared it's that gang again. Can you help?'

'I'm sorry to hear this, Stefan. You're right to be worried. Do you have a description of the men? Did they say anything?'

'I didn't really see their faces. They both wore caps. But I did get the van's number.'

He recited it.

'That's brilliant. Hang on a sec while I check it on the computer.'

'That's odd,' said Mel, a few minutes later. 'That number belongs to a pink Fiat registered to a woman who lives in Sunderland. Are you sure you got it right?'

'Of course. It was a white van, a Nissan, and the plate was clean and clear.'

'Then I think you should probably be worried. The plate must have been cloned, and that's usually done with criminal intent. I'll log this on our system as an assault and

I'll ask our patrols to keep an eye open for the van. I'm sorry I can't do more, but, as you probably realise, we're even more short-staffed than usual. Don't hesitate to ring us again if anything else happens. And be careful.'

'Yes. Thank you. I will,' Stefan replied, mentally calculating whether he could employ security guards at all five of his Mexton Minimarts.

Stefan's fears were realised when he was dragged from his bed in the early hours of the next morning and told that one of his shops was on fire.

Chapter Four

Day 3

THE SMELL of smoke lingered in the morning air as Mel stopped the police car a few metres from the outer cordon of police tape.

'You know what this is, don't you?' she said, gazing at the blackened ruins of Stefan Paweski's Minimart.

'What?' replied Martin.

'Those bloody Albanians. They're taking revenge for the arrests and for him not paying up last time. It would be bad for business to let it go. People wouldn't take them seriously.'

Her suspicions were confirmed when Stefan rushed over to the car, brandishing a brick to which a note was taped.

'Look at this, DC Cotton. It was thrown through the window of another of my shops. Those bastards are back.'

In crude capitals the note said, 'Twenty percent tax. We will collect. No police tricks.'

Mel reached for an evidence bag into which Stefan dropped the brick.

'I'll get this to forensics,' she said, while filling in the label and sealing the bag. 'I doubt that they'll find anything, but you never know. We'll need a sample of your DNA again, for elimination. Is that OK?'

Stefan nodded dejectedly.

'Let me clear this mess up and I'll come down to the station. You were right. I was worried, but I never expected this. What the fuck should I do now?'

'We can give you some advice on crime prevention, but much of it's common sense. Shutters on all the shops, not just a few, and more CCTV. Keep away from dark alleys, check under your car in the morning, try not to be alone in the shop. It's terrifying, I know. I wish we could help more but we just don't have the resources.'

'OK. I have friends. I will be ready for them. Next time they'll wish they'd...'

'Can I stop you there, Stefan? You can defend yourself using reasonable force. That's OK. But you cannot start a war. And, please, don't carry weapons. If you carry a baseball bat in the streets, intending to hit someone, you will be arrested for carrying an offensive weapon.'

'That's bullshit. Total fucking bullshit. They're trying to destroy my livelihood. What am I supposed to do? There's no police on the streets, and it was an hour before anyone turned up last night.'

'Look. I feel for you. You've already been through a lot.

I'll talk to control and ask them to prioritise any calls from you. I'll see if we can get patrols to drive past your shops a bit more often. You have my card so you can contact me, too. We're desperately overstretched at the moment, but we'll do what we can.'

Stefan looked far from mollified as he returned to his shop. Mel approached the senior fire officer who was supervising the scene.

'I take it that was arson?'

''Well, the accelerant didn't pour itself under the door, did it?' he replied sarcastically. 'Sorry, I didn't mean to be rude. We'll carry out a proper investigation when the site's safe, but, yes, I'm sure. We found no human remains, so that's a relief. We'll let you know when your SOCOs can attend.'

'Thanks,' said Mel. 'I'll leave you to it.'

'How's Tom?' asked Martin, as they drove away.

Mel grimaced. 'Not good. They woke him from the coma yesterday and they don't think he's suffered any serious brain damage. But he can't hear much, and he'll need a prosthetic hand, I guess. The psychological damage could be fucking horrendous.' She wiped her eyes with her sleeve. 'I can't stop thinking about it. If only we hadn't left those sodding flowers in the car. I can see why people in the Job turn to drink. Or religion. You probably understand better than anyone, because of the stabbing, but, honestly, I feel so fucking alone.'

Martin rubbed at the scar where Dwight Marlow's blade had nearly taken his life.

'You're not, mate. We're all rooting for Tom, and for you.

This shit could happen to any of us, so don't be afraid to ask for help.'

'Thanks, Martin.' Mel smiled weakly. 'I know. For now, I'm just trying to keep as busy as possible. I need to help to nail these bastards before they kill anyone else, but I'm stuck on this cold case.'

'You had dealings with the shop owner before, didn't you?'

'Yes. He was hospitalised by the OCG last year when he refused to pay protection. We only just stopped them from torching one of his shops. He's a brave guy, but I'm worried he'll get into trouble if he fights back.'

'Can't blame him, can you?'

'S'pose not. Right, I've got some pathology reports to read. I'll collect them from the station and take them home. It's quieter there. Apart from the parrots.'

Martin grinned.

Mel had taken to cycling between the temporary police station and the home she shared with Tom Ferris. It was good exercise, and the path along the canal was usually quiet, apart from a few other cyclists and joggers. Cycling into a tunnel, she was overtaken by a similarly dressed young woman who was clearly in a hurry. Mel nearly scraped her handlebars on the tunnel's brickwork as the woman shot past. No manners, she thought, but as the woman reached daylight, the back of her T-shirt bloomed scarlet and Mel heard the crash of a shotgun blast. She froze at the mouth of the tunnel as the other cyclist's bike slid from under her and she tumbled into the canal, her blood adding a darker hue to the murky water. Terrified, Mel rummaged in her bag for her phone, and as she did so, she heard a vehicle speeding away with a squeal of tyres. Fumbling with the keypad, she couldn't shake a thought embedded in her mind. 'That was meant for me.'

Chapter Five

Day 4

All eyes were on DCI Farlowe as he opened the morning briefing.

'Ladies and gentlemen,' he began, straightening his immaculate jacket and approaching the whiteboard. 'We have another murder in Mexton. Sarah Collis, an IT consultant, was shot on the canal towpath yesterday evening as she cycled home. Another team, based at County headquarters, is dealing with it, but they are keeping us in the loop. They have found no motive for anyone to kill Ms Collis, who had no connection with criminality, and was widely liked. She had no enemies,'

'Not being funny, boss,' said DC Adeyemo, 'but why are we involved?'

'Because it was almost certainly an attempt on DC Cotton's life, Addy. The killer shot Sarah by mistake. She was wearing similar clothes to Mel and overtook her in the tunnel. When she emerged, she was hit by the shotgun blast, which killed her outright.'

Shock rippled through the team. Several officers swore. Mel stared at the floor, trembling slightly and fidgeting with an earring Tom had given her.

'How sure are we that Mel was the target?' asked Trevor Blake.

'There's little doubt,' replied the DCI. 'The shooter would have seen Mel enter the tunnel and fired at the victim, who looked much the same, as she came into view. He or she must have known Mel's route home and simply got the wrong person. The County team got nothing from the crime scene, not even tyre tracks from the road above the tunnel mouth. No witnesses, either.'

Farlowe cleared his throat and stood up even straighter.

'I have a warning for you all,' he began. 'We are under siege. You must, each and every one of you, consider yourselves at risk.

'From now on, nobody goes to take statements or interview witnesses on their own. I know you've been doing that because we're short-staffed, but this must stop. Please use your cars to travel between home and work, and check underneath them each time you use them. If you are out in the community, check in with control at least every half hour. Vary your routes between work, home and any other regular destinations. Warn your families and partners to be on the lookout for suspicious vehicles or individuals. We will be increasing armed patrols in the area, paying particular attention to police premises and officers' homes. A sergeant from the PSNI will be here tomorrow to provide further advice, drawing on his experiences in Belfast during the Troubles. Don't forget there is counselling available for anyone who needs it, although there is a bit of a queue. Are there any questions?'

'Look,' said Martin, 'it's pretty bloody obvious that those Albanians are behind this shitstorm. I agree with what Jack said the other day. They even announced themselves to Mr Paweski. We did them a lot of damage last year and they're not forgiving types. Mel was involved in the raid on the computer scammers and so was Tom. He's in danger, so we'd better alert the hospital. Trevor was at the scrapyard and Addy was involved in arresting Delvina. And if I were DI Thorpe, I'd go somewhere else to have the baby. At least Karen Groves has left. They're obviously not satisfied with the results of the bomb, and, frankly, I'm shit-scared for all of us. Including you, guv.'

'I'm afraid you're right, Martin,' said Farlowe. 'I've already spoken to our colleagues in Drugs and Vice, who were involved in raids on the OCG's premises, and warned DI Thorpe. The NCA has been in touch with Interpol, who report that several members of an Albanian gang have disappeared from their homeland recently. The suspicion is that they are here, but the Border Force has no record of them entering the country. Interpol will be sending over photos later today.'

'Is it worth talking to the gang members in prison?' asked Addy.

'Pointless,' replied Farlowe. 'They were too scared to talk to us when we arrested them and they're going to be even less communicative when they're banged up with their criminal compatriots. And, before you ask, there's no way we can send someone undercover to infiltrate the gang. They're far too tight for that; they only use their countrymen and we don't have any Albanian detectives anywhere in the country. Also, we don't know where they are at the moment.'

Farlowe's briefing was interrupted by a uniformed officer who poked her head round the door.

'Excuse me, sir. I thought you might want to know this. A member of the public reported a body in a wheelie bin, first thing this morning. A young man. He'd been badly beaten. And the thing is, his tongue was cut out.'

Chapter Six

Half a dozen onlookers stood at the end of the malodorous and litter-strewn alley, hoping to get some juicy footage on their phones. They were disappointed, as they were pushed back beyond the outer cordon surrounding the crime scene. Within the red-and-white inner cordon, a tent had been erected to protect the scene from the fine drizzle that had recently begun to fall, and SOCOs were busy with cameras.

'What can you tell me, Mark?' called Jack. 'DCI Farlowe's asked me to come along in his stead.'

'Suit up and sign in,' replied the Crime Scene Manager. 'There's not a lot to go on.'

Jack complied and followed the stepping plates towards a commercial waste bin that lay on its side. The body of a dark-haired young man lay on the ground, his legs still entangled in a pile of packaging and food waste from the adjacent restaurant. A smell of rot pervaded the alley and the occasional rat scurried along, looking for snacks.

'The guy who found him tipped the bin over,' said Mark. 'He thought he might still be alive. When he saw the mess the victim's face was in, he called 999. Uniforms were here within ten minutes and the witness went off to be sick, considerately, some way away.'

'Any forensic evidence likely?'

'Not a lot. There's no point looking for DNA or fingerprints on the wheelie bin. Too many people have handled it. Similarly, there are too many overlapping footwear marks in the dirt around the bin to be of any use. He must have been carried down the alley to the bin, as it's too narrow for a car, so no tyre marks. It would have taken two people.'

'Did you get anything at all?'

'We've had a preliminary look at the body. There's no ID on him, at least not in his pockets. We did find this, though.' Mark held up a plastic evidence bag containing a small silver coin. 'It says 5 lek on one side and Republika e Shqiperise on the other, around a picture of an eagle. Any idea what it is? I've probably got the pronunciation wrong.'

Jack thought back to a recent pub quiz round on foreign currencies.

'It's Albanian. The lek is the Albanian currency. OK. We need to get the PM done as soon as possible. Have you got much more to do?'

'Nearly finished. A paramedic confirmed death shortly after we arrived. I'll notify the undertaker when we're ready.'

'Thanks, Mark. I need to get back to the station. The DCI needs to know all about this.'

DCI Farlowe had a headache. A metaphorical one, related to his workload, and a physical one, which was probably linked. Swallowing a couple of paracetamol, washed down with Earl Grey tea from a china cup, he decided to forego lunch.

'Come in,' he said, when Jack knocked on his office door.'

'Guv,' said the DS, 'that body in the wheelie bin. SOCOs found an Albanian coin in his pocket. Given that his tongue was cut out, I'm thinking he could be the drunken caller to the radio phone-in. He obviously spoke out of turn and was punished for it.'

'You could be right, Jack. I'll ask the pathologist to check for alcohol in his blood, although he'll probably do that routinely. Can you get the lab to look for traces of explosives on his clothing? I suppose there's an outside chance he was involved with the bomb.'

'Will do, boss. There was no ID on him, but we've sent his prints to Interpol and a DNA sample's being processed. For the moment, we're calling him Mr Wheelie.'

'Hardly tasteful, Jack.'

Jack flushed.

'Neither is the mass murder of police officers.'

'OK, OK. I'll hold a briefing when we've had the results of the PM. Can you organise the usual trawl of CCTV and potential witnesses? Just in case someone saw something.'

Jack nodded and left the room. Taste, for fuck's sake, he thought. What was the matter with him? He should have heard what they wanted to call the little shit.

The man with pale grey eyes, secure in his lodge near Tirana, watched and listened intently to the Zoom call with his footsoldiers in Mexton. He preferred the face-to-face contact provided by a conferencing system to audio calls. Even though the images were sometimes blurred or jerky, he found it easier to tell when he was being lied to. No-one was lying at the moment, he believed, and felt reassured.

'So the bomb worked and that shitty little shopkeeper has had a warning, yes?'

'Yes, boss,' Fisnik Hasani, a gym-pumped thirty-year-old with a shaven head, replied. 'They've had to move out of the station and they've no fucking clue about us. The operatives were careful. We will collect from the shopkeeper soon. The sums are small but he was disrespectful.'

'Good. Any problems?'

The man hesitated.

'A junior employee got drunk and spoke out of turn to a radio station. He no longer speaks. Or breathes.'

'Damage?'

'Only to him.'

'What about the individual police? You had names from court and coroner's hearings and newspapers.'

'They all survived, it seems. They were in a different part of the building. We have special punishments lined up for them.' He omitted to mention the failed attack on Mel.

'And the other operations?'

'We've acquired three new premises and expect the first load of girls later this week. Fisnik and his boys have been explaining to local dealers that they will be buying drugs from us in the future. We've had to hurt a couple of their suppliers, and we don't expect any more difficulties. They weren't serious players. Computers should be running soon, but we've had problems getting reliable internet connections. Altin is expected in a few days and will start scamming soon, but we have something else for him to do first.'

'Good. Keep me informed. And no mistakes. Remember what Nikolla did to Kreshnik.'

'Yes boss. No mistakes.'

Even though the connection was shaky, the look of fear on the gangsters' faces was unmistakeable.

Chapter Seven

Mel knocked on DCI Farlowe's office door and entered in response to his summons.

'I've been through those reports, guv, and I think this is one for us. Dr Fox, says that the bones are modern, male and from someone in their late sixties or seventies. Dental work and a hip replacement suggest that they're British and, in her opinion, they were deposited around seven to twelve years ago. The lab looked at the pieces of clothing she found and the dates roughly match up.'

'OK. That certainly puts them in our timeframe. What did the pathologist have to say?'

'Well, Dr Durbridge examined the skull. I'd noticed some damage to it, and he confirmed that it was a depressed fracture, consistent with a blow from a blunt object. It could have been fatal but, of course, the victim might have been killed by some other means and the skull fractured after death.'

'Definitely murder, then.'

'He said that was our job to determine, but he did suggest that the injury was unlikely to have been accidental.'

'Any clues to the victim's identity?'

'Dr Durbridge got the serial number of the replacement hip and tried to trace it, but it seems some records were lost and he couldn't find out who it was fitted to. He also retrieved DNA. But I've had a thought.'

'Go on.'

'When we looked at the house, the estate agent said that the previous owner had disappeared in Australia, and had only recently been declared dead. Maybe he never left Mexton.'

The DCI thought for a moment, tapping a pencil on the side of a teacup.

'Look into it, will you? It's highly irregular for an officer who may be considered personally involved to be part of an investigation, but the remains seem to have been there long before you bought the house. Also, I simply can't spare anyone from Operation Fieldmouse, so these are exceptional circumstances. I'll be the SIO, but you'll have to do the legwork, reporting to me constantly. I'm sure you know what to do.'

'Sure, boss. What about Mr Paweski?'

'You've given him advice, I presume. We can't do much more at the moment, but feel free to check in with him from time to time.'

'Will do, guv.'

Mel stood up to leave but Farlowe motioned her to sit down again.

'I'm afraid we have a serious matter to discuss,' he said.

Mel complied, looking worried.

'We have had a complaint of assault against you.'

Mel immediately thought of the Albanian with the knife. She had lost it with him, hitting him with her baton repeatedly. But he was dead, so how could he complain? She looked at Farlowe defensively.

'Who is it?'

'Ricky Marriott.'

'What? I saved the bastard's life. What's he on about?'

'Apparently, you injected him with the antidote to the poison he'd taken without his consent. Technically, that counts as assault.'

'He's got to be kidding.' She nearly included the word 'fucking' but thought better of it.

'Did he, at any time, tell you to stop?'

'No. He was pretty out of it. He struggled, but I put that down to the poison.'

'Are you absolutely sure?'

'Yes. And Jack will back me up. Jenny Pike might be able to, as well. I think she was still conscious. And, for the record, the doctor didn't instruct me what to do, he just indicated what a medic might do in the circumstances. He didn't want to lose his licence to practise.'

'OK, Mel. I believe you, and most of us would have done the same in those circumstances, if we'd had the wit to do so. It hasn't got as far as the CPS yet, and I'm sure they won't take it forward. The IOPC may want to talk to you, and take a sworn statement, but I will make it clear to them that you did nothing unprofessional or illegal. I had to raise this with you, as I'm sure you realise, but you have my full support.'

'Thank you, sir,' she said, preparing to leave. 'Something's occurred to me about the bones, but if it's all right with you, I'll leave that till later. I need some air.'

Farlowe nodded and Mel left, closing the office door with exaggerated care. What the fuck was wrong with this job, when you save someone's life and end up in the shit for it? She screamed silently to herself. She really didn't know how much more she could take. She longed to put her arms around Tom and have him reassure her, but he was still in hospital, woozy from painkillers. He was improving but she missed him dreadfully. Anyway, he had enough problems of his own. So, after she'd visited him, it would be a bottle of wine in an empty house, with only the parrots for company. Perhaps she should phone her dad. He could always cheer her up.

Three hours later she dialled her father's number. He was always in at this time of night, ready to chat and share policing anecdotes. But there was no reply.

Chapter Eight

Day 5

Jack caught up with Mel before the morning briefing and led her into an empty room.

'How are you coping?' he began, speaking gently.

'OK,' shrugged Mel.

'Really? 'Cos you've had more shit to deal with in the past couple of years than many officers get in their whole careers.'

Mel said nothing for a while as she gathered her thoughts.

'I'm coping when I'm busy,' she said, slowly. 'But I'm still not sleeping and I have bursts of anger, sometimes over trivial things. I'm anxious much of the time, but my training helps me to overcome it.'

'What about the counselling?'

'Yeah, the guy seems good. He's explained all about PTSD and how it's affecting me. He calls it psychoeducation. He keeps getting me to relive the sword attack. Not nice. It's to help me confront it. He says avoiding stops my brain processing it, or something. I think it will help, but I've had the bombing, Tom and the shooting on top of it.'

Her voice quavered slightly.

'When I'm working, I'm focused and I've got mates around me. It's at home that it's worse, especially with Tom in hospital. You needn't worry about my performance.'

'Don't be bloody silly,' replied Jack. 'It's you I'm worried about. You know we've all got your back. Talk to me if you want to, and if you need time off, don't hesitate. OK?'

'Yes. Thanks, Jack.' She smiled weakly. 'But I'm not the only one fucked up by recent events, am I?'

The morning briefing did little to lift the gloom in the incident room. Farlowe began with an update he'd received from the officers investigating Sarah Collis's murder.

'Someone saw a white van near the canal at around the time Sarah Collis was killed. She noticed it because it ran a red light at some roadworks a few hundred metres away and almost forced her into a ditch. She got the number, and guess what, it's the pink Fiat.'

'Promising,' said Trevor. 'They must be getting careless. I'd have thought they would have changed the plates again by now. Still, we can track it on ANPR.'

'That's where the news isn't so good. The last sighting was along the Highchester Road, heading out of town. It must have taken back roads after that. Anyway, we can tag it and see where it turns up.'

The DCI turned to the report from the pathologist on the dead man found in the wheelie bin.

'According to Dr Durbridge, the victim was badly beaten before he was killed. His tongue was cut out while he was still alive.'

Several officers shuddered. Farlowe continued.

'Cause of death was most likely damage to his brain. He had a large haematoma and there were contrecoup injuries suggesting that repeated blows to the head had rocked his skull backwards and forwards. Our assumption is that whoever did it is sending a message to other gang members to keep silent. He had been drinking, but Dr Durbridge couldn't say whether he was killed immediately after the radio show or subsequently.'

'Is the killer the same person who tortured Kreshnik Osmani?' asked Addy.

'I asked him that. He doesn't think so. The damage was much cruder and the tongue removal was amateurish. Whoever killed Osmani was much more skilled.

'We do have an ID for the victim, though. Interpol had his prints on file. His name is Skender Shelia. He comes from a small town in Albania and has convictions for violence and importing drugs into various EU countries.'

'No loss, then,' muttered Trevor.

The DCI looked at him sharply, then carried on.

'We need to canvass possible witnesses, check local CCTV, put out noticeboards near the scene and alert the local media. You know the ropes. Can you sort this, please, Jack?'

'Yes guv.'

'One other thing. The lab got back to me this morning.

They found traces of diesel and ammonium nitrate on his clothing. If he didn't make or plant the bomb, he certainly came into contact with the explosive. Unless, of course, there's another one being prepared.'

No-one said anything. They didn't need to.

Mel sat at her desk, her coffee cooling, and sketched out a plan of action for the bones investigation. Her first job was to contact the Australian embassy to ask for their help in tracing the previous owner of the house, an Alan Michael Fearon. Within a couple of hours a helpful attache confirmed that Fearon had arrived in Melbourne on the eighteenth of June 2013. He had stayed at the Victoria hotel for two nights and then disappeared. The state police had no record of him being involved in any kind of crime or accident and neither did the Australian Federal Police. The Australian Border Force had no record of him leaving the country.

He was a bloody ghost, thought Mel. He clearly went to Australia, presumably with his lottery win, and disappeared. But why would he?

Mel's next call was to the estate agent, Robbie Biggs.

'Good afternoon, Mr Biggs. It's DC Mel Cotton. You sold 42 Craven Street to me and my partner. Do you remember?'

'Yes, of course. I'm really sorry about what you found in the garden. Obviously, we had no idea the bones were there.'

'No, of course not. That's why I'm phoning. I need to

get in touch with the owner's relatives. Can you give me their names and, if possible, their addresses?'

'I'm not sure I can. GDPR and all that.'

'I'm afraid I'm investigating a suspicious death, Mr Biggs. The bones didn't get there by accident. I can get this information by other means if I need to, but you can save me a lot of time and trouble if you co-operate.'

Biggs thought for a moment.

'I'll see what I can do. As a purchaser I suppose you have a right to know who you bought the property from, rather than just the estate of Mr Fearon. Leave it with me. I'll email you what I can.'

'Thank you, Mr Biggs. I appreciate it.'

Mel hung up and, on a hunch, Googled Alan Fearon. She sat back in surprise. His Wikipedia entry ran to several pages and revealed a startling history, hardly consistent with the owner of a slightly run-down semi in Mexton. Alan Fearon had been a rock star, at the top of his game in the late sixties and early seventies. Known as Johnny Fear, his bands had won gold discs and awards, topping the album charts regularly. Suspecting that the entry might have been sanitised somewhat she had an idea and reached for her phone.

'Steve,' she queried, when the call was answered. 'It's cousin Mel. You're an old music guru, aren't you? What do you know about Johnny Fear?'

'Bloody hell, Mel. Haven't heard from you for ages. Seen your picture in the papers, though. Bombs and things.'

'Yeah, sorry I haven't been in touch. Demands of the job, I'm afraid. It's about time we had a family get-together. Anyway, I wonder if you can help me. Johnny Fear has disappeared, and it's possible his remains were buried in our garden. I need to talk to someone who knows about him.'

'What are you gonna do? Put up a blue plaque? I don't know, Mel. Last time I helped the police with their inquiries I got cautioned for possession of dope.'

There was a brief silence, then Steve chuckled.

'Only teasing. But it will cost you a curry, though.'

Mel laughed and they agreed to meet at a local Indian restaurant that evening.

'Jack. We've had a possible sighting of the killers of Skenda Shelia.' Trevor caught up with the DS as he was trying to make the new coffee machine work.

'A taxi driver saw one of our notice boards. He said he saw two men carrying another into the alley where Shelia was found, at around three a.m. He assumed they were helping a drunk mate. There was a white van nearby but he didn't get the number.'

'Right. I'll tell the DCI. He's taken this inquiry into Operation Fieldmouse since the lab found those explosive traces. We must find that bloody van before they change the plates or respray it. Get on to Traffic will you, and make sure foot patrols keep an eye open.'

'Sure thing. Oh, you press that button there to get the coffee.'

Jack turned back to the machine with a grunt.

Chapter Nine

'YEAH. JOHNNY FEAR. INTERESTING BLOKE,' said Steve, wiping vindaloo sauce from his chin. 'Bit of a weathervane, following whichever style was popular at the time. He was a decent guitarist though. You reckon he's dead?'

'I didn't say that,' replied Mel. 'It's just that he's disappeared and a set of bones was found in our garden. We bought the house from his estate, so it seems likely. We're waiting for proof. So, tell me about his career. The condensed version.'

'OK. He left school half-way through his A-levels, changed his name and formed a blues band, just as the British blues boom was starting. He drew on the Stones, John Mayall and various other artists popular at the time. He called the band The Fearsomes, and their first album, Twelve Bar Fear, got into the lower reaches of the charts. He was a bit of a dick, though, and the band soon broke up. He did a stint with The Graham Bond Organisation and various session jobs, earning a regular, if modest, income. Can I have another pint?'

Mel ordered another couple of Cobras and Steve continued.

'By late 1966, he could see psychedelia was happening, so he collected a bunch of stoners from North London and formed Electric Amnesia. He wanted to call the band Maxwell and the Houses but the coffee company threatened to sue. They gigged at the usual underground clubs – Middle Earth and UFO – and their demo records were played by John Peel on Radio One in 1967. Their breakthrough came when they were featured on a BBC documentary that attempted to expose the "hippie plague". A couple of their tunes were broadcast, and one of the big record companies offered them a contract. They had two singles in the charts, and their debut album, Flying through the clouds of cosmic soup, reached number one.'

'Impressive. So he became rich.'

'Not exactly. The contract gave them little in the way of royalties, and their agent took a large chunk of what was left. Still, they were on their way. When the hippie dream faded Johnny turned his attention to prog rock. He recruited a few ex-students from UCL, including a biochemist who played synthesiser, and formed The Pentose Phosphate Shunt. Fuck knows what that's supposed to mean. They put out a series of albums with pretentious titles and fantastical covers, and did the whole touring thing, playing in America, Europe and Japan. They actually made some money for a while, but spent it on all kinds of crap, including cocaine. By the mid-seventies, the whole prog genre was losing popularity. In an attempt to cash in on the punk market they bought all the safety pins and ripped clothes and so on and rebranded themselves as the Swamp Adders. It didn't work, and by 1978, Johnny was officially bankrupt.'

'A bit sad. What happened to him then?'

'Not sure. He had some genuine musical talent, so he may have done a bit of session work, cash in hand, using an alias. I think I saw him in our local Tesco car park, pushing a trolley. Whether he was working there or shopping, I couldn't be sure.'

'Hmm. We should be able to find out what he's been doing from HMRC. If the bones in our garden really are his, he died about eight and a half years ago, so he may not even have claimed his state pension. Do you know anything about his relationships?'

'Loads of girlfriends early on, as per usual in those days. He was with that model, Saffron Flowers, for a while, but they broke up. He married eventually, but it was a bit on/off. One or other of them would stray for a while, but they always got back together. I think she died about ten years ago, or thereabouts.'

'Right. Thanks so much, Steve, you're a mine of information. You should do pub quizzes like my sergeant, Jack.'

'I do sometimes, but questions on sixties rock rarely come up. Did you say Jack? Jack Vaughan?'

Mel nodded.

'Blimey. I didn't know he was a copper. He's lethal.'

'Well, please keep it to yourself. It would spoil the whole thing for him, if everyone knew.'

'Will do. Thanks for the curry, Mel.' He burped. 'And the beer. G'night.'

Chapter Ten

Day 6

DCI Farlowe tapped his fountain pen on a teacup to call the team to order.

'We have a possible lead on the Albanians, ladies and gentlemen,' he began. 'Yesterday, a container lorry broke down on the M25 and a Traffic Officer stopped to help. The driver's behaviour made him suspicious, so he called the police. When the container was opened, they found twelve young women inside, in dreadful conditions, some looking no older than thirteen. The driver was arrested and the women were taken to safe accommodation.'

'Bastards,' muttered someone.

'How does that help us?' asked Trevor.

'The driver had a piece of paper in his wallet with an address just outside Mexton. A disused timber warehouse. So, it looks like the women were destined for brothels in our area. The driver swore he was carrying pickles and other foodstuffs from Poland and the manifest bore this out. He denied any knowledge of his real cargo. He was lying, of course. The Polish bit was true – the women were loaded into the container in Poland – but the number plates were Albanian. Someone from the NCA Modern Slavery and Human Trafficking Unit managed to talk to a few of the women, who told them where they came from, and the unit is currently helping to look after them. So it's definitely linked to Operation Fieldmouse.'

'So Oktapod is really back in business here,' said Jack, referring to the Albanian international OCG they had dealt with during the previous year. 'I assume they'll also be importing drugs and running cyberscams again. But why Mexton? We're hardly the hub of the universe.'

'The NCA think they're establishing a beachhead in southern England,' replied Farlowe. 'They don't want to challenge the established gangs in the big cities but can build up their influence down here and then move up when they are strong enough.'

'So what do we do now?' asked Martin. 'Raid the warehouse?'

'Not yet. I'll seek authorisation for surveillance and we'll keep an eye on them. It's notable that the white van involved in the shooting by the canal was last picked up heading in that direction. As yet, we have no addresses for premises they may be using as brothels, but some of our civilian investigators are going through the Land Registry to see if anything raises a flag.'

'What about the drugs?' asked Addy.

'DS Palmer, the drug squad officer who worked with us before, is asking his informants to look out for new players moving in to the Eastside and elsewhere in town. Anyone arrested for possession or low-level dealing will also be asked, with a guarantee of anonymity. Already, two known dealers have left town and a third was admitted to A&E with multiple fractures. He claimed he'd fallen off his bike, but it looked more like he'd fallen off a building. Oh. One other thing. With DC Ferris still in hospital I've asked for help in tracking any possible computer scams. We've been assigned a civilian expert, a Robbie Edwards. You look pleased, Jack. Do you know him?'

'Yes, guv. He saved Mel and Tom's lives when a gunman burst into their flat and also helped us bring down a paedophile network, some of it unofficially, shall we say. He's brilliant.'

'Glad to hear it. I'll look forward to meeting him. One last thing. The remains found in DC Cotton's garden are recent and the result of foul play. The investigation has been upgraded to a murder inquiry, Operation Ezekiel, and DC Cotton is the case officer, with me as SIO. Fieldmouse is the priority, but if anyone has the time to lend her a hand, please feel free to do so. I'm sure she would appreciate it. Carry on.'

'How are you doing, love?' Mel asked, loudly, sitting by Tom's bedside.'

'Mustn't grumble,' he said, in a fake cockney accent. 'They don't expect to keep me here much longer. My hearing's improved in one ear – the one next to you – but I may need a hearing aid in the other one. They're still talking about a prosthetic hand, but that's a long way off. Apparently, there's a firm near Bristol that 3D prints them, which could be promising. My guvnor has been in to see me and he assures me my job's safe as long as I can pass the fitness test. How about you?'

'Missing you. The house is so empty with just the parrots.'

'You are looking after them, aren't you?'

'Of course. But I think they miss you, too. They're unusually quiet. I can't wait for you to come home and things to get back to normal.'

A tear ran down Tom's cheek.

'I wanted to ask you something, Mel, and please tell me the truth.'

'What?' asked Mel, nervously.

'Do you still want me? I mean, I'm not the man you proposed to. I've lost a hand, I may be deaf in one ear and I've got these horrible scars on my face. I'm damaged goods.'

'Oh you fucking idiot,' Mel replied, pushing aside wires and tubes to hug him. 'Of course I do. You're still my Tom and I love you. How could you think I wouldn't? I've no idea when we will eventually get married, though. It seems to be jinxed. But we can think about that when you're better.'

Tom smiled.

'We will. And I love you too. So what are you working on? The bomb?'

'No, they think it's too personal, what with you being injured, although I expect I'll end up helping. I'm looking into the bones in our garden, virtually on my own. It's possible they belong to a faded rock star who used to own the house, but we need to take DNA samples from his relatives unless there's something on the database. If they allow phones in here, you could look up a couple of his bands on YouTube – Electric Amnesia and also The Pentose Phosphate Shunt. Enjoy!'

Tom grinned and then looked worried.

'For fuck's sake be careful out there, Mel. I was lucky, but you're in danger too. You're not exactly anonymous.'

'I will, don't worry. See you tomorrow.'

She kissed him and waved goodbye as she left the side room on the ward. Should she have told him about the attempt on her life? Or the warning from the DCI? Not now, she thought, but she would do in time. When she got home she would pour herself a beer, heat up a ready meal and try, again, to phone her dad.

Chapter Eleven

Day 7

'So has anyone got anything to report?' asked DCI Farlowe at the start of the morning briefing.

The silence was broken only by the sound of workmen dealing with a broken water main outside the building.

'Nothing? Nothing at all?'

'We've had some intel from the community officers on the Eastside,' said Jack. 'Apparently, there are some new players on the local drugs scene. They don't say much, but they're foreign, apparently. A black SUV has been seen on the estate, and it's unlikely to belong to anyone who lives there. Also, one of the PCs confiscated a wrap of heroin and it's been sent to the lab to check if it resembles the stuff we recovered from Oktapod last year. It'll take a few days for the results to come back.'

'That's something, I suppose. Anything else?'

'I spoke to Robbie,' said Martin. 'He's been looking

around for new scams, but unless someone reports a fraud attempt, he doesn't have much to go on. But if anyone can find something, he can.'

'We may have a lead on that,' said Farlowe. 'The Border Force tipped off the NCA about a person of interest entering the UK via Stansted. Altin Hoxha is flagged as a hacker who Interpol have been tracking for several years. He has no convictions but has come under suspicion in several major computer frauds. We don't know where he went after the airport, but we're watching out for him.'

'Perhaps Robbie could befriend him online?' suggested Addy.

'Not a good idea,' replied Jack. 'It could be dangerous, and Robbie already risked his life with those paedophiles. And these people don't make friends with strangers. We can't put a civilian at risk.'

'I agree, Jack,' responded Farlowe, 'but the name might give him something to go on.'

At that point the DCI's phone rang and he answered it irritably. When the call finished he addressed the team.

'The lorry driver they picked up with the trafficked women. He was found dead in Maidstone Prison while on remand. Murdered. No witnesses.'

'Fuck,' said Trevor, almost inaudibly. 'He failed, didn't he? And they don't like failure. I saw what happened to Guzim Marku. The sight of his smashed-in face still haunts me.'

'Can I make a suggestion, guv?' asked Mel, who had just entered the room to report on Operation Ezekiel. 'They're clearly going after Stefan Paweski again. The arson was a warning to pay up. Can we put some surveillance in place and track them back to their base?'

'If we had the resources, yes. But we haven't. And I can't have officers posing as shop assistants in all four of his remaining premises, on the off chance that one of them will be targeted.'

'I realise that, boss. But perhaps we could put some of our own cameras in place. His own CCTV is rubbish.'

'That's more reasonable.' Farlowe thought for a minute. 'You know the man. Could we get him to play along with them, give them some money and put a tracker in the package?'

'He won't like it, but I may be able to persuade him. He's all for getting his mates ready to beat the shit out of them, but I've tried to explain that he'd be in trouble if he did.'

'OK. We'll work on that. You're our liaison with Mr Paweski. Reassure him that we are trying to help him. Now, can you bring us up to date with Operation Ezekiel?'

'Yes, guv.' Mel wheeled a whiteboard from the side of the room and addressed the team.

'The remains found in my garden almost certainly belong to an Alan Michael Fearon, who won the lottery and disappeared to Australia some eight and a half years ago. There is no record of what he did in Australia or of his returning to the UK. He was probably killed by a blow to the head – his skull was partly caved in. We have a familial DNA match with a Sarah Denise Fearon, who was arrested for a public order offence at a climate change protest a couple of years ago. She confirmed that he was her father but knew nothing about what happened after he left the country.'

'What do we know about Fearon?' asked Martin.

'He was a reasonably well-known rock musician in the sixties and early seventies,' replied Mel. 'He performed under the name Johnny Fear and was arrested a few times for drunkenness, possession, trashing hotel rooms and doing various other bits of rock star nonsense. This was all before DNA, and he never served time, so we have no profile on the system. There's a rough match with dental records – a couple of fillings – but his teeth were in a bad state, possibly because of drug use. He married in 1980 and fathered four children. His wife died in a car crash in 2009. We don't know how he made a living since the mid-seventies, although some royalties would have still been coming in. I'm still trying to trace him from then onwards.'

'OK, keep at it, Mel,' said Farlowe. 'I suppose we have no suspects?'

'A bit too early, guv. The estate agent mentioned something about him not sharing his lottery winnings with his children, so they could be in the frame, but it's hard to see how they moved him from a hotel in Melbourne to a semi in Mexton for the purposes of killing him. I've put his photo on the whiteboard – back when he was a hippie type. I'm trying to identify, and get pictures of, his children and any siblings, but I'm afraid it's not like on a TV programme. We don't have photos from the actors' agents to display.'

Mel's attempt at humour brought the first smile in the incident room since the explosion.

'Thank you, Mel, said Farlowe, turning to address the whole room. 'Look, I realise things are awful and I do appreciate all the work you are doing. Can I invite you all to the pub this evening? I'll put some money behind the bar at the Cat and Cushion and I'll try to join you when my meeting with the Chief Super finishes.'

Murmurs of appreciation ran round the room and the mood lightened. But only slightly.

Chapter Twelve

ALTIN HOXHA LOOKED around the room with disdain.

'So I'm supposed to work in this shitty dump, am I?' he complained, in Albanian. 'And what's that crap over there? Looks like it's still running Windows 5. How am I supposed to do my job with shit like that?'

'Don't worry,' his companion said. 'You tell me what kit you need, and I'll get it for you. We're using this house because it's out of the way. There are no nosy neighbours and no cops driving by. You can get back to the high life in Tirana when you've set things up and a kid can run it. Did they tell you about the special project? The cop?'

Altin nodded.

'There's food in the fridge and freezer and plenty of beer.'

'I don't drink.'

'OK, there's fruit juice as well. The bed's not too bad. If you need anything else, let me or one of the guys downstairs know. Oh, one bit of advice. Don't complain too much and don't fuck up. Nikolla's in the country.'

At the mention of Oktapod's enforcer, Altin shuddered. He sat down and drew up a list of equipment, which he handed to the other man.

'Get me this and I'll do what's needed. Don't involve me in dealing with the women. That kind of work makes me sick. And I don't fuck up.'

'So, what do you think of the idea, Stefan?' asked Mel, closing the door on the men installing additional CCTV cameras outside the shop.'

'I think it's shit. But I suppose I have no choice. Do you really think it will work? Tell me the truth, please.'

'It should do. I can't guarantee it, of course. If they get suspicious and switch the money to a different bag, we've lost the tracker. But we can't have officers watching your shops day and night. It's the best chance we've got.'

'All right. Tell me what to do.'

'We'll provide a bag with the tracker built in. We'll also fit hidden cameras in your shops, and outside them to pick up any suspicious vehicles. You should tell your staff what's happened, and that you're too scared to resist any more. If someone demands money from them, they should send them to whichever shop you're working in. The gang'll probably know anyway, but just in case. When they leave, phone us and we'll do the rest. We'll give you a spare phone in case they think of taking yours.'

'OK,' said Stefan, reluctantly. 'But if this doesn't work,

I'll employ my friends as security guards. And when they come, bang!'

'Please don't, Stefan. You'll put them at risk of assault and, probably, arrest.'

Stefan shrugged and showed Mel out, muttering to himself about the British police being too soft.

In a soundproofed room below Altin and his companion, two men sat talking and drinking rakia. A third sat on a couch, facing the door, an Albanian newspaper on his lap. He didn't seem to be listening, but his eyes were constantly flickering around the room.

'Tirana is unhappy,' said Fisnik Hasani. 'They say we should have made more progress by now. Losing the women wasn't our fault and the driver has paid the price, but we're not making money until we get replacements.'

'Are they not pleased with the bomb?' asked Zamir Prifti.

'Yes, but several key cops survived. Other measures are being taken, but they would be most displeased if they found out about the missed hit on the woman.'

'Are they satisfied with anything? For God's sake, we're working hard and keeping under the radar.'

'They are pleased with the heroin sales. We have taken over much of the trade on that shitty estate and will be moving into night clubs with ecstasy, when supplies arrive from our Dutch friends. But they would like more progress on the shopkeeper. We will visit him again soon. If he still refuses, perhaps we could send Nikolla.'

The third man switched his attention to Fisnik.

'I answer to Tirana, not to you. I am not your employee.'

'No, sorry, Nikolla,' Fisnik stammered. 'It was just a thought.'

Nikolla ignored him.

'What are the cops doing?' asked Zamir.

'We don't know much. The bugs we had in the police station were destroyed or will be found in the wreckage. They've moved to other places and we haven't had time to put new ones in, though this will happen. We've planted people in work crews, but they've reported nothing. There seem to be more cops on the streets, and people have been asking questions around the estate, but I don't believe they know anything.'

'I hope you are right. Tirana won't forgive any more mistakes.'

Zamir nodded meaningfully towards Nikolla.

'So do I. We will have another drink.'

They chuckled and chinked their glasses.

'A toast to tomorrow,' Fisnik grinned, 'when we begin to destroy an interfering policeman.'

Chapter Thirteen

Day 8

'Good morning, everyone,' began DCI Farlowe. 'May I introduce DI Geoff Chidgey. He's been loaned to us while DI Thorpe is on maternity leave. I'm sure you'll all make him welcome. Would you like to introduce yourself, Geoff?'

'Of course. It's a pleasure to work with you, ladies and gentlemen. You have an excellent reputation and some of my former colleagues still talk about Mel and Jack saving two people's lives in the disused bogs in Weston. Mind you, one of them should probably have been flushed away long ago. Not Mel or Jack, that is.'

A few officers chuckled at Chidgey's joke. Most didn't.

'I've nearly done my thirty years and I've tackled all kinds of villainy in my career, but, I have to say, I have never been involved in such a horrific incident as this bombing. You have my deepest condolences for the loss of your colleagues.'

He paused for a few seconds before his West Country burr resumed.

'I'm a Somerset man, as you can guess from the accent, and I worked all over the Avon and Somerset force area, in a number of roles, before I moved to Mexton. My career has not consisted of just chasing sheep-shaggers, as I heard someone remark in the gents. I've handled numerous murder investigations, dealt with Bristol drug gangs and worked on complex fraud cases. Rural policing – tractor thefts, livestock rustling and so on – was only a small part of it. I hope that's cleared the air, and we can get on with chasing these fuckers.'

Some of the detectives were taken aback by Chidgey's earthy language, used as they were to Farlowe's more restrained vocabulary.

'I need to spend some time with Mr Farlowe this morning, catching up with what's been going on, but I'd like to sit down with you later on. Bring your ideas along with your coffees. I'll bring biscuits. Thank you, all.'

The DI's portly frame suggested that he was no stranger to snacks, although his florid complexion indicated that at least some of his calorie intake was in the form of duty-paid liquids.

'What do you think, Martin?' asked Trevor, as they queued for coffee. 'Bit of a contrast, eh?'

'The DCI's tailored suit and Chidgey's rustic tweeds, you mean? Chalk and cheese.'

'Not just that. He looks like he's on his way out. Not

exactly the epitome of modern policing. How the hell is he going to cope with these Albanian bastards?'

'Well, he said he'd tackled Bristol gangs, didn't he? Our lot can't be any worse. Anyway, I think his slow speech and Somerset accent may be deceptive. He looks pretty shrewd behind that.'

'I hope you're right. With this shitstorm going on, we need all the brains we can get. How's your arm, by the way?' Martin asked.

'Still hurts like fuck, but it's mending. The thing is, Suzy wants me to pack in the job. She thinks it's too dangerous. So far, I've been nearly burned to death, had a pile of cars collapse on me and been blown up. I thought public order policing was dangerous, but it was nothing like this. I'm beginning to agree with her, especially as we've got a kid.'

'I sympathise, mate. I got the same from Alice when the Maldobourne gang tried to kill me by sabotaging my brakes, and then stabbed me.' Martin smiled. 'But when we get a result, catching murderers, nailing paedophiles and preventing terrorist attacks, it's the best job in the world. I couldn't give it up.'

'I suppose so,' said Trevor, not completely convinced. 'We'll keep talking about it.'

'Yeah, well, chat anytime. I'm in the same position, with a young family. Nobody would blame us if we left, but I'm fucked if I'm gonna let these bastards get away with blowing us up and killing our own.'

Trevor smiled and walked back to his desk, a thoughtful expression on his face.

Where the hell could he be, Mel asked herself, when yet another call to her father failed. If he was ill, surely he would have told her. Oh shit. Perhaps he'd had a stroke or an accident, and couldn't phone. Then a chilling thought paralysed her. Could those bastards be trying to get to her through him? She wouldn't put anything past them, but how would they know about her dad? Then she recalled a photo in his local paper, when she completed her training – the daughter following in her proud father's footsteps. Should she call the local police and ask them to check on him? No. They'd hardly be likely to send a patrol car just because he wasn't answering his phone. Then she had an idea. She had a number for his neighbour somewhere. Rummaging in her bag, she found it and dialled.

'Hello, Shirley, it's Mel. Mel Cotton. D'you think you could do me a favour and check on my dad? I've not heard from him for days.'

'Sure, love. I'll pop round in a minute,' the woman replied. 'I haven't seen him for a while either. I've got a key and I'll call you back.'

Mel paced around the incident room, unable to concentrate, her stomach full of concrete. She'd lost one parent to violent crime; she couldn't bear to lose the other. As the minutes dragged by, she became more and more convinced that something dreadful had happened. He was dead. He must be. She was on the point of calling Shirley again when the phone rang.

Chapter Fourteen

Five days previously

Philip Cotton contemplated the warmed-up stew in front of him and decided it needed a decent bottle of wine to make it more edible. His widowed neighbour was very kind, providing him with home-made meals, although he was perfectly capable of cooking for himself, a point he had gently reiterated on several occasions. He did wonder whether she had romantic inclinations towards him, feelings he didn't reciprocate, but he didn't want to hurt her feelings by refusing the food.

Absorbed in these thoughts, he didn't hear the stealthy approach of two balaclava-clad young men, or the click as they picked the simple lock on his back door and eased their way into the house. He didn't switch on the alarm until he went to bed or went out, believing that nobody would attempt burglary at an occupied house during the daytime. Had he read the stories in the local paper about daytime home invasions, he might have been more careful. He unlocked the door to the cellar, turned on the light and made his way down the creaking stairs. He had just selected a reasonable bottle of Rioja from his modest collection, when he heard the door slam behind him. Bloody draught, he thought, and started to climb the stairs.

Five minutes before

'This'll be a piece of piss, Vin,' said Del, as they approached the house. 'One old geezer, on 'is own, and the only neighbour's out walkin' the dog. A quick smack and we can 'elp ourselves.'

Vin grinned and flexed his hands around the baseball bat, while his mate picked the lock. As they entered, they saw Philip going down to the cellar, clearly unaware of their presence. Vin was about to follow when Del held him back.

'No need to 'it him. Just lock 'im in. Less DNA that way. Help me shift this cupboard thing.'

Somewhat reluctantly, Vin slammed and locked the door, then the two burglars dragged a heavy antique sideboard across the hall and shoved it against the door. They moved from room to room, ignoring the hammering from the cellar, grabbing what portable valuables they could find and stuffing them into rucksacks. Del was about to seize a pair of silver sporting cups from a mantelpiece when he stopped.'

'Fuck me. Look at this photo. All England police rugby championship 1985 winners. He's a fuckin' cop.'

Del smashed the framed picture on the floor and swept the two cups into the fireplace.

'D'you want me to give 'im a doin'?' asked Vin, eagerly.

'No, leave the bastard where 'e is. He's locked up enough people in 'is time, I guess, so 'e can have a taste of it.'

'What if no-one finds 'im?'

'Tough shit. We'd better go before doggy gets back next door.'

Pausing only to urinate on the carpet, the two thieves dashed out the back door and climbed over the garden fence, dropping into the lane at the rear where they had parked a stolen, almost silent, Renault Zoe.

Philip soon realised that the door hadn't shut accidentally. Draughts don't lock doors when they slam them and this door was undeniably locked. He hammered on the door, calling out to whoever was in the house to let him out, threatening all kinds of dire retribution. As he expected, no-one answered, despite the muffled conversations and occasional crash that reached him. When things were finally quiet, he found an old toolbox and retrieved a pair of long-nosed pliers, a screwdriver and a couple of wood gouges. In a few moments he had managed to unlock the door, and, pleased with himself, he tried to open it. It wouldn't budge. Shit! Dejectedly, he sat on the steps and analysed his situation.

On the negative side, he had no phone and no means of communicating with anyone. The cellar had no window, so there was no point trying to send Morse code messages by flashing the light on and off. He was expecting no callers, as Shirley had only recently dropped in with the tub full of stew. No-one would be able to hear him in the road, no matter how loudly he shouted or banged. His blood pressure medication was by his bedside, but he could go without it for a while as long as he didn't exercise over much. As if that was likely to happen.

On the positive side, he had bottled water set aside for emergencies, some local cheeses ripening menacingly in the corner and plenty of empty bottles to pee in. And thank God for screw-topped wine bottles. He thought of his daughter, too busy chasing scrotes, miles away, to ring him regularly. He didn't blame her – he had done the job too. But would she know something was wrong? Probably not. He didn't believe in telepathy. But someone would realise he was missing, and come looking for him. Wouldn't they?

Chapter Fifteen

Present day

'He's all right. I've found him. He's fine. Paramedics are on their way.'

Mel almost sobbed when she heard Shirley's voice.

'What happened? Can I speak to him?'

'Some burglars locked him in the cellar. He's been there since Friday night. Here. I'll pass him the phone.'

'Dad! Dad! What's been going on?'

'I was in the cellar getting a bottle of wine when two local shits broke in, locked the door and shoved the sideboard in front of it,' he said calmly. 'I've been living on wine and cheese ever since. Very French.' He chuckled.

'Did they hurt you? Did you see who it was? Did they leave any forensics?'

'No, no and I don't know, in that order. A proper detective you are, my girl.'

Mel could almost hear his smile down the phone.

'Shirley came round. She said you phoned. She couldn't move the sideboard but she called 999 and a couple of PCs came and shifted it. The buggers have made a right mess of the place, but nothing's gone that can't be replaced. Apparently, there've been a few like this locally, and CID have got a team on it so they might get a result. The two lads insisted on calling an ambulance, although I'm fine. All I need is a good, long shower. I stink. And the cellar needs cleaning out.'

'Probably all that weapons-grade cheese you keep down there,' joked Mel, glad that he seemed reasonably cheerful. 'I'll come up and see you as soon as I can.'

'That'd be great. But you've got young Tom to look after. How's he doing?'

'Mending. But traumatised. He reckons he'll go back to work, but it's a long road to travel.'

'I'd better go. There's an ambulance in the road. You take extra care, OK.'

'I will. Promise. And we'll come and see you soon. Bye.'

'Bye, love.'

Mel put the phone down, waves of relief flooding over her. She would send some flowers to Shirley to thank her. A horrible experience for her dad, she realised, but nothing like he would have suffered at the hands of the Albanians. Should she have warned him and told him about the attempted shooting? Maybe. Perhaps that was something to talk about when she finally managed to visit. In the meantime, she had to carry on piecing together what had happened to the skeleton in her garden.

Detective Sergeant Derek Palmer hadn't served seven years in Mexton Drugs Squad without developing an ability to see when something wasn't quite right. And something about the parcel on his doorstep, from the usual online retailer, was definitely off. For a start, he hadn't ordered anything from them, and there were no emails alerting him to an impending delivery. Maybe his wife had, but she would normally mention it. Also, the tape that held the parcel together was standard brown parcel tape, not the tape with multi-lingual phrases printed on it that the retailer normally used. He could see a small hole in the side of the packaging and was just about to pick the item up when something stayed his hand. A name flashed into his mind. Airey Neave.

An hour later, the street had been cordoned off, houses had been evacuated and Army explosives technicians, in blast suits, were working on the package. A military drone hovered overhead, filming everything they did and relaying images to a monitor in the control point. Derek watched as the technicians X-rayed the package without moving it, conferred and slowly sliced open the top. He couldn't see exactly what they were doing, but a few minutes later, one of the soldiers gave a thumbs up while his colleague picked up the remains of the bomb.

'What is it with you chaps?' asked the lieutenant in charge of the operation. 'This is the second nasty, aimed at police officers personally, that we've dealt with in the last couple of years.'

'Just doing our jobs,' shrugged Derek, 'but clearly pissing off the wrong people.'

'Well, you can reopen the road and let people back into their homes now. We'll get the bomb components to a lab and you'll have my report by the morning. Any questions?'

'No, no. Thanks very much for what your guys have done. We'll need a full forensic examination of the bits. If they got careless, we may get something on them.'

'Absolutely. Cheerio.'

Derek thanked the officer again and waited for the military vehicles to leave before phoning the station. Uniformed officers reopened the street and guided people back from the nearby church hall to which they had been evacuated. Derek's path and doorstep remained cordoned off with crime scene tape until SOCOs could examine it.

Feeling sick to his stomach, he phoned his wife.

'Alison, it's me. There's been bit of a situation. Someone put a bomb on the doorstep, so when your course finishes, we'll find a hotel to stay in for the night, if the SOCOs haven't finished. Everything's fine.'

'No, it fucking isn't,' she whispered. 'It's only the fact that I'm in the coffee lounge that stops me from screaming at you. What the hell have you been doing?'

'I don't blame you. This sort of thing's never happened before. Sure, I've put away some nasty people, but planting a bomb in a busy street is a line they wouldn't cross. I'm guessing it's something to do with the Albanian gang that blew up the police station, though why they would target me, I don't know.'

'But you led the drugs raid, didn't you?'

'Yes, a good result, but hardly crippling.'

'Perhaps they're sending a message. One you'd better bloody listen to. Christ, talk about prodding a hornet's nest. It's more like you've stuck your dick in a nest of scorpions.'

'I know, love, I know. We'll talk about it when you get back.'

'Too bloody right, we will. Meet me at the station at six-twenty, don't be late.' Her tone softened; there was a catch in her voice. 'I'm glad you're OK. Take extra care. I couldn't bear to lose you. Gotta go, we're starting again. Love you.'

'Love you too.'

A hundred miles from Mexton a woman answered a call on her burner phone.

'You right wrongs. I have a job for you. Are you interested?' the voice said.

'It depends on the job. And who you are.'

'I'll tell you my name when I know you're on board.'

'Sorry. I don't work like that.' She paused. 'Is this a burner?'

'Of course.'

'Then, I'll call you in a day or so, from a different number. Be prepared to identify yourself.'

There was a short silence.

'All right. But there is something you should be aware of. I know who you are.'

The woman cut the call and for the first time in her career, felt real fear.

Chapter Sixteen

Day 9

DI Steve Morton joined the team for the morning briefing and kicked off proceedings.

'You may already know that someone left a bomb on DS Palmer's doorstep yesterday. The bomb squad dealt with it and I've just read the report from the lieutenant in charge.'

The team, exhausted from hours of overtime, suddenly looked more alert.

'The device contained about two hundred grams of TATP, which would have blown your colleague to pieces had it detonated. It was made to look like an ordinary parcel, but DS Palmer was suspicious and didn't touch it. It was just as well he didn't because it contained a mercury tilt switch. The slightest tipping motion would have set it off. You may remember that the IRA used such a switch in the car bomb that killed Airey Neave MP at the House of

Commons in 1979. It looks as though they put it in place and then armed it by pulling a string out through a hole in the box. DS Palmer was extremely lucky.'

'Thank you, Steve,' said DCI Farlowe. 'Does SO15 have any thoughts about who planted it?'

'It doesn't match the style of any known groups. The triggering mechanism and other gubbins are unusual. I'll talk to colleagues in the Security Service, but my feeling is that it's probably the Albanians again.'

'Fuck,' someone muttered, amidst a general hubbub of consternation.

'Are there any forensics?' asked Addy. 'I mean, this one didn't go off.'

'Too early to be sure, but the lab did find a hair inside the box. They are also hoping for shed skin cells, especially on the tape that sealed the box. There were no retrievable fingerprints. Anyway, I'll hand you back to DCI Farlowe, but, before I go, I would urge you all to be extremely careful. You've had the briefing from the PSNI sergeant, so please take it to heart. DS Palmer was probably targeted because his team disrupted the drugs side of the Albanian operation, so anyone else involved is at risk. We've warned DS Idle, and DI Thorpe has moved up north to stay with family for the duration, but everyone should be on full alert.'

As he spoke, Mel suddenly wondered whether Tom was still at risk. His injury had been mentioned in the local press. Surely, they would leave him alone now?

'Anyway,' said Morton, 'if you need to talk to me, my door is always open, not least because it doesn't shut properly.'

The SO15 officer's reference to the dilapidated state of the building provoked a few wry grins but did little to lighten the mood.

Farlowe restarted the briefing once Morton had left, with DI Chidgey at his side.

'It looks as though we may get a lead from traces left on the bomb,' he began. 'But it will take some time before the lab gets back to us.'

'That's all very well, guv,' interrupted Martin, 'but knowing who they are doesn't help us much, if we don't know where they are.'

'Quite right, and I'm sorry to say that the surveillance camera aimed at the timber warehouse produced nothing. No-one seems to be using it, so it could have just been a transfer point, from which the women would have been moved off to brothels in town.'

'Do we have enough for a search warrant?' asked Trevor.

'Probably not,' Farlowe replied. 'It's also possible that the gang realised it was compromised, once we arrested that driver, and cleared everything out. It may be worth taking a look at the premises from the outside. Jack, can you organise that?'

'Yes, guv.'

'Do we have anything from the Land Registry? Any suspicious names on house sales?'

'Nothing, boss,' replied one of the civilian investigators. 'There are a few foreign names, but they seem OK. Many of the recent purchases seem to have been by companies, presumably buying to let. We're checking them out at Companies House, but nothing looks odd so far.'

'Thank you. Please keep at it.'

'How about estate agents?' suggested Addy. 'They may have seen some OCG members face to face. Perhaps they would remember them?'

'That's a good idea. We have a couple of photos of possible Albanian suspects from Interpol. Jack, organise teams to canvass all the local firms. We're looking for purchases or rentals of houses with several bedrooms, in run-down areas where people mind their own business. If purchases are involved, they would most likely go through without mortgages or surveys. If the places are rented, they would probably use forged references.'

'What about online estate agencies?' asked Martin. 'They wouldn't have met the clients in person.'

'Someone would need to meet a renter,' said Jack. 'They wouldn't just post the keys to them. There might be problems with GDPR in getting hold of details, but we can try. We wouldn't get a warrant to go fishing through their records, though. Trevor, can you check these out, and also look for recent sales in likely areas on Zoopla?'

'OK, Jack.'

'Right, then,' said Farlowe. 'Plenty to do. Ask for help from uniform if you need it. One piece of good news – a uniformed officer is being seconded to CID, temporarily, to replace DC Groves. If it works out, it could be permanent. From now on, DI Chidgey will be running things, but, if anything major comes up, I need to know immediately. Thank you.'

PC Sally Erskine pulled the marked police car onto the forecourt of the disused timber warehouse. Weeds grew through the cracked concrete, what few windows the building had were broken and leaking guttering had enabled a coat of moss to build up on one of the walls. A weather-beaten sign proclaimed that A.B.Grange and Sons imported the finest timber from around the world.

'What do you think, Reg? Waste of time?'

PC Reg Dawnay grunted and heaved himself out of the passenger seat, rubbing his back.

'Still getting trouble?' Sally asked, adjusting her stab vest and collecting a torch from the car.

'Yeah. Chasing after villains is getting too much for me. Still, I'm retiring in a few months. What will you do without me?' he joked.

'Well, life will never be the same, Reg.' Sally smiled. 'But I'm being seconded to CID, and hope to stay there, so I suppose I'll get over it.'

'You've got a friend there, haven't you?'

'Yes. Mel Cotton. We trained together. Right, let's take a look at this place and then go somewhere for a cuppa.'

As the two officers approached the building, Sally cast her eyes over the scene. She noticed several sets of tyre tracks where vehicles had recently parked close together. Debris had piled up against the huge roller shutter that formed the main entrance to the warehouse, but there was a smaller door, to the side, that looked as if it had been opened recently and was slightly ajar.

'Sally, look at this! Bring the torch,' yelled Reg, who had walked round the side of the building. 'Through this window.'

A shaft of light from missing roof tiles shone directly onto a chair, in a ghoulish parody of the *Mastermind* TV set. Instead of a receiving a gentle interrogation from Clive Myrie, someone had been tortured. Straps dangled from the arms of the chair and a pair of secateurs lay on the floor, next to a pool of dark, long-congealed, blood. More bloodstains were visible on the chair and the floor, as Sally played the torch beam across the scene.

'Fuck,' she said. 'That's horrible. I'll call it in. We have grounds for entry so let's take a look inside in case there's anyone alive in there. We'd better keep well away from the chair.'

They returned to the front of the building and Reg was about to push open the small door when Sally shouted.

'Stop, Reg! Get back.'

'What's the matter?' he said, puzzled.

'It doesn't seem right. Why would they leave evidence like that in full view and the door ajar? It's almost as if they're inviting us in.'

She approached the door cautiously and shone her torch through the narrow gap.

'Look. On the floor. There are clippings of electrical wire. The copper's still bright, so they weren't cut a long time ago. And see, here.' She shone a torch upwards. 'There's some sort of wire running from the door to what looks like a switch on the frame.'

'A booby trap, you think?'

'Well, it's not a bloody Christmas decoration. OK, keep well away from the door. I'll phone Mr Farlowe. He'll call the bomb squad. Thank God we didn't just charge in.'

'Quite the detective, aren't you?' said Reg, trembling

slightly. 'Thanks. I want to retire gracefully, not end my career with a bang. You'll do well in CID.'

'Thanks, Reg. Now, let's get well clear of this building in case they can blow it up remotely. We'll wait in the road until the cavalry arrives and then we'll go for that cuppa.'

Chapter Seventeen

MEL LOOKED up from a pile of printouts and smiled.

'Hi, Sally. What brings you to CID? I heard about you finding that booby trap. Brilliant spot!'

'Thanks, Mel. I've been seconded to help out, replacing Karen. I want to move to CID so the DCI is giving me a kind of trial. I'm to help you with the bones, and if it works out, I'll move on to other things.'

'That's brilliant! I'm up to my arse in this stuff and really need a hand. What do you know about the case?'

'Only that you got your garden dug over for free,' she grinned. 'The remains seem to be of a former rock star who went missing some years ago, after winning the lottery. It looks like he was murdered with a blow to the head. That's about it.'

'That's pretty much true. We've tracked him to a hotel in Melbourne, where he stayed for a few days. Then he disappeared. There's no record of him returning to the UK.'

'How about his family? Surely, they should have an idea

about what happened to him? And aren't they the obvious suspects?'

'Well, all his children benefited from his death, but not his siblings. He had a brother, a part-time lecturer in history at the university, and a sister with dementia who lives in a care home. His children, though – they're a mixed bunch. Let's get some coffee and I'll take you through them.'

With coffees in front of them, and a biscuit each, pinched from Trevor's stash, Mel began.

'Let me give you a potted bio of each of them, then we'll go and interview them together. I'll start with the oldest, Sarah Denise. She's forty, a social worker and environmental activist. She was arrested at a climate demo, which is why we have her DNA. She got off with a fine. She's married with two children, a girl of twelve and a boy of ten. I've spoken to her on the phone, to confirm she's Fearon's daughter, and she seemed quite open.

'Next, Grenville Malcolm. He's thirty-eight, a solicitor specialising in business and commercial law. I don't know much about his personal life but I know he's unmarried and, as far as I know, has no children. He has no social media profile and doesn't appear to be a member of any clubs or societies.'

'Mr Boring, then,' said Sally.

Mel chuckled. 'Maybe he has hidden depths. Anyway, bachelor number two is David Stephen, who likes to be known as Davvi. He's an IT entrepreneur, although I couldn't quite work out what his company, Davvitech Cyber, actually does. No children, although he seems to have had a number of girlfriends, judging by the press coverage. He's thirty-seven.

'Finally, there's Nicola Claire, a businesswoman who runs two companies. One operates an upmarket dating site and the other is an executive recruitment service. She's thirty-six and married to a stockbroker. Their only child, a six-year-old boy, is at prep school.'

'Do we know anything about their finances?'

'No, and we can't get a court order or warrant to look, unless we have evidence of potential wrongdoing. We can look at data on the businesses on the Companies House website – there's a job for you. Could you also set up interviews with the children? It might be worth talking to the brother, as well. The details are in this folder. Sorry to disappoint you, but CID work is mainly like this. Digging and collecting and recording information.'

'Really, Mel? I've been looking at re-runs of *The Sweeney* and I thought it was just like that.' Sally looked wide-eyed and innocent. 'And when do I get my shooter?'

'Daftie,' laughed Mel. 'I'm off to visit Tom. He should be out of hospital soon. Give me a call if you need anything. It's great to be working with you. We'll have a drink soon.'

'You're looking good, love. How are you feeling?' Mel kissed Tom and sat down on the chair beside his bed.

'Not so bad. My hand still hurts like fuck even though it's not there. They call it phantom pain. It should subside in time. My hearing's getting better in my left ear, but the right one is still buggered. They'll fit me up with a hearing aid in a few weeks when they know exactly how much damage was done. The good news is that I'll be out in a few days. I can't wait to get back to Sheila and Bruce. And you, of course.' He grinned.

'Tease,' Mel smiled.

'They'll give me some heavy-duty painkillers for a while, but it won't be for ever.'

'Well if you run out, I'm sure Derek Palmer could put you in touch with someone on the Eastside who can sort you out,' she joked. 'Did you hear that someone tried to blow him up?'

'Shit. No. The Albanians, I presume.'

'Most likely. We've all been told to be extra vigilant, and I guess that includes you.'

Tom looked worried.

'How about you?'

'There was an incident.' Mel spoke slowly. 'Someone looking like me was shot and killed on the canal towpath where I cycle home. It might have been meant for me.'

'Why the fuck didn't you tell me?'

Tom's expression was a mixture of shock, fear and anger.

'Because you had enough on your plate, recovering from being blown up. Anyway, I was fine and I doubt they'll try that again. I drive to work these days.'

'Mel, please, promise me you'll tell me if anything like that happens in future. I know danger comes with the job, but I couldn't bear the thought of losing you.'

Tom's eyes moistened and Mel put her arm round his shoulder, almost dislodging a lead that connected him to a monitor.

'I promise. And I felt the same about the prospect of losing you.'

They held each other for a few minutes, then Mel straightened up.

'I've got to get back to the station. Sally Erskine's joined us on secondment and I need to see what she's found. Can't wait to get you home. I'll tell the parrots you're coming back soon.'

'Twit,' laughed Tom. 'And for fuck's sake be careful.'

They exchanged goodbyes and endearments, and Mel walked slowly down the hospital corridor. She had made light of the murder attempt on her. She realised she was lucky and was scared the gang would try again. Oktapod, she knew, did not forgive.

Chapter Eighteen

'How did you get on, Sally?' Mel asked, when she returned to the station.

'Not too bad. I've contacted Fearon's children and set up a schedule for interviews, starting tomorrow morning. I've been checking out the businesses at Companies House, as you suggested, and have a list of directors. They're keeping it in the family, a bit. Grenville is a co-director of both Davvi's and Nicola's businesses, presumably because of his legal expertise. Sarah has no involvement with the companies. I'm looking into the other directors but, so far, nothing odd has come up.'

'Great, Sally. That's a good start. Anything else?'

'Yes. I've been digging around on social media. Nicola's dating site, Yourmatch.org, has come in for some stick. There are some posts from satisfied customers on Facebook and Twitter – wedding photos and so on – but also quite a few complaints. Several people said the fees were too high and a couple of blokes demanded refunds because, in their words, "they set me up with a cheap hooker".'

'Did they want expensive ones, then?' grinned Mel.

'I think it was the principle, not the price, they were complaining about,' Sally chuckled. 'Also of interest are some posts and tweets from former employees. On her websites Nicola emphasises how important her staff are to her. "They are the heart of the company", she claims, but, according to people who have left, she's a tyrant, imposing impossible workloads and creating a climate of fear in the office. This applies to the executive recruitment company, as well, although there've been no customer complaints about that one. Apparently, she threw a cup of coffee at one woman who dared to question her judgement and had to pay her compensation. It wasn't reported to us as an assault.'

'Hmm. Might be worth talking to some of the aggrieved workers, then.'

'OK. I'll try and get in touch with a few of them.'

'How about Davvi's company?'

'He's got a much larger web presence, as you'd expect. He seems to be presenting his company as a laid-back Californian-style outfit, where staff are encouraged to be creative and, in his words, "think outside the box". According to the website, they are encouraged to look after their mental welfare and enjoy being part of the organisation.'

Mel winced at the business cliché.

'However, there are complaints about long working hours from ex-employees, and the need to take stimulants to cope, so the image could be a sham. The company's certainly been profitable in the past year or so, though it was just scraping along until recently.'

'What about Nicola's companies?'

'They seem to be profitable. They've expanded in the last year and profits have increased.'

'It looks like the legacy from their father gave them both a boost. I bet they couldn't wait to have him declared dead. I noticed that Grenville handled the probate and other legal bits.'

'Of course. Why buy a dog and crap on the pavement yourself?'

Mel laughed. 'Don't you mean bark?'

'Not where I live,' replied Sally, grimly. 'Anyway, the new DI wants to see us all in the incident room at four, so we'd better grab some coffees and make our way there.'

'A really good start, Sally. It's going to be brilliant working with you.'

Sally blushed slightly and headed for the coffee machine.

'I've talked to Lieutenant Foxbury, whose team dismantled the IED in the timber warehouse,' began DI Chidgey. 'The device would have killed anyone within ten metres of the door, had it gone off. There were several drums of petrol next to it, so the warehouse would have been destroyed, along with any evidence. Well done Acting DC Erskine for spotting it.'

Sally blushed as the team applauded.

'What about the crime scene, guv?' asked Martin. 'Sally said it looked like someone had been tortured there.'

'She's right. SOCOs confirmed the presence of blood, a

couple of teeth and other bits of tissue around the chair. We are matching the blood with DNA from the young man found dead five days ago.'

'Did they find his tongue?' asked Addy.

'No. I expect rats took that,' replied Chidgey, 'unless someone kept it as a souvenir.'

Two detectives made exaggerated gagging sounds and the DI smiled slightly.

'Anyway,' he continued, 'the Crime Scene Manager described the scene as a "forensic feast". There were documents found there, bottles and cans that should yield DNA and fingermarks, and a number of other articles, some of which may give us leads. He said there were signs of at least four individuals there. It looks like they were careless this time, and we'll have the buggers for it.'

'But it's not just who,' said Martin, 'it's where.'

'I agree, but the documents might give us something there. Jack – you had people canvassing estate agents, didn't you?'

'Yes, guv. Martin and Trevor. They've done about half the firms in Mexton, with no joy. They should finish the rest tomorrow. We've got nothing from the Land Registry search.'

'OK. The bastards must have got hold of houses for their brothels somewhere, unless they are cuckooing.'

A couple of civilian investigators looked puzzled.

'Taking over someone else's premises to use as a base, like county lines drug gangs do,' explained Jack. 'I'll talk to the handlers of our informants. Ask them if anyone's heard anything.'

'Thanks, Jack.' Chidgey's tone became more sombre. 'I

understand that some of you appear to have been targeted personally by this bunch of shits, because of what you did to them last year. I get the general idea, but can you give me the details?'

Jack answered.

'Derek Palmer led a drugs raid on the Albanian OCG's premises. Mel Cotton retrieved a laptop with details of the gang's activities throughout the county, when we did a warrant on a house from which they were running cyber-scams. Tom Ferris led that raid.'

'But Tom wasn't targeted. He just happened to be closer to the bomb than the rest of us when it went off,' said Trevor. 'I was knocked over by debris, hence the broken arm. We think that was a non-specific attack on the police. They had already shot up the Environment Agency after one of their officers helped us shut down a scrapyard handling stolen car parts.'

'So, if they are going after specific officers, who else is at risk?'

'Me,' said Trevor, 'for one. I was involved in searching the dodgy scrapyard. They tried to kill me on site.'

'DI Thorpe and I arrested the scrapyard owner,' said Addy. 'And Jack chased the car that sprang him from custody to the farmhouse where they died. There's also DS Idle, from Vice, who led the raid on their brothels.'

'Fuck,' said Chidgey. 'Anyone else?'

'Obviously Mel, since they failed the first time. And Tom Ferris. They probably don't know how badly he was injured, but they'll realise he wasn't killed.'

Chidgey pursed his lips and exhaled noisily.

'Looks like you've all got bloody targets on your backs.

And from what I gather, after talking to Mr Farlowe, finding these bastards is like looking for a wedding ring in a slurry pit. But I'm told you're the best. Right, we're adjourning this meeting to the Cat and Cushion – that is your local, isn't it? Here's a few quid, Jack. Get a round in. Mine's a pint of Thatchers. I'll join you when I've spoken to the DCI.'

Chapter Nineteen

'"WILL THE CHARGES STICK?" a new DC on the team asked me. "Stick? They'll stick like shit to a blanket," says I. Not only did the daft twat post a photo of himself, in the stolen car, on Instagram, it was parked next to a CCTV camera when he nicked it. He tried to pretend it wasn't him, but how many other local scrotes have E-N-G-A-L-N-D badly tattooed on their forearm?'

The others laughed at Chidgey's anecdote.

'Anyway, putting him away was a job well done. He'd been twocking and burning cars since he was fourteen, but he'd always been more careful and we'd never managed to get enough evidence, even though we knew who he was. We found some cannabis on him, so maybe he just got a bit silly. So, go on, you've heard enough of my war stories. Give me some of yours. The dafter the better.'

Chidgey took a deep draught of his second pint of cider and waited expectantly.

Martin was the first to speak.

'We once arrested someone for stealing a donkey.'

'Go on,' said the DI.

'This idiot had been on the brew all evening, in a pub near the city farm. The landlord confiscated his car keys, as he was obviously unfit to drive, so he needed another form of transport to get home. He spotted a donkey, in a field at the farm, and decided that would do.'

'Oh, aye. Palm Sunday, was it?'

Martin grinned at the comment.

'Anyway, the donkey had other ideas. We spotted the man pulling the poor creature along the road, and when he tried to climb on its back, it kicked him in the balls. I've never seen someone sober up so fast.'

A couple of male officers winced, but most chuckled.

'So, we arrested the drunk and my mate calmed the donkey down, by giving it his sandwich, and led it back into the field.'

'So, what were the charges?' asked Mel.

'Breaking and entering and theft of the donkey. We considered animal cruelty, but we reckoned the donkey was crueller to the drunk than vice versa, so we didn't bother with that.'

'Nice one, Martin,' said Chidgey. 'Who's next?'

Emboldened by Martin's tale, Sally took a swig of her drink and smiled.

'We had reports of a flasher in one of the parks, so we drove there in an unmarked car. I put on a coat to cover my uniform and strolled around for half an hour or so. I'd just about given up when this bloke jumped out in front of me and whipped open his raincoat. I burst out laughing.'

Sally took another gulp.

'Instead of the scrawny tackle I expected, the bloke was wearing a fancy pair of scarlet knickers.'

'You're joking,' said Trevor.

'No, it's true. We arrested him but it clearly wasn't indecent exposure. All we could do was take him in for the theft of the pants, which he admitted stealing from Marks and Spencers.'

'His name wasn't Arnold Layne by any chance?' asked Jack, smiling.

'No, Derek Fontaine. Why?'

'Nothing.'

'So, you nicked the knicker nicker,' giggled Mel.

'Oh, that's bloody awful, Mel. You can get the next round in,' Sally groaned.

With new drinks in front of them, the others racked their brains for stories.

'I've got one. Well, sort of,' began Trevor. 'It was when Covid was starting and all sorts of scare stories about shortages were going around. We were called to a warehouse that supplies convenience stores with stock. It had been broken into and the manager couldn't believe what had gone.'

'So, what was stolen? Booze? Fags? Batteries?' asked Martin.

'Toilet rolls.'

'You're joking.'

'No. It's true. We did a quick calculation. Enough toilet rolls had been taken to keep a family of four supplied for around three years. Of course, the thief could have been planning to sell them on, expecting black market bog rolls to command a premium when everyone else was resorting to the *Daily Mail*, but, of course, the only shortages were because people were buying too many. There was a media panic about shops running out.'

Jack muttered a comment about the most appropriate use for the *Daily Mail*, and Mel asked if the thief was caught.

'Yes, he was. He was stopped by a traffic patrol outside town in the early hours because his car was so full of toilet rolls that he couldn't see out the back, and he was driving erratically because they were obstructing the gear lever. They'd originally meant to give him advice, but he looked guilty and wouldn't explain where the rolls had come from, so they took him in. We heard about it when we got back to the station and put two and two together.'

'I suppose he spun you a tissue of lies.' Mel, again.

'Yes, but he rolled over and told the truth.'

'Christ,' said the DI. 'Is that the standard of humour around here?'

'You'll get used to it, guv,' replied Jack. 'Some of us are getting their second childhood early.'

Mel grimaced at him. 'OK, I've got one,' she said, 'The giant meerkat of Mexton.'

'What?' asked Trevor. 'I didn't think we had any mythical beasts round here'

'Ah, well. I was a uniformed PC, on the night shift with Reg Dawnay. We were driving along this country lane, following up a report of sheep in the road, when this wild-eyed bloke came running out. We nearly hit him, but Reg managed to stop in time. He was clearly pissed and was babbling about a giant meerkat he'd seen, looking over a hedge at him. Reg asked him if it was trying to sell him insurance, in a Russian accent, but he didn't seem to understand. Then we saw the sign. Jim Peters' Alpaca Farm. It turned out that the bloke had been to a gin-tasting event at his local and had come off his bicycle on the way home. He'd looked up and seen an alpaca peering at him. The gin did the rest.'

'So, what did you do?'

'We put his bike in the car and gave him a lift home, then went looking for the sheep.'

'Well, I've heard of pink elephants. May have seen a few meself,' said Chidgey. 'But giant meerkats are a new one on me. Anyone else?'

'I've got to get back, guv,' said Trevor. 'Suzy is expecting me and I want to say goodnight to the youngster.'

'Same here,' said Addy. 'Victoria's waiting dinner for me.'

'OK,' replied the DI. 'Leave it till next time. And I'll tell you about the naked saxophonist of Nether Stowey.'

'We'll look forward to, it, boss,' said Mel, also getting up to leave. 'See you tomorrow.'

Left alone, Geoff Chidgey stared at the last drops of cider in his glass. Another pint perhaps? Maybe not. The solitary drinker in the corner of the pub usually looked pathetic, and he was way past eavesdropping on villains' conversations. No, he would phone for a taxi and have a drop of Scotch at home. At least, there, his loneliness wouldn't be so obvious.

Chapter Twenty

Day 10

Grenville Fearon, slim and dapper, ushered Mel and Sally into a meeting room at his firm's offices, exuding an air of urbanity and expensive aftershave.

'How can I help you? My secretary said you wanted to discuss my father's disappearance.'

'Yes, Mr Fearon. Thank you for seeing us,' replied Mel, showing her warrant card. 'I'm DC Mel Cotton and this is DC Sally Erskine. I'm afraid we have found a body, here in Mexton, and, after having carried out tests, we have identified it as your father. We are trying to establish how it got there, given that there is no record of him returning from Australia.'

'Good lord,' said Grenville, paling under his suntan. 'The family assumed he had died there. We had him declared dead once he had been missing for seven years.

Can I ask,' he weighed his words, 'is there anything suspicious about the remains?'

'I'm afraid so, sir,' said Sally. 'The evidence strongly suggests that he was murdered.'

'How?' Grenville asked, his voice trembling.

'We're not at liberty to say, at the moment,' interjected Mel. 'The coroner opened an inquest and adjourned it immediately, while we gather evidence. Do you recall when you last saw your father?'

'It was shortly after his lottery win. Sometime in June 2013. The exact date is in the papers presented to the court. I can find it if you need it.'

'Thank you. That would be helpful. How was he?'

'Elated, obviously. He was a successful musician, some years ago, but had spent most of the money he earned. He had been doing casual jobs, teaching guitar, and just about scraping by. Mum's earnings, as a local government officer, had supported him for a while, but she died in 2009. He was looking forward to spending his remaining years in comfort.'

'Why do you think he went to Australia?' asked Sally

'I believe it was something he'd always wanted to do. The beaches and the wildlife appealed to him, I think.'

'How did you get on with your father?' Mel asked

'OK, I suppose. I won't say we were particularly close. My career contrasted somewhat with his former lifestyle, but there was no particular disagreement.'

'I understand he refused to share his lottery winnings with his family. How did you feel about that?'

'How did you know that?' Grenville responded, sharply.

When Mel didn't answer he continued. 'It was his money. It was up to him what he did with it.'

He looked at his watch.

'Now, if you'll excuse me, I have a meeting with a client shortly and need to prepare. My secretary will see you out.'

'Thank you for your time, sir,' said Mel. 'We may need to talk to you again.'

'Of course. Please make an appointment in advance. Good day, ladies.'

As soon as the detectives left the room, Grenville picked up his phone and dialled. It was answered in three rings.

'We need to talk,' he said, closing the meeting room door.

'What did you think of him, Sally?' asked Mel as they walked to their car.

'I don't know. He didn't seem upset about his dad's death. More on edge than distressed. How did you know the father wouldn't share his winnings with his children?'

Mel chuckled. 'When we bought the house, the estate agent was indiscreet and told us so.

'Well, they've clearly got a motive for killing him, but, if they did, they waited a long time to collect. How much was it, anyway?'

'About four and a half million. They ended up with just under a million each, when duties and fees had been paid.'

'So why is Grenville still working? It can't be the excitement of the job, surely.'

'A good question. One for another time, I think. Now, let's see what Nicola has to say for herself.'

Mel and Sally were offered coffee by a blonde receptionist with armour-piercing fingernails and an orange tan that would have put Donald Trump's to shame. They declined.

'Nicola will be with you in a moment,' she said. 'She's just on the phone.'

A few minutes later, Nicola Fearon, tall, curvy and fashionably dressed, swept into the reception area, a frown on her face. She invited the detectives into her office.

'What's this about? I'm afraid I'm extremely busy. I can only spare you a few moments. Is this a formal interview?'

'No, no,' reassured Mel. 'You're not under caution or anything. We just want a quick chat about your father.'

'Well, I know he's dead and probably murdered. I've just spoken to Grenville. I don't see that I can tell you any more than Grenville did. He won the lottery, banked his winnings and buggered off Down Under. We never saw him again, so how he ended up back in Mexton, I've no idea.'

'How did you get on with your father?' asked Sally.

'OK, I suppose. He wasn't exactly a hands-on parent, but he was never violent or neglectful. We always had enough to eat, although Mum's income from the Council was partly responsible for that.'

'And when you grew up?'

'Didn't see him much. I was too busy setting up the business. There was the odd family get-together, and, for a while we went to Mum and Dad's for Christmas, but we were never a really close family.'

'How did you feel when he wouldn't share his winnings?' asked Mel.

'Well, how would you bloody feel?' snapped back Nicola. 'Just a small part would have helped grow my business, but the selfish...' She reined herself in. 'We all felt let down, but, I suppose, he had the right to do whatever he wanted with his own money.'

'Did you argue?'

'No. I suppose I was too proud to plead with him. Is that all?'

'Just one more thing,' said Mel. 'You say you weren't a very close family. How do you get on with your brothers and sister?'

Nicola looked puzzled.

'Fine. Grenville is a co-director of my companies and also of Davvi's. Sarah's OK but a bit of a snowflake. We meet up for a meal from time to time. Now, I really must be going. There's a glitch in the recruitment software and the IT guy will be here any minute.'

She stood up, wished them goodbye and left the receptionist to show them out.

'A charming woman,' said Sally. 'Do you buy that story about the software glitch?'

'No,' replied Mel. 'She wanted to get rid of us. I'd be interested to know how they really got on with their father, and with each other. I doubt that we'll get a straight answer, though. Who's next?'

'Sarah can't see us until after work and Davvi is busy until two thirty. Lunch?'

'Yeah. Coffee and soup at the Ace of Spades?'

'Good idea. I need a change from the excuses for sandwiches they sell at work.'

'OK. My treat.'

Chapter Twenty-One

WHILE MEL and Sally were interviewing Fearon's family, Trevor and Martin were trudging round the town's estate agents. Last on their list was Edwards and Biggs. When they arrived, Lester Edwards was out with a client, but Robbie Biggs invited them into his office.

'How can I help you, gentlemen?' he said, having inspected their warrant cards. 'I take it you're not here to buy or sell a house.'

'I'm afraid not, sir,' replied Trevor. 'We are investigating a serious matter and we need some information about some people who may have been clients of yours.'

'Well, I'm not sure I can help you. Confidentiality and all that. But ask away.'

Martin showed him the, by now dog-eared, photos of the OCG members that Interpol had sent.

'Have you had anyone looking like these men enquiring about properties in Mexton? They would be houses with several bedrooms, not necessarily in the best condition, and in the less salubrious parts of town. The men would probably have had eastern European accents.'

Something flickered across Biggs's face as he handed the photos back.

'Sorry. I can't help you. If you need access to confidential information, you'll need to get a warrant. Now, I have a viewing, so I must leave you. Please feel free to look at the properties on display. You may see something you like.'

Biggs grabbed his car keys and coat, and left the office without looking back.

'What did you say to him?' asked the receptionist, a neatly dressed young woman with a diamond piercing in her nose and an impish grin. 'He shot out the door as if you'd shoved a stoat up his arse. I've never seen him move so quickly.'

The detectives laughed.

'He wasn't very helpful,' said Martin. 'Quoted confidentiality and told us to get a warrant.'

'What did you want to know, anyway?'

'We're trying to find if these eastern Europeans,' he proffered the photos, 'have enquired about slightly iffy houses in dodgy areas of Mexton in the past few months.'

She looked at the photos and grinned.

'I know why the old bastard blanked you. This guy, the one on the left, came in a couple of times. He leered at me a lot but I didn't like looking at him. He had a tattoo of a snake peering out above his T-shirt. I'm not a fan of snakes. I'm Josie Norwood, by the way.'

'You're not a fan of Mr Biggs, either, Josie,' said Trevor.

'No, I'm not. The dirty sod keeps patting my bum and

brushing up against my tits. I'd tell him where to go if I could find another job.'

'Do you want us to arrest him for sexual assault?' asked Martin. 'What he does is illegal.'

'No, but I'm happy to help you. Let me look in the files. I think I can remember the guy's name.'

A few minutes later the office printer disgorged several sheets of paper.

'This is the property he bought,' said Josie. 'And he was also interested in these. There's no reason why Robbie couldn't tell you. All sales should be recorded on the Land Registry, though I suppose someone could forget to do so.'

'Was there anything odd about the sale? And can you tell me which solicitor acted for the buyer?'

'I remember thinking it went through very quickly. No mortgage, no survey. And Biggsy was very furtive about it. Not long after, I took him some coffee in his office and he shut his desk drawer in a hurry. I caught a glimpse of a roll of notes. He wasn't pleased to see me. This was the solicitor.'

She scribbled a name on the printouts.

'Josie, you've been incredibly helpful,' said Martin, tucking the papers into his coat pocket. 'At some time, we may need a formal statement from you, but not at the moment. Oh, it might be wise not to mention you've spoken to us.'

'Don't worry. As I said, I need this job. It's a treat to get one over the old sod.'

Trevor and Martin left Josie with a huge grin on her face. As soon as they were out of sight Martin punched the air.

'A result! At last, a result.'

Trevor grinned and waved the cast on his arm in agreement.

'We'll drive past the property on the way back to the station,' said Martin. 'Just to check it out. Then we'll break the good news to DI Chidgey.'

Number 37, Jubilee Terrace, had clearly seen better days. Paintwork was peeling, the garden was a repository for rubbish and an assortment of flora was growing in the gutters. The windows were blocked out by thick curtains, and the front door was warped, although a modern looking mortice lock, its keyhole cover still shiny, had been fitted recently.

'A typical modern knocking-shop,' said Trevor. 'No-one can see what goes on, the neighbours mind their own business and I'll bet the women never leave the house.'

'You're jumping to conclusions a bit, aren't you?' countered Martin. 'There is one odd thing, though. That's a fibre broadband wire going into the building, the only one in the street. I wonder what's going on there?'

'Maybe we'll find out, if we can find probable cause to do a warrant. Let's get back to the nick. I could murder a cuppa and a biscuit.'

As Martin put the car into gear and pulled away from the kerb opposite the building, neither of the officers noticed the smartphone poking around the edge of a curtain, photographing their number plate.

Chapter Twenty-Two

'Look, I really don't think I can help you,' said Davvi Fearon. 'I know why you're here. My brother phoned me. And I'm busy. Really busy.'

Mel and Sally looked around the open-plan office at Davvitech Cyber, taking in a dozen employees working at computers, their eyes not leaving the screens. Coffee cups and energy bar wrappers overflowed from waste baskets and the whole place smelled slightly of unwashed bodies and despair.

'May we speak in your office? It won't take long, I promise,' said Mel.

Davvi grudgingly led them to a glassed-in area at the back of the room. He offered them neither seats nor coffee and perched on the edge of his desk with his arms folded.

'Get on with it, then.'

'We are trying to understand,' began Mel, 'how your father got back from Australia without leaving a record of his journey and ended up dead in a garden in Mexton.'

'No idea.'

Davvi's left knee was jerking up and down and his eyes flitted around the room, barely looking at the detectives.

'How did you get on with your father, Mr Fearon?'

'Fine. Fine. We weren't particularly close, but we had no major disagreements. I was much closer to my brother and sisters, if you must know.'

'So that's why Grenville is a co-director of your company.'

'Yes. And he's on the board of Nicola's. We all try to support each other.'

'How about Sarah? She seems to be the odd one out.'

Davvi shrugged. 'She's a bit hippydip. Not interested in business. She's OK, though.'

'How did you feel when your father refused to share his winnings?'

'Disappointed, obviously, but it was his and he could do what he liked with it. There was no point arguing with him.'

'What exactly does your company do, Mr Fearon?' asked Sally.

'Look, I haven't time to explain. Take one of these brochures when you go and look at our website.' He thrust a glossy booklet at them. 'Have you finished? Can I get back to work now?'

'Thank you, Mr Fearon. That will do for the moment. We may want to talk to you again.'

'Well, please make an appointment if you do. You can detect your own way out, I'm sure. Good day to you.'

Fearon turned his back on his visitors and started to fiddle with a coffee machine.

'Well, he was either seriously scared or on something controlled,' said Mel. 'I bet we'd find traces of white powder by the sink in the gents.'

Sally chuckled.

'What do we know about his background?'

'Apart from his degree in applied rudeness, you mean? He's unmarried, lives alone and appears a lot on social media in the company of young women, but rarely the same one twice. Judging by his haircut and clothes, I reckon he tries to look younger and cooler than he really is. Part of the thrusting IT entrepreneur image, I suppose. He did an IT degree, worked for a number of firms and set up his own company shortly before his father left the country.'

'Well off?'

'He must be, with the legacy from his father. After a slow start, the company seems to be doing well, although it's not spectacular. Anyway, so far we've heard from the business-oriented members of the family. We'll see if Sarah has a different perspective. It would be useful to talk to Alan's brother, Peter, too.'

Sarah Fearon ushered them into an empty room at the Mexton Social Care offices and collapsed into a chair.

'Do, please, sit down,' she said wearily. 'There's machine coffee if you'd like some, but I wouldn't recommend it.'

The two detectives declined.

'A difficult day?' queried Mel.

'Every day's a difficult day in this economic climate,' Sarah replied. 'I've spent the last hour with your DC Cathy Merritt, discussing four urgent child protection cases. One child will be removed from a dangerous environment in the next hour or so, but I'm desperately trying to find placements for three others. I'll probably be up all night. It's heartbreaking. Anyway, what did you want to talk to me about?'

'Your father, Ms Fearon,' answered Sally. 'We're trying to establish how his remains came to be in a garden in Mexton when he was supposed to be in Australia. I'm sure you know we believe he was murdered.'

'Yes. And the first suspects are his family,' she said, ruefully. 'I'm afraid I can't help you. I haven't seen him since he called us together one evening in June 2013, announced he was leaving for Australia and told us he wasn't going to share his lottery winnings with us.'

'Can you tell us about that meeting?' asked Mel. 'Your brothers and sister didn't say much about it.'

'I'm not surprised. There was the most almighty row. Nicola and Davvi said they needed the money to expand their businesses, Grenville wanted money because...well, he just likes money. I wanted nothing to do with it and went for a walk in the garden.'

'Did it look as though things were getting violent?'

'Not really. Well, I don't think so. Davvi was very whiney, saying he deserved it more than the others. Grenville was coldly furious – he can convey an awful lot of hate without raising his voice – and Nicola had a screaming fit, arguing that her businesses were more deserving.'

'That's interesting,' said Sally. 'Davvi said you were close.'

'Well, I've no idea why he would say that. Those three were always at each other's throats, competing for attention and trying to borrow money from Dad, even though he barely had any. I kept out of it. As you can see from my profession, I'm more interested in people than money.'

'So what did you do with your share of the legacy?' asked Mel.

'Paid off my mortgage, invested in a few green energy companies and donated some to environmental charities. I kept enough to ensure I won't starve in my old age.'

'Right. Getting back to that evening, when did you leave?'

'Before the others. I interrupted their argument and said goodbye to Dad. I told him I wasn't interested in the money, that he should enjoy himself with it and that he must let us know how he was getting on. Then I went home.'

'And he was perfectly well?'

'Yes. I tried to phone him later, to ask for contact details, but there was no answer. I assumed he'd worked his way through the bottle of champagne I saw on the table.'

'What time was this?'

'I can't remember exactly. It was about eight years ago. Late evening, I guess.'

'And did he keep in touch?'

'No, I'm afraid not.'

'OK. Thank you, Ms Fearon. We'll let you get on,' said Mel. 'Here's my card. Please give me a ring if you think of anything else relevant.'

'Well, that was an eye-opener,' said Sally, as they walked back to the car. 'If Grenville, Nicola and Davvi weren't exactly lying to us, they were certainly being economical with the truth. Assuming Sarah was telling the truth, that is.'

Mel grinned. 'It certainly was. But remember the detective's ABC.'

'ABC?'

'Assume nothing, believe no-one, check everything.'

'OK, clever-clogs. So, do we believe there was a big row the evening before Fearon left for Australia? And was Sarah lying about relationships in the family?'

'Well, there may be one way of checking whether there was a row or not. I'll talk to my neighbour who lives at the back of us. I think he was living there eight years ago. Come on, and I'll even make you a decent cup of coffee when we've finished.'

Chapter Twenty-Three

HENRY FOLDSWORTHY WAS the sort of man who, within ten minutes of meeting you, would regale you with details of his bowel issues and other medical problems. This need to share was not only inappropriate but embarrassing to most people. His urge to talk incessantly was complemented by a deep interest in things that happened around him; things that almost invariably displeased him. People not sorting their recycling, failing to clean up after their dogs or parking, albeit legally, outside his premises – all these prompted his ire, and he was widely suspected of being the author of the passive-aggressive notes posted regularly through his neighbours' letter-boxes.

Unsurprisingly, when the forensic anthropologist and the SOCOs were excavating Mel's and Tom's garden, he was a near-permanent fixture, standing on a chair and peering over the fence, attempting to interrogate the people working there. He questioned the couple repeatedly, despite being refused concrete information every time, and sought more details of the delicious drama from the local press and the internet.

He was, therefore, an ideal witness to what might have happened to Alan Fearon, and he was only too willing to share his thoughts when Mel and Sally called on him. He buttoned up his cardigan and smoothed his thinning hair when he heard the knock, a frisson of excitement running through him. They wanted to talk to him about the bones, he was sure. He would be a witness in a real murder inquiry. How exciting!

'Good afternoon, Mr Foldsworthy,' said Mel, showing her warrant card. 'This is my colleague, DC Erskine. May we come in?'

'Yes, please do. Would you mind taking your shoes off?'

The two detectives complied and followed their host into a fussily furnished sitting room that faced the street. A nineteen fifties style three-piece suite, complete with antimacassars, dominated the room, while a small table beside the window held a pair of binoculars and a notebook. China sculptures of dogs, milkmaids and anthropomorphised rodents decorated a tiled fireplace, of the same vintage as the suite, and the floral wallpaper was clearly a relic of many decades ago. His mother's taste, surmised Mel. A bookcase in the corner contained two shelves of identical notebooks, as well as a number of true crime books, and a faint smell of lavender permeated the room.

'Do sit down. Would you like some tea? And perhaps a biscuit? I have some Rich Teas in the pantry.'

'No thank you, Mr Foldsworthy,' replied Mel, as they sat, uncomfortably, on the overstuffed sofa. 'I'd be happy to chat to you another time, but we're here on official business.

We wondered whether you could help us with our inquiry into the remains found in my garden.'

Foldsworthy perked up like a dog offered its favourite treat.

'Yes of course. What do you want to know?'

'We have identified the bones as belonging to Mr Alan Fearon. I'm sure you remember him.'

'I most definitely do,' replied Foldsworthy. 'An unkempt individual, always playing his wretched electric guitar whenever he was at home. Sometimes as late as ten o'clock at night. He never bothered to keep his garden tidy or maintain the house like you and Tom do. I wasn't sorry when he went away. To Australia, his daughter said. I spoke to her over the fence. But how come he was buried in the garden? What are your theories?'

'I can't divulge details of our investigation, I'm afraid, but I wonder whether you can remember anything about the day he left. That would be the seventeenth of June 2013.'

Foldsworthy looked disappointed but then stood up and pulled a notebook from the bookcase. He riffled through the pages and looked up.

'That's right. The seventeenth. Nothing much happened during the day. Two youths were playing football in the park in the afternoon, and Mrs Colton's dog chased them. She should have kept the stupid animal on a lead, otherwise it wouldn't have ended up under that lorry. It survived, but the vet's bill must have been enormous.'

'How about the evening?'

'Now that was interesting. Fearon was playing his guitar in a back room, through some sort of amplifier. It was seven forty. I was trying to watch a documentary, so I went round, banged on his door and complained. He just laughed and said he was going to turn the volume up. I was leaving when I saw several cars pull up at the front, in quick succession, and four people got out. I didn't recognise them, but I later found out one was his daughter. I've got the car numbers, if you're interested.'

'Was there any more noise?' asked Sally.

Foldsworthy looked again at his notebook.

'All was quiet until about eight o'clock when there was a lot of shouting. It went on for a good few minutes.'

'Could you hear what was being said?'

'No. I recognised Fearon's voice, and there was another man and a woman. It didn't last long and his visitors left about half an hour later, although I think one had already left, slamming their car doors and revving their engines. Most inconsiderate.'

He turned the page.

'It was quiet then, but I heard a car at about half past eleven. My bedroom's at the back and I hadn't yet dozed off. I didn't get up, and went to sleep soon afterwards. Once I'm asleep, I stay that way. The sleep of the just, my mother used to say.'

'Did you see any of his family members later?'

'Yes. I saw his daughter. A smartly dressed woman. She came round the following day, told me where he'd gone and asked me to keep an eye on the house. I assumed that the noise in the night was him leaving.'

'Well, you've been extremely helpful, Mr Foldsworthy. Thank you very much,' said Mel, closing her notebook.'

'Delighted to...er...help the police with their inquiries.

Isn't that the phrase? Do pop in for a cup of tea, soon. And how's your Tom?'

'Getting better, thank you. He'll be home in the next few days. Please let me know if you think of anything else.'

Foldsworthy showed them out, a satisfied smile on his face. He had a lot to put in his notebook and he would even delay having his tea to do it.

'What a weird neighbour you have,' said Sally, as they sat in Mel's kitchen. 'He's like one of those busybodies in *Midsomer Murders,* but sent back in time to the nineteen fifties.'

'Yes,' chuckled Mel. 'He lived there with his mother until she died and seems to have changed nothing in the house since. He was a park keeper until he was made redundant and then a council traffic warden for a while. He retired with stress-induced illness years ago and keeps himself busy monitoring the neighbourhood. I'm surprised he heard the last of the vehicles, but it's a quiet area and sound carries. Still, at least we know there really was a row the night before Fearon left. More coffee?'

'No thanks. I'd better be off. I'll leave you to the parrots.'

Some checking to do, thought Mel, as she closed the door. What really happened during the row? Which daughter made a point of telling Foldsworthy that Fearon had gone to Australia? It sounded like Nicola, judging by Foldsworthy's comment on her dress. Plenty to think about – and there was also the brother to interview.

Chapter Twenty-Four

Day 11

Dr Peter Fearon met Mel and Sally in the foyer of the University history department and led them to his office. He shifted piles of journals off a couple of chairs, invited them to sit down and apologised for not offering them coffee. An old Adler electric typewriter sat on a table at the side of the room, next to an elderly computer, and there was no laptop visible.

'How can I help you, officers?' he asked, steepling his fingers, with his elbows on his desk. 'I presume this is something to do with my brother?'

'Yes, sir,' replied Mel. 'I'm sorry for your...'

Dr Fearon brushed aside her condolence before she could complete it.

'Don't worry. We were never close and we hadn't spoken in years. There was no particular animosity between us; just a mutual lack of interest in each other. Our paths diverged many years ago.'

'So when did you last see him?' asked Sally.

'Probably at my sister-in-law's funeral, in 2009. I think we exchanged a few words, but we were really strangers.'

'Have you had any contact with your nieces or nephews?'

'I used to get Christmas cards from them, probably out of a misplaced sense of obligation. I didn't bother to reciprocate so they stopped sending them.'

'So you've no idea what they do? You haven't followed them on social media or anything?'

'I don't go in for that TwitFace stuff. Total waste of time and I don't understand it. I use email and some specialist historical websites for my research, but that's the limit of my competence with online stuff.'

'Can I ask what you do here, Dr Fearon?' asked Mel.

'I give a few lectures and take some tutorials. Much of my time is taken up with research. I'm something of an expert on the effects of the Russian revolution on that country's neighbours.'

'Do you travel much?'

'I have done in the past, but I'm a bit too old for extensive field trips these days.'

'Getting back to your brother, have you any idea who might want to kill him?'

'That's a rather silly question, officer, given that I've already told you I've had no contact with him for years.'

'I'm sorry, sir. I had to ask,' Mel said. 'So you didn't know about his lottery win?'

'No. But I'm not surprised he paid the stupidity tax. He

always was careless with money. I take it he was one of the lucky few?'

'Yes, sir. He won a substantial sum. He died shortly after but his remains were only found recently.'

'Didn't do him much good, then, did it?'

'I'm afraid not. Just one more question, if you don't mind. Can you tell me where you were on the seventeenth of June 2013?'

'I probably can, but I don't see why I should. Are you accusing me of being involved in Alan's death?'

'No sir. It's just routine.' Mel attempted to reassure him.

The academic drummed his fingers on his desk, then pointed over Sally's shoulder to a row of faded posters on his office wall. One, headed 'Revisiting the Russian Revolution: A historico-geographic perspective', advertised a conference, held in Budapest, over three days covering the date of Alan Fearon's last sighting. His brother was listed as a keynote speaker.

'I was there for the whole conference,' Dr Fearon said, starchily. 'I flew out the day before and returned the evening after it finished. There are numerous well-respected individuals who can confirm that, as can British Airways. Good enough for you?'

'Yes, sir. Thank you. We won't take up any more of your time.'

'Well good day to you, then. I'm sure you can find your way out. Turn right out of my office and follow the corridor to the lifts.'

Mel nodded in response, left her business card and wished him good bye.

As soon as the detectives had left, Dr Fearon pulled a

laptop from his desk drawer, switched on his VPN and headed straight for his favourite social media groups. Then, using Tor, he visited a site that provided him with some very specific services. Services that he would never admit to using.

'Not much brotherly love there, was there?' commented Sally.

'Nope. Not a lot,' replied Mel. 'Do you believe that he's had no contact with his brother since his sister-in-law's funeral?'

'Seems a bit improbable, although Alan Fearon has been out of the limelight since the mid-seventies. I suppose some families are like that. Is it worth talking to Sarah Fearon again? See if she knew of any rows between the brothers? She seemed to be the most open of the siblings.'

'Yes, we should. And could you check with the airlines whether he took the flights we think he did? Just in case the Australian Embassy got it wrong.'

'Will do. God, are all university lecturers that unpleasant?'

'I'm sure they're not. I met DI Thorpe's husband, Mike, at a Christmas do, once. He's lovely. But I can't help feeling there was something a bit off about Dr Peter.'

'Police 101. How can I help you?'

'Oh, hello. I'd like to report someone carrying a rifle.'

'Indeed, sir. Can I have your name and address?'

The operator noted down the caller's details.

'Was this in a public place sir? If so, you should have called 999.'

'No. It was on farmland outside Mexton.'

The caller gave the grid reference.

'It's not illegal to own a rifle on private land, sir, as long as a firearms certificate is held. Many people have rifles for pest control or hunting.'

'Yes, but this was a Kalashnikov. An AK-47. It's an automatic weapon. Surely you can't get a licence for one of those?'

'No, sir. But may I ask if you are a member of the armed forces?'

'No. I'm a birdwatcher. I was watching a peregrine stoop on a pigeon when I saw it.'

'So how can you be sure it was an AK-47?

'I've seen it on the films. The curved magazine is distinctive. I know what I saw.'

'Well thank you for informing us, sir. I'll log your call and we will get back to you if we need anything more. Have a good evening.'

The operator took off her headphones, stretched and addressed her colleague.

'Daftest call of the shift so far. Bloke thinks he saw someone with a machine gun on a farm near Mexton. Honestly, he watches a couple of *CSI: Wherever* programmes and reckons he's a gun expert. It was probably an old shotgun.'

'Better log it anyway,' her colleague advised. 'Just in case.'

Chapter Twenty-Five

Day 12

DI Chidgey coughed loudly and the incident room fell quiet.

'First off,' he began, 'we've had some forensics back from the timber warehouse. There was a DNA match between blood on the floor and Shelia, so we can be pretty sure that's where he was tortured. Several additional profiles were recovered, from blood, hair and other tissues, but, as yet, they've not been matched to anyone. There were prints on drinks cans and bottles, but they were generally smudged. Some ridge details in blood on various implements could be useful when we have suspects in custody, but they didn't match anyone on our system. We're sending what we have to Interpol to see if they can help.

'That's me done, so what have you got to report, folks? Can we start with Operation Fieldmouse?'

Martin was the first to speak.

'A couple of months ago, one of the Albanians whose photos we got from Interpol was involved in buying number 37 Jubilee Terrace, a slightly run-down property not far from the centre of town. Trevor and I took a look at it, and all the indications are that it's being used for something dodgy, probably a brothel.'

'You didn't go in did you? Sample the wares?' Chidgey joked.

Martin looked affronted.

'No, boss. We just looked at the place and took pictures. I'll put them on the board later. There's a couple of other properties the suspect was interested in. I'll check who bought them with the Land Registry.'

'OK. Anything else?'

'Well, the sale went through suspiciously quickly. It's possible that the estate agent was bribed to move things along, keep quiet about the sale and, possibly, undervalue the property. It belonged to an elderly lady who died. And the most interesting thing is that the solicitor who handled the conveyance was Vernon Chawte. He was the brief who got bail for Guzim Marku, who, you will remember, was killed shortly after he left the court, by his Albanian confederates.'

'I heard about that,' said the DI. 'I bet he wished he'd been remanded.'

'They'd have probably got to him inside,' said Jack, morosely.

'OK. Can we take a look at this dodgy brief, then? See what else he's been up to. Look at other court cases and so on.'

'I'll do that,' volunteered Trevor. 'Are we going to raid the brothel?'

'No. I don't think so,' said Chidgey. 'Jack – talk to Vice and see if they've heard anything about the premises. My feeling is that if we move against them too soon we'll only chop off one head of the bloody hydra. I shouldn't think there'd be evidence linking anyone to the bomb there.'

'What's counter-terrorism doing?' asked Addy.

'I don't know and I think it's time we had a chat with them, and also with the NCA. We're supposed to be working together, but I haven't heard a peep. I'll speak to DCI Farlowe. Is there anything else on Fieldmouse?'

When no-one answered he turned to Mel.

'Can you summarise where you've got to with the bones?'

'Yes, guv. In brief, at least three of his children had a motive for murdering him for his money. They hated the fact that he wouldn't share his winnings, and according to the daughter who said she wasn't interested in his money, and the next-door neighbour, there was an argument on the evening before he left. Later that night the neighbour heard a car and assumed it was Alan Fearon going to the airport. We still don't know how he got back from Australia undetected or exactly when he was killed.'

'Right. Thanks, Mel. If they killed him, couldn't they have made it look like a car accident or something, instead of concealing his body and waiting for him to be declared dead? Anything else?'

'Sally and I did manage to talk to the victim's brother. He claims not to have had any contact with Alan Fearon for years, or any knowledge of his activities, for that matter.

He's a social media denier, apparently. We thought there was something a bit odd about him. When we asked him where he was when Alan was last seen in the UK he got quite shirty but then told us he was at a conference in Hungary.'

'I checked,' interjected Sally. 'Alan took the flight we thought he did and arrived in Australia on the eighteenth.'

'So, who the fuck do we have as suspects, then? Anyone from his past? Someone who he crossed or upset after his career collapsed? We don't really know what he's been doing these past thirty years or so.'

'I still reckon it has to be one of his children. Or a conspiracy. None of them liked him, although Sarah seemed a bit more favourably disposed towards him than the others. I suppose she could have been hiding a burning hatred, but I didn't think so. Three of them didn't mention the row, and there are inconsistencies in their accounts. Maybe it was an accident and they panicked.'

'But if they killed him for his lottery win, it was a bloody long wait before they collected,' Martin observed, 'and, anyway, he was alive when he travelled so they couldn't have killed him on the seventeenth.'

'True. But perhaps they could afford to take out loans, knowing that they would inherit in the end.'

'Bit of a gamble,' said Chidgey. 'He could have left the lot to a donkey sanctuary or something. But, I agree, they're the favourites. You'd better re-interview them, under caution.'

'Already planned, guv.'

'OK, keep at it and keep me informed. Carry on, everyone.'

As Mel left the incident room in search of coffee her phone rang.

'DC Cotton?' an unfamiliar voice asked.

'Yes. Who's this?'

'DS Lauderdale. Independent Office for Police Conduct. Can you meet me in reception? We need a chat.'

Chapter Twenty-Six

MEL GREETED DS Lauderdale with icy politeness, barely concealing her fury.

'Good morning. What can I do for you?'

The IOPC officer led her into a side room and shut the door behind them.

'Please sit down. This won't take long. And I must make it clear that this is an informal discussion and not part of any disciplinary process. You can have a Police Federation rep present if you like, but I can assure you it won't be necessary.'

They both sat, Mel feeling puzzled and still furious.

Lauderdale opened a cardboard file and leafed through a sheaf of papers.

'I presume this is about Ricky Marriott,' said Mel, wanting to get things moving.

'Yes, it is. Saving his life earned you a commendation, but, as you know, he's claimed you assaulted him by giving him an injection without his consent. I have spoken to your

DCI and to DS Vaughan. They confirm that at no time did Mr Marriott tell you to stop. Indeed, he was probably incapable of doing so, they told me. So, as far as the IOPC is concerned, you did nothing wrong. You acted professionally, with compassion, and discharged your duty as a police officer to preserve life. The CPS agrees.'

'So why,' asked Mel, both relieved and aggrieved, 'did you summon me down here and scare the shit out of me?'

'Because of an oddity. Mr Marriott said nothing about an assault complaint while on remand or during his trial. He only raised it after he'd been sentenced and placed in a long-stay prison. No-one at the hospital, the custody suite or the remand prison reported him expressing any animosity towards you, or DS Vaughan, for that matter.'

'So?'

'So, we think he was put up to it by someone he met in prison. Someone who does bear a grudge. Can you think of anyone that might be?'

'Well, I've arrested quite a few people, both as a PC and a DC. I suppose there are two groups who may bear grudges. The right-wing terrorists and paedophiles we took down a couple of years ago and the Albanian gang we disrupted last year. Of the two, the Albanians are the more likely. They have a reputation for vengeance and tried to shoot me a few days ago, as well as planting that bomb.'

'Can you give me a list of likely names?'

Mel nodded her agreement.

'You mentioned Jack,' she said. 'Did Marriott complain about him as well?'

Lauderdale hesitated then came to a decision.

'As there are no disciplinary proceedings happening, I

can tell you that Mr Marriott complained that DS Vaughan assaulted him by knocking him down. Jack's argument was that his actions were reasonable, in the circumstances, given that a firearm was potentially involved. They may have been somewhat foolhardy, but, as far as the IOPC is concerned, they were certainly entirely acceptable. That is why we didn't ask you for a witness statement.'

'I see. Is that all?'

Lauderdale stood up and shook Mel's hand.

'It is. You can forget about all of this. There is no blemish on your record and I believe you're a credit to the force. Please be careful.'

Mel left the room in a whirl. Those bastards just didn't stop. She hadn't mentioned the assault complaint to her dad, as he'd had enough to deal with following his captivity. At least she wouldn't have to, now. But what other shit could Oktapod throw her way?

Chapter Twenty-Seven

'Is THERE anything counter-terrorism can tell us?' asked DCI Farlowe. 'Anything at all?'

DI Morton looked sheepish.

'A couple of things, but I'm afraid they're not a lot of use. The Security Service told me that an Albanian national known to be a proficient bomb-maker disappeared from Tirana shortly before the Mexton attack. The Border Force has no record of him entering the country, and Interpol doesn't know where he went, but it's reasonable to suppose he came here. I'll circulate a photo to all officers, but it's a bit blurred.'

'So, do Five think the bugger's planning something else?' asked DI Chidgey.

'They wouldn't speculate, but I'm worried. If he hasn't returned home, he could well be working on another attack. It's possible he built the bomb left on DS Palmer's doorstep as well as the bombs at the station and the timber warehouse. I would be extremely vigilant, if I were you.'

'Everyone's been briefed on personal security measures,' replied Farlowe. 'They check their cars before every journey, and so on. What more can we do?'

'Not a lot. We can't warn the public to look out for suspicious Albanians. It's racist, apart from anything else, and could lead to hate crimes. Infiltrating their local community would be impossible. They're too tight. We are building up a list of local leaders, priests etcetera, so we can, perhaps, have a word with them, but I doubt that it will come to anything. The OCG is too ruthless for anyone to gossip.'

'So, is there any good news?'

'Possibly. We've been liaising with the Met over the use of facial recognition software. There are no dedicated facial recognition cameras in Mexton, but we could use the software to interrogate footage from other cameras. It may be possible to track the movements of the two individuals we're already looking for. That could give us a lead to their base.'

'How about the bomb maker?'

'The photo's not really good enough,' said Morton. 'There are some recognisable details but nothing that would stand up in court. You can't take a blurred photo and magically make it crystal clear, with a few clicks on a keyboard. If the image isn't there, you can't create it.'

'I suppose that's something. Get DC Blake on to it, Geoff. He's good at examining video recordings, and his broken arm shouldn't hamper him too much. Anything else?'

'One thing. Our tech guys did a bug sweep of the old police station, once the SOCOs had finished and it was declared safe. They found surveillance devices in both the male and female toilets on the CID floor. They were made in eastern Europe. There were no recoverable fingerprints – the devices were too small – but we sent them off for DNA testing, just in case. I'm not hopeful.'

'That explains how they know which officers to target. I seem to remember having a plumber in shortly after the raids. He must have fitted the bugs then. Can your guys sweep this building as well?'

'They do. Regularly. But you need to impress on people the need to keep conversations about operational matters to a minimum outside meeting rooms. Remember the wartime slogan "Walls have ears".'

Farlowe nodded.

'They're all pretty sensible, but I'll reinforce the message and so will DI Chidgey. Thank you, Steve. I'll let you get on. I've a Teams meeting with the NCA in a moment. Please keep me informed.'

'Will do,' said the SO15 officer, closing the door as he left.

'Ten percent of bugger all,' snorted DI Chidgey, hauling himself to his feet and leaving the DCI's office without waiting for a reply.

Farlowe looked around his office, straightened a couple of files on his desk and switched on his computer.

He recalled something his grandmother had said about her experiences in London during the blitz. You had a brief respite when the bombers returned to Germany, but you never knew when they would come back. Everything you did was coloured by the thought that the next bomb would have your name on it. He knew, logically, that it was a bit ridiculous, but Colin Farlowe was beginning to feel like that in peacetime Mexton. Effectively, he realised, the force was at war with the OCG, and he had no idea when and where the next blow would fall.

Chapter Twenty-Eight

Day 13

DESPITE TOM PROTESTING that he could make his own way, the hospital insisted on sending him home in an ambulance car. The paramedic led him into the house, carrying a bag full of dressings for his wrist and details of how to care for it. There was also a leaflet on prosthetic hands.

'It's so brilliant to have you home love,' said Mel, hugging him once the paramedic had left. 'You've no idea how much I've missed you. Come and say hello to Bruce and Sheila and I'll make you a cup of tea.'

The parrots seemed interested to see Tom again, making gentle noises and, in the case of Bruce, perching on his head. But just as Tom was settling down with his tea, the doorbell rang.

'I'll get it,' called Mel.

A few minutes later she led two stony-faced police officers, brandishing warrant cards, into the room.

'Thomas Ferris?' the older one asked.

'Yes, what's this about?'

'Come with us please. I'm arresting you on suspicion of engaging in sexual activity with a minor. You do not have to say anything...'

Tom barely heard the rest of the caution, and it was all he could do to prevent himself from vomiting.

'What the fuck is going on?' yelled Mel. 'Tom would never do anything like that. He loathes paedophiles.'

'You're DC Cotton, aren't you?' the younger officer said. 'You should know we wouldn't arrest someone without evidence.'

'What sort of evidence?'

'I'm not at liberty to say, but it will be disclosed to Mr Ferris's solicitor in the normal way, prior to interview. She reached for her handcuffs.'

'Don't even think of handcuffing him,' Mel snarled. 'Can't you see he's lost a fucking hand?'

The officer thought for a moment and cuffed Tom's good wrist to one of her own.

'I'm coming with you.'

'I think that's a good idea, DC Cotton. We will need to ask you a few questions as well, although you are not under arrest. But you'll have to make your own way to the station. We don't want you talking to Mr Ferris until we've interviewed him.'

Tom looked despairingly at Mel as he was led away.

'You know I'm innocent, don't you?'

'Of course. You're being fitted up and I'll find the shits who are doing this. And they will fucking pay.'

Mel crashed her way through the doors of the police station, waved her card at the security guard and headed for the makeshift custody suite. News of Tom's arrest had obviously got out, as she received some odd looks from officers she encountered on the way. Even Cathy Merritt, who she counted as a friend, blanked her. So much for innocent until proven guilty, Mel thought.

The custody sergeant was adamant.

'You cannot see him. You know that, so stop wasting my bloody time. If he's remanded, you can visit him in prison during official visiting hours. If he's bailed, you can see him then. Now go away.'

Mel sat, seething, in the staff canteen, an untouched cup of coffee in front of her. How could she help Tom if she was unable to talk to him? Firstly, she had to discover what evidence they had against him. Then she would find a way to disprove it. It must be convincing, otherwise he wouldn't have been arrested so quickly. She would obviously need help, but who could she turn to if other officers didn't share her certainty that Tom was innocent? Waves of despair swept over her and she began to cry.

Mel found a spare computer and logged in, thinking she would at least try to do some work. It might take her mind off the horror of Tom's arrest. The custody sergeant had promised to let her know when Tom had been interviewed, so she spent the intervening time desultorily Googling the

Fearon family and Johnny Fear's career. Nothing much came of it, and she was relieved when her phone pinged with a text telling her that Tom had been returned to the cells.

The two detectives who had arrested Tom declined to talk to her, but Tom's solicitor, Raymond Marchbanks, took her aside.

'Is there somewhere we can talk?' he asked.

Mel led him back to the canteen and found a quiet corner.

'What's happening?' she asked, anxiously.

'I've seen the evidence against Tom,' began the solicitor, gloomily, 'and I'm afraid it's damning. It's a video of Tom, naked, and a young girl. I would say she's about twelve. I won't describe what he's doing to her, but, suffice it to say, he would be facing a long prison sentence if found guilty. And there is every chance he will be. I'm sorry.'

Mel fought back the urge to vomit.

'What did Tom say about it?'

'He denied it was him in the video. He swore he had never had any contact, sexual or otherwise, with the girl, or with any other underage child. He was very convincing, I must say, but these people often are.'

Mel exploded.

'How dare you include Tom with those bastards? You're supposed to be on his side, for fuck's sake. He would never do anything like that. He would kill himself sooner than abuse a child. How fucking dare you?'

'I hear what you are saying, and I will certainly support any "not guilty" plea. It's my job, as you imply. But proving his innocence will be extremely difficult in the light of the video. Can you give him an alibi for the afternoon of the seventh of May this year? There was a time and date stamp on the video and a copy of the *Mexton Messenger* in the shot.'

Mel thought for a few seconds.

'Shit. I was on a training course in Bristol from the sixth to the eighth. No, I can't.'

'Did you have any telephone conversations?'

'Not during the day. We were told to keep our phones switched off. We talked in the evenings, though.'

'That's unfortunate. The video seems to have been taken during the hours of daylight, and a clock beside the bed showed ten past four.'

Mel began to panic.

'Surely there's some way of challenging it? Did Tom say anything else?'

'He maintained he was being fitted up. A deep fake. Does that mean anything to you?'

'Yes, it does. Sophisticated computer software is used to manipulate images so that people seem to be doing or saying things they never did. The whole thing started when people photoshopped Princess Diana's face onto other women's naked bodies. It was crude and easily detectable, but it's much more sophisticated now. An expert could create a video of you, in a bikini, shooting a pensioner, if they wanted to.'

Marchbanks paled and made a quick note on a legal pad.

'How can we prove this is what happened to Tom?'

His manner indicated he had begun to change his view about his client's guilt.

'I can't,' replied Mel. 'Tom possibly could, but he wouldn't be allowed access to the equipment and programs he would need. Look, can you find an independent computer expert who would take a look at it as a witness for the defence? It doesn't matter how much it costs. I'll sell the bloody house if I have to. I'd rather we were homeless than see Tom banged up for something he didn't do.'

'I'll ask around, Miss Cotton. It looks as though there is something we can do after all. He will be re-interviewed tomorrow, and if he is charged, I will argue at the Magistrates that he should be given bail, or kept in police cells rather than in prison. Try to remain positive. I'll be in touch.'

Chapter Twenty-Nine

Mel sat at the kitchen table, a ready meal congealing in front of her and a bottle of wine repeatedly finding its way to her glass. She had spent over an hour feeding and cleaning up after the parrots, after letting them out to fly around the room for a while. Any other domestic tasks had seemed pointless. Her heart was like lead and her eyes were scarlet from crying at the prospect of being without Tom. Even worse, if that were possible, was the thought that Tom could spend years in jail for a crime he hadn't committed – a crime he found particularly abhorrent. A police officer in jail always had a hard time, but one convicted of child abuse would get it ten times worse.

She would do everything she could to prevent that happening. But what could she do? Her eyes fell on the space where Tom usually charged his laptop, now empty since the police had confiscated all his IT. The image of a similar machine, flying through the air and hitting the gunman who was about to execute her and Tom, flashed into her mind. Yes! He was the one! She scrolled through the contacts on her phone and prayed to the goddess of IT that her call would be answered.

'Mel! Long time no hear. How are you?'

Robbie Edwards's cheerful tones lifted Mel's spirits a fraction.

'Dreadful, Robbie. Tom's being fitted up on a child abuse charge and we need your help.'

'What? What do you mean?'

'Someone made a deep fake video of him with a young girl and sent it to the police. He's been arrested and his brief thinks he'll be convicted. It's fucking awful. He would never do anything like that.'

'I know, Mel. I know. How can I help?'

'I need you to prove that the video is a fake. Can you do that?'

There was a pause.

'I'm still at work. I'll come over as soon as I can. You can tell me more then.'

'Thanks, Robbie. Thank you.'

Mel dumped her uneaten meal in the bin, resolutely put the cork back in the wine bottle and made herself a strong coffee. She would need a clear head for the next few hours.

Robbie turned up within half an hour of Mel's phone call, a laptop under his arm and a worried expression on his face.

Mel hugged him and led him into the kitchen. He accepted coffee and listened while Mel repeated what Marchbanks had told her.

'First off,' he said, 'who could be behind this? It may give me an idea for tackling it.'

'I suppose there's two possibilities. The paedophile ring you helped us bring down and an Albanian organised crime group we went after last year. Tom was involved in shutting down their cyber scams, and they seem to be targeting people who damaged their operations. They were behind the bomb at the station and also tried to shoot me.'

'Shit. I knew about the bomb, obviously, but not about the shooting. What happened?'

'I'll explain later. So, what do you think about this video?'

'I can't imagine those local perverts having the expertise to produce a deep fake video that would convince the police. They weren't particularly computer-savvy. They just used stuff, and children. So my money's on the Albanians. We know there are many proficient hackers in eastern Europe and several nation states are conducting cyber warfare. It would be quite a challenge to prove the video is a fake.'

'Can you do it?'

'There's a problem. Firstly, I work for the police and I don't have any lawful reason to examine the video as part of my duties. If I was an independent consultant, the defence could engage me to do it, but given my job, they can't. Secondly, I'm friends with you and Tom, so my objectivity could be challenged. I'm not sure what I can do.'

Mel looked despairingly at her friend.

'Surely, there's something you can do? Unofficially? My

dad used to joke about the Ways and Means Act being used to collect evidence when normal procedures wouldn't work.'

Robbie looked uncomfortable then appeared to come to a decision.

'Officially, Mel, I have to say I can't help.' He winked. 'But, who knows, something may turn up.'

Mel nodded slowly.

'Well thank you for your advice, Robbie. Would you like a drink?'

'No. No thanks. Ollie's cooking and I don't want the dinner to spoil.'

'That's fine. Do keep in touch.'

'Don't worry. I will. Bye.'

After Robbie left, Mel sat at the kitchen table thinking. He had helped with an investigation before, unofficially and illegally, using his hacking skills. Would he do so again? She didn't want him to lose his job, but she was desperate to free Tom. Robbie's wink suggested he was going to help, and this gave her comfort. All she could do was wait. But she could try to help Stefan in the meantime.

Chapter Thirty

STEFAN WAS EXPECTING THE VISIT. It was nearly closing time and the manager of one of his other shops had told him the gangsters were on their way. He had a shabby sports bag ready, full of loose notes and two-pound coins. He had memorised the instructions from the police and had been assured that the tracker, concealed in the base of the holdall, was working and undiscoverable unless someone took a knife to it. He was nervous, but angry at the same time, and wished he'd been able to deal with the problem in his own way.

The door crashed open and two men stood in the doorway of the empty shop.

'Turn that fucking camera off,' shouted one of them, pointing to the CCTV lens mounted above the counter. Stefan complied, and the men approached.

'Time to pay tax,' the other one grinned. 'Twenty percent.'

Stefan looked at him with loathing and dumped the holdall on the counter.

'What's this shit?' one of the men snarled.

'Twenty percent,' replied Stefan. 'I make three thousand a week from my shops. That's six hundred. You can do the maths, can't you?'

The Albanian drew back his fist to hit Stefan, then dropped it.

'Don't be fucking funny. Next time we want tens and twenties. No fifties. No rubbish.'

He pulled out a cigarette lighter and flicked the wheel.

'You know what happens if you piss us about. See you next week.'

He threw the lighter at Stefan, who ducked as it flew past his head.

As soon as he heard the gangsters' car drive off, Stefan phoned the direct number he'd been given.

'They've taken the bag. And there's something else. One of them threw a lighter at me and he wasn't wearing gloves. There could be fingerprints.'

'Thank you, Mr Paweski,' said DC Clive Newton, in the control room. 'Please don't touch the lighter. We'll send a SOCO to retrieve it. That was a good spot. We're tracking the bag now. We've also got some footage of one of the offenders, which should be useful. Thank you for your co-operation.'

Stefan relaxed slightly and closed up the shop. He would drop his car off at home and then walk to Mexton's

Polish Club for a few vodkas. He considered himself British first and Polish second, but the camaraderie he found with expatriates from his ancestral homeland nourished him. He would tell them what had happened, and he knew he would have plenty of volunteers if he decided to take matters into his own hands.

While Stefan was closing up and driving home, officers at Police Headquarters were tracking the bag. Mel had insisted on joining them, partly because she knew Stefan but also because she couldn't bear to be at home while Tom was in custody. Keeping busy gave her mind something to focus on, and she desperately wanted to see the Albanians arrested.

'Where is it now?' she asked, not for the first time.

'Not much further than when you asked the last time,' Clive patiently replied. 'Hang on, it's stopped.'

'Where?'

'On Swarbrick Street.'

The street name made Mel shiver. Tom and Robbie had nearly lost their lives to the paedophile gang when they tracked them to a disused night club there. Surely Oktapod couldn't be using the same premises?'

'Can you see where on Swarbrick Street?'

'I'll call up Google maps. Yep. Here it is. A snooker club and pool hall.'

'OK. Thanks.'

Mel flinched when she saw the image. Its use might have changed, but it was still the same shabby building she remembered.

For the next two hours, detectives watched for further movements from the tracker, but it remained in the same place. Suddenly, it started moving again, but within a minute it was, once again, stationary.

'So, what do you think's happened?'

'My guess,' replied Clive, thoughtfully, 'is that they counted the money in the snooker club, perhaps laundering it through the till, then drove off to their HQ, disposing of the bag on the way. We may not have identified their base, but we have found some premises that they use. So, a result of sorts.'

Mel nodded her agreement, but a frightening thought occurred to her. If the gang had discovered the tracker and ditched the bag as a result, Stefan was as good as dead. And her team had condemned him.

Chapter Thirty-One

Abas Sayyid had slipped out of the country half an hour before the police came for him, although he hadn't known they were coming. He had made his way across Europe and ended up in Britain, without a visa or money. He had given the last of his cash to a so-called transport broker who had driven him, and a dozen other asylum seekers, to a beach in France. There they had boarded a flimsy boat that crossed the Channel at night, dodging the other vessels using one of the busiest shipping lanes in the world. Weak, starving and cold, he hadn't expected to be welcomed with open arms, but he had hoped to be able to plead his case and be allowed to stay. He hadn't realised he would be locked up in what was, basically, a prison, albeit a more civilised one than those in his home country.

He had been in Loders Way Immigration Removal Centre for four months when he was informed that his application to remain would be turned down. He lodged an appeal but the lawyer who took his case held out little hope.

It was only a matter of time before he would be sent back, and dread was his constant companion. Dread and a loathing for one of the guards.

A notice pinned up in every corridor pledged that the private company that ran the centre was committed to treating detainees with "Respect, Decency and Compassion", but Abas saw mainly indifference, often laced with hostility. Some of the guards were OK, he thought, but Officer Hannick was vile. Thick-set, with a neck wider than his shaven head, Hannick stalked around the centre as if it was his own personal kingdom. The other guards kept out of his way, particularly when he was abusing the detainees. If anyone complained of rough treatment, they would back him up. The management either didn't know, or turned a blind eye, since their principal objective was to provide an efficient, and profitable, service. One day, Abas vowed, he would strive to expose the conditions at Loders Way. But who would listen to him?

Chapter Thirty-Two

Day 14

ABAS, a gentle, peaceful man, had always tried to avoid Hannick, terrified of what the guard would do if he found out about him. But when he heard his only friend's screams coming from a recreation room, he had to do something. Throwing open the door, he saw Hasan pinned on the ground, his trousers round his ankles, while Hannick brandished a cigarette lighter towards his genitals.

'You're disgusting,' shouted the officer. 'You can fuck right off back home. We've got enough of your sort here already, you dirty bastard.'

Abas thought for a couple of seconds. Decision time. What had he got to lose? He picked up a chair and swung it at Hannick's head, catching him on the temple. Dazed, the guard rolled sideways and his victim crawled away. Abas struck again, and when the semi-conscious officer was on his back, he straddled him, forcing a leg of the chair against the man's throat. Hannick struggled, but Abas bore down on him with all the force his wiry frame could muster. Gradually, the guard's struggles grew weaker and then ceased. Abas kept the chair leg in place for a while longer, pulled himself off the dead bully and waited for the inevitable beating from the man's colleagues. He had made a choice in the heat of the moment. But he realised he would have done the same thing if he'd had time to think it through. He didn't know what life would be like in a British prison, but he was certain it would be better than his fate back home.

'Good morning, all,' began DI Chidgey. 'Last night, as some of you know, we placed a tracker in a bag of protection money that two heavies took from Stefan Paweski's premises. We tracked it to a snooker and pool establishment in Swarbrick Street. The bag was discarded shortly after and we don't know whether or not the gang discovered the device. In any event, we will be keeping an eye on the snooker hall, which, I gather, is a former night club.'

Mel and Martin exchanged glances at this.

'We hope to be able to follow vehicles, using ANPR, to the area where the OCG's base is located. Unfortunately, we didn't get the number of the SUV that the gang used last night, but we are looking at movements in that area. We are also looking at vehicles seen around the brothel in Jubilee Terrace, so we may be able to match sightings and identify which car they use. Trevor – can you get on to this?'

'Yes, guv.'

'How are you getting on with the facial recognition software?'

'Nothing so far,' Trevor replied. 'The bomb-maker's image is too blurred. I'm still working on the other two Interpol sent over, and I'll look at last night's CCTV recordings from Stefan's shop.'

'Good man.'

'How about Operation Ezekiel, Mel? Anything to report?'

'No developments, guv,' she replied, listlessly. 'I'm setting up fresh interviews with his family and I've been looking at stuff on the internet. I'll let you know the results.'

'OK. Thank you. One more thing. There's been a suspicious death, possibly murder, at Loders Way Immigration Removal Centre. As if we haven't got enough on our plates already. Jack, can you nip out there with Mel and see what's what? Uniforms are already in attendance. Before we finish, DCI Farlowe would like a word.'

Farlowe stood up.

'DI Morton has informed me that listening devices were discovered in the gents and ladies lavatories in the old police station. This, we assume, is how the OCG knew which officers were involved in the actions we took against them last year. We don't know if they have any names other than those of the officers who have already been targeted. We have swept this building, and HQ, for devices and, so far, have found nothing. We will do this regularly, particularly as outside contractors are working on site. I must impress on you the need to be discreet about any conversations you have outside police premises. I know some of you like to meet up in the Cat and Cushion and toss around ideas, but please make sure you're not overheard by anyone else. And, as ever, be vigilant about your own safety. Thank you. Carry on.'

The team dispersed looking collectively gloomy.

'Are we ever going to nail these bastards?' Mel asked Jack, as they queued for coffee.

'Eventually,' he replied. 'But I've no idea how much damage they'll do before we get them. By the way, I've heard about Tom's trouble. It's appalling. For the record, I believe he's innocent. The truth will come out eventually.'

'Thanks, Jack. That means a lot.'

She smiled weakly and her eyes began to water. Then her phone rang, and she stepped into a quiet corner. It was Raymond Marchbanks.

'Bad news and good news, Miss Cotton,' the solicitor said. 'Tom's been charged, but I managed to persuade the magistrates to grant bail rather than remanding him in custody. However, a condition of bail is that he must have no contact with any police officers unless he is being interviewed. So, you will have to live apart for the time being and not speak on the telephone or exchange emails. They will check call records if they deem it necessary.'

'Thank you for your efforts, Mr Marchbanks. I'll miss him, but it's better than fearing he's getting the shit kicked out of him in prison. Have you found anyone who can analyse the video?'

'There's a couple of companies that think they could do

it, but, unfortunately, they are booked up solidly for eight or nine months.'

'That's no bloody good. He'd be tried and convicted by then. Is there anyone else?'

'I'll keep looking, so don't give up hope. Tom sends his love.'

'Well give him mine when you next speak to him. Tell him I'm not alone in believing him innocent.'

'I will. Don't worry. Good bye.'

Mel hung up, feeling desolate. On the one hand, Tom being on bail was good news, but, on the other, the lack of an expert to prove, officially, that the video was fake was a blow. She hadn't told the solicitor that Robbie was going to help, as it could have caused trouble for all concerned. She was hanging on desperately to the hope that he would come up with the goods. The problem, then, would be how to get it to the right place without compromising Robbie. She walked slowly back to her desk and collected her jacket for the trip out to Loders Way. Then she would try, once again, to get to grips with the murder of Alan Fearon.

Chapter Thirty-Three

THE SECURITY GUARD at the gate checked Jack's and Mel's warrant cards, then directed them to a parking space. The two detectives approached the bleak, dirty, concrete building and, despite the sunshine, shivered as a chilly wind blew across the forecourt of the converted prison.

'Welcome to Britain,' muttered Mel.

Jack simply nodded.

A harassed-looking woman in a smart trouser suit met them at the door and ushered them past the reception area once they had introduced themselves, had their photographs taken and been issued with visitors' badges.

'I'm Carina Ford, senior manager here. This is a terrible business. I've never encountered anything like this before. We've had the occasional fight, but never this.'

'Can you tell us what happened, please?' asked Jack. 'We've had reports of a suspicious death, possibly murder, but no other details.'

'Of course,' said Ford. 'Come into my office. Please sit down.'

She indicated two hard chairs opposite her cluttered desk.

'One of our detainees, Abas Sayyid, killed a guard, Carl Hannick, by crushing his throat with a chair. By the time our doctor saw him, Carl was already dead. Another asylum-seeker was present, but refused to say what happened. For some reason, the security camera had been moved so it didn't cover the area where the incident occurred. A member of my staff looked in, as he was passing, and found Sayyid holding the chair. He admitted what he had done, but wouldn't say why.'

'Has he done this sort of thing before?'

'No, never. He has always been co-operative and quiet. He became depressed for a while, when his application to remain was turned down, but he lodged an appeal. I doubt it would have succeeded. I had expected him to be on his way back to Afghanistan before long.'

'Where is Mr Sayyid now?' asked Mel.

'He's in a segregation room. He's received first aid for injuries received when he struggled with the guards.'

'How about the room where it happened?'

'It was locked as soon as Sayyid was removed. No-one's been in there since and there are two of your officers outside the door.'

'That's good,' said Jack. 'We'll need to get SOCOs in there to collect evidence. I presume Mr Hannick's body is still there?'

'Yes, it is.'

'What was Carl Hannick like?'

Ford pursed her lips and answered carefully.

'He was a hardworking, loyal member of staff who commanded the respect of his colleagues. He had been with us since the centre opened.'

'Ms Ford,' said Mel, 'I sense a "but" somewhere.'

Ford flushed slightly.

'There have been complaints from detainees about the way he treated them. Accusations of violence and abusive behaviour. However, these were investigated and his colleagues confirmed that they were false. In this line of work, spurious complaints are not exactly rare, as I'm sure you realise.'

'You say he was respected by other staff members. Was he liked?' asked Jack.

'I wouldn't like to say.' Ford looked at the papers on the desk. 'I suppose you'll have to ask them.' She paused. 'I think it may be true that he could have been a little intimidating at times. He was forthright in his views about how things should be done.'

'And did his views coincide with the principles on the posters on the wall – Respect, Decency and Compassion?' Mel asked.

'These principles are drummed into all our staff, Detective Constable, and I have no evidence that Carl Hannick ignored them. Now, let me show you the crime scene.'

After glancing briefly through the window set in the door of the recreation room, and refraining from entering so as to avoid further contamination, Jack requested that the room remained locked until SOCOs arrived and left the two uniformed officers on guard. The detectives were shown into the segregation room where Abas was waiting. They told the guard to leave, asking him to ensure no CCTV was recording, and turned to the prisoner. He had a split lip and a swollen eye, and winced when he stood up to greet them. His expression was calm and his speech was polite.

'You have come to arrest me,' he said, when Mel and Jack introduced themselves and produced their warrant cards.

'Yes, we have, Mr Sayyid. But are you hurt? Have you been assaulted?' Mel asked.

Abas shrugged.

'It's what I expected. Even though they didn't like Mr Hannick, they have to put us in our place. There is no point reporting it.'

'We can look into if it you wish. But now, I am arresting you on suspicion of murder. You do not have to say anything...'

'Stop!' Abas held up his hand.

'I know about your cautions but I want to say something first. I will give a proper statement later.'

Mel looked at Jack, who nodded.

'Hannick was a racist, homophobic thug and I found him torturing my friend because he was gay. I had to stop him so I killed him. He deserved it. That's all. You can caution me now and I'll speak again when I have seen a lawyer.'

As they led him through the centre to the exit, his head erect and his demeanour dignified, other detainees caught sight of him and cheered. By the time they reached the door the cheers had given way to applause, prompting a furious glare from Carina Ford. As they crossed the forecourt, detainees shouted from their windows and banged items on the glass in support. A small smile played across Abas's face and, just before he was placed in the police car, he raised his handcuffed wrists above his head and shouted, 'Peace be with you!'

Chapter Thirty-Four

'Mr Sayyid,' began Mel, after switching on the recording equipment in the interview room, introducing those present and repeating the caution. 'You have been arrested on suspicion of murder. I understand you have consulted your solicitor, Mr Galloway, and wish to make a statement. Is that correct?'

'Yes, it is,' replied Abas. 'I, Abas Sayyid, admit to the murder of Carl Hannick. I killed him deliberately by hitting him on the head with a chair and crushing his throat with the chair leg. No-one else was involved. I accept full responsibility for my actions. I have nothing more to say.'

Mel glanced at Sally, a confused look on her face.

'But Mr Sayyid – Abas – you said when we spoke that you were protecting a friend who was being tortured. Has your solicitor not advised you that this could be a mitigating circumstance?'

'No comment.'

'May I remind you, Detective Constable,' interjected

the solicitor, 'that statements made when a person has not been cautioned are inadmissible?'

'You do not need to remind me, Mr Galloway. But I am concerned that your client doesn't fully understand the situation.'

'I can assure you he does. He trained as a lawyer in his home country. And I have not failed in my duty to him, as you appear to suggest,' Galloway said, starchily.

Mel turned back to Abas.

'Is there anything else you can tell us about this, Abas? Had Carl Hannick attacked you or abused you in the past?'

'No comment.'

'Can you say anything about Mr Hannick's behaviour or attitudes to detainees at the centre?'

'No comment.'

Sally spoke up, her expression as exasperated as Mel's. 'Is there anything, anything at all, you can tell us, Abas, that might help your defence? Now is your chance.'

'No comment,' Abas said, and smiled.

'All right,' said Mel, 'Sally will escort you to the custody sergeant and you will be put back in a cell. Once we have approval from the Crown Prosecution Service you will be charged with murder. Interview terminated at 16.49.'

'I don't understand,' said Sally, as they walked back to the incident room. 'You said he told you and Jack that he was protecting his gay friend and that Hannick was a racist bully. Why didn't he say so under caution?'

'I've no idea,' replied Mel. 'He didn't seem at all worried about a trial and a long prison sentence. Still, I suppose an early guilty plea, instead of a long and expensive trial, will knock a few years off it.'

'It should do. But he'll still be away for a long time. Right. Coffee, then some notes to type up.'

'It was blocked, boss. That car number.'

Fisnik frowned as Zamir reported the results of his DVLA enquiry.

'What does that mean?'

'Cops, security services – anyone who doesn't want people to know who owns the car. They make sure no-one can find out.'

'Are you sure about this? Could the licence people just be refusing to give you anything?'

'I'm sure boss. I registered the garden as a car park and told them the car had overstayed. They have to give the details to car park owners, so they can get the penalty charge money. I tested it with a different car number and it worked. I'm sure.'

'So you're saying the fucking cops were snooping round the house?'

'They parked over the road for two minutes then drove off. They haven't been back. What do you want to do?'

'Nothing, for the moment. Just keep watching. If they come back again, maybe Nikolla should have a talk with them.'

Zamir shuddered at the mention of Oktapod's enforcer.

'OK, boss. I'll tell the others to look out for it. Should we pass it on to Tirana?'

'No. We can't afford to shut this down or look incompetent. You know what happened to Marku and Osmani. Keep it between ourselves for the moment. Now go and check on the girls.'

When his subordinate left, Fisnik lit a cigarette and thought. A suspicious car outside the house so soon after they had started operations was disturbing. Had somebody grassed? A dissatisfied punter, maybe? The lawyer? The estate agent? Surely not. The punters knew they would suffer if they gave anything away, and, anyway, the services the girls provided were difficult to obtain elsewhere in Mexton. As to the other two, they were too well paid, and frightened, to give anything to the authorities. Perhaps it was a coincidence, but he didn't like coincidences – and neither did the boss in Tirana.

Mel sat in front of the Ezekiel whiteboard, turning over scenarios in her head. She discounted a number of possibilities, such as an obsessive fan of Johnny Fear, someone he impregnated in his rock star days, a jealous husband or an attack by a random stranger. There was no-one with an obvious motive for revenge. This left three main possibilities. Firstly, there could have been an accident. Alan Fearon could have got drunk, fallen over and cracked his skull. A person or persons unknown could then have concealed the body, for reasons best known to themselves. This scenario didn't seem likely, and Dr Durbridge said that the damage to the skull was more consistent with a blow from a hard object than a fall.

Secondly, one of his children killed him, when he somehow returned from Australia, and buried him in the garden. Digging the grave would have been hard work for one person, but the soil in the garden was deep and free from tree roots and large rocks.

Thirdly, there could have been a conspiracy between two or more of his children, to kill him and, eventually, inherit the lottery winnings. It could have been all of them, although Sarah didn't seem to be the murdering type.

There was, she supposed, a fourth possibility. The neighbour, Henry Foldsworthy, could have got so incensed by Fearon's noise that he snapped and killed him, again after he returned. Highly unlikely. Foldsworthy was the type to rehearse, endlessly, elaborate scenarios in his head for removing people, but he would never put them into practice. So, it had to be one or more of his children. Unless, of course, the brother had a motive, as yet unknown. He didn't inherit anything, but perhaps there was something else.

A major problem with all these explanations remained. When and how did Alan Fearon return from Australia undetected? He couldn't have been killed on the night of the row, so when was he actually murdered? She stared at the whiteboard with its unclear images of individuals, spidery writing and crime scene photos. Something started to niggle at her, and she began to get the glimmerings of an idea.

Chapter Thirty-Five

'THANK YOU FOR COMING IN, Ms Fearon,' said Mel, guiding Nicola into the interview room.

'I didn't have much bloody choice, did I?'

Mel didn't reply, but recited the caution, switched on the recording equipment and named those present.

'Are you sure you don't want a solicitor?'

'No. I've not done anything wrong. If I need advice, I can talk to Grenville.'

'As you wish. My colleague, DC Erskine, and I have a few questions for you, particularly relating to the last night anyone saw your father in the UK. I know we have discussed this before, but we need to get things on the official record. Also, you may have had time to reflect on your previous answers.'

A frown passed fleetingly over Nicola's face at Mel's last remark.

'You said that your business could have done with some of your father's money. How desperate were you?'

'I'm not sure that's any of your business, but, for your information, I was doing all right. An injection of capital would have helped me expand, which it did when my father's will was proved and the money distributed. In the meantime, things were OK and I was making a living.'

'You said that you hadn't argued with your father over his intentions. Do you still maintain that?'

'Yes. Yes, I do. I may have spoken a little harshly, but that's all.'

'Ms Fearon, we have two witnesses who stated that there was a major row going on at some point in the evening. Would you like to reconsider your statement?'

'I suppose it was goody-two-shoes Sarah, who likes to consider herself above earning wealth. Yet it's taxes from people like me who pay for her bloody social work job. And she's not as bloody squeaky-clean as she makes out. OK, I'll admit there were a few words exchanged.'

'More than a few words, according to our other witness, who was outside the premises.'

Nicola didn't reply.

'Did these few words escalate into violence?'

'No. Of course not. I would never hit my father.'

'How did your siblings react?'

'Grenville stayed calm. Davvi made a fuss. Sarah was outside, no doubt feeling superior.'

'How much rivalry was there between you and your siblings?'

'A bit at first, I suppose. Three of us wanted to succeed in business, so there was some competition, but we weren't trying to get on *The Apprentice*. We're OK, though. As you know, Grenville works with both me and Davvi.'

'Did you return to the premises later that night, after everyone had left?'

Nicola twitched slightly.

'No. Frankly, I didn't want to see him again. It would have only led to an altercation. There was no point pleading with him.'

'One last thing, Ms Fearon. How do you think your father got back to Mexton after he went to Australia? We know which flight he took out but we found no trace of a return journey.'

Nicola's jaw tightened and she drummed her fingers on the table.'

'I have absolutely no idea. Can I go now?'

'Yes, Ms Fearon. That's enough for the time being.'

As Nicola was being signed out at reception, she turned back to Mel.

'Am I a suspect?'

'Ms Fearon. You and your siblings have all benefited from your father's death. It would be remiss of us if we did not consider everyone in such a position as a potential suspect. But nobody is under arrest. At the moment.'

Nicola glared at the two detectives and stalked out of the building.

'How did you think that went?' asked Sally. 'I didn't say anything, as you obviously had everything in hand.'

Mel smiled. 'How about you tell me what you thought?'

'OK,' began Sally, cautiously. 'She obviously resented being here, but I suppose most people do. She was worried when you said she could think about what she said before and suspected a trap.'

'Go on.'

'She didn't like it when you caught her out in the lie over the row. She obviously has no time for her sister and is clearly money-oriented.'

'Yes. Anything else?'

Sally thought for a moment. 'She definitely reacted when you asked her about her father's return from Down Under. I think she could have been lying. Also, the question about returning to the house seemed to provoke a reaction. She could have been right about not wanting to see him, though.'

'Well done, Sally. I agree with you on all points. I wonder what she meant about Sarah not being squeaky-clean. Might be worth looking into. If your transfer to CID is permanent, and I hope it will be, you should go for specialist interviewer training. I think you'd be good at it. Coffee?

Chapter Thirty-Six

WHEN MEL and Sally returned to the office, Mel spotted a familiar figure by the coffee machine. She pretended she hadn't seen him for ages.

'Hi, Robbie! How are you?'

'Not so bad, Mel. And you?'

'Pretty shitty as a matter of fact. You know about Tom?'

'Yes. Dreadful. I'm sure he's innocent. He wouldn't do that sort of thing.'

'Oh, this is Sally Erskine. Our acting DC. Sally – this is Robbie, a computer whiz. He saved our lives by flinging a laptop at a gunman. Quite a useful chap to know.'

Robbie smiled and greeted Sally.

'Didn't I see you on the Pride march?' he asked.

'Probably. I was there with my girlfriend. Great fun, wasn't it?'

Mel left Robbie and Sally chatting and took her coffee back to her desk. She found a piece of paper, just poking out from under a coaster, that she knew wasn't there earlier. It read C&C 7 R. She smiled and screwed the note up. Robbie must have found something and she would meet him in the Cat and Cushion at seven. Before that, she would re-interview Davvi Fearon.

She had barely touched her coffee when DI Chidgey called the team into the incident room.

'Listen up, everyone. We have some progress on these Albanian buggers. This is Robbie Edwards and he's got something to tell us.'

Robbie moved to the front and began to speak, diffidently at first but growing in confidence.

'Hi, everyone. I'm Robbie and I work in computer crime. I've been tasked with leading a team looking at possible scams and frauds perpetrated by the Albanian gang. They were doing this sort of thing last year and we suspected they may be starting up again. This was a bit like looking for an invisible needle in a haystack the size of Yorkshire. But, two days ago, we had a break. A woman reported an attempted scam to ActionFraud. Someone phoned her, impersonating her bank's security department, and said her account had been compromised. She was advised to transfer her funds to a new, so-called safe, account until the problem was sorted out. She played along, got the details of the new account, then pretended that her phone was running out of charge. The bank in question is in Mexton.'

'A smart woman,' said Addy.

'I wish there were more people like that,' said Trevor, coughing as a biscuit crumb lodged in his windpipe.

'Anyway,' continued Robbie, 'we got a warrant and have the name and address of the account holder. It's a Mr Albert

Squire – presumably a false name – and the address is Jubilee Terrace. Number 37.'

'That's the knocking shop,' said Martin. 'We found it the other day. It was the only house in the street with fibre broadband.'

'Well, they'd need that for their scamming,' replied Robbie. 'So, we're working on identifying the IP address, and then we'll be able to get a better idea of what they're up to.'

'Thanks, Robbie. Well done,' said the DI. 'Last time they were using different premises for scamming and selling sex. This time it will be easier to take them down. The bad news is that the NCA want us to hold off until they get more information on the extent of the OCG's activities, and SO15 don't want us to spook them while we're trying to build a terrorism case. So, keep away from Jubilee Terrace, please.'

Several people groaned but most seemed to see the sense of the instructions.

'Could we put some surveillance on the place?' asked Martin. 'A helpful householder letting us use a front bedroom or something?'

'A good idea,' replied Jack, 'but it's not a very police-friendly neighbourhood and strangers there might raise suspicions.'

'What about street sweepers or weed controllers? Could one of us pose as a Council employee?' Trevor suggested.

'That would look odd,' replied Mel. 'The Council doesn't sweep the streets or spray weeds in that area any more, because of the cuts.'

'How about utilities?' asked Addy. 'Could we pretend

there's a gas or water leak? Set up a tent, dig a hole and watch?'

'That might work,' said Chidgey. 'Anyone here know how to use a pickaxe?'

'I did some labouring as a summer job once,' Martin said. 'I could look convincing.'

'So did I, but I couldn't,' said Trevor, waving his arm in the sling. The others laughed.

'Right. Let's look into that,' said the DI. 'Martin, you're in charge of hiring any equipment, workwear etcetera you'll need. Borrow a couple of badged hi-vis jackets from the water company and check where the mains run. I'll speak to the Council and get permission to dig a small hole. We'll get a contractor to fill it in when we've finished. I'll also get an authorisation for the surveillance.'

'There's just one problem, guv,' said Mel. 'We can't go digging holes at night.'

'I know, but it's not the punters we're after, it's the OCG members. Hopefully, they'll visit during the day and we can get some vehicle registrations and pictures.'

'Hang on,' said Jack. 'We'll have to put cones and flashing lights around any hole at night to stop cars falling in. Could we fit a camera in one of those, like in the wildlife documentaries when they're filming bears or lions?'

'We have a new David Attenborough,' teased Mel, 'filming the lesser spotted gangster in its natural habitat.'

'Worth exploring,' replied Chidgey, when the chuckles had died down. 'Jack, can you talk to the technical guys? If they can't help, talk to Steve Morton. Those SO15 folks are accomplished buggers.'

More laughter.

'Right. Let's do this,' said the DI, his West Country tones unusually animated. 'You're in charge, Jack. I'll let you know when I've heard from the Council and spoken to the Super about surveillance. Before we finish, did you get anything from the camera in Stefan Paweski's shop, Trevor?'

'Yes, guv. The heavy who did the talking was one of the individuals whose photos Interpol sent us. His name's Vjosa Dibra and he's got previous for violence and supplying drugs in several countries. We don't know who the other one is, but I hope to use the facial recognition software to track both of them. Fortunately, they were too arrogant to wear balaclavas or masks. I guess they didn't mind being recognised.'

'Good man. Keep at it. OK, everyone. Get to it.'

Chapter Thirty-Seven

DAVVI FEARON ENTERED the police station with Grenville Fearon accompanying him.

'I don't know why you're wasting more of my time,' he complained. 'I've given you all the help I can. This is a complete waste of public money.'

'There's a couple of inconsistencies in your account that we need to clear up, sir,' replied Mel. 'Before we start, are you sure you want your brother here as your legal representative? There could possibly be a conflict of interest.'

'Nonsense. I trust Grenville completely. Now, can we get on with this nonsense? I've things to do back at the office.'

Mel switched on the recording equipment, recited the caution and introduced the two men, as well as Sally Erskine.

'The first thing I wanted to clarify with you, Mr Fearon, is the nature of the meeting you had with your father just before he left for Australia.'

Davvi, by now sweating profusely despite the moderate temperature in the interview room, exchanged glances with his brother.

'What do you mean?'

'You stated that you got on with your father fine and that there was no point arguing with him about his decision not to share his lottery winnings. However, we have accounts of a serious row between Mr Alan Fearon and his children during that meeting. Would you like to comment?'

'I expected you to ask that. You've talked to Nicola, I understand, and snowflake Sarah. Yes, there were raised voices. Understandable, in the circumstances, Dad was taunting us, waving the champagne bottle he'd just opened, without offering us any, needless to say, and telling us to piss off. There was never any physical violence. Nicola told you this, and I'm telling you the same thing.'

'Did you return to the premises later that evening?' asked Sally.

'No. Why would I? His mind was made up.'

'The money would obviously have been useful to you,' she continued, 'and your business seems to have taken off since the legacy came through. How did you manage for investment in the intervening years?'

'I got by. A few friends lent me some money. Obviously, I couldn't expand as much as I would have liked, but we survived OK. My business affairs are confidential, and if you want any more information you will have to get a court...'

'Have you ever been to Australia?' interrupted Mel.

A silence lasted for a couple of seconds.'

'No, I bloody haven't. I don't like the heat and it's full of lethal wildlife. Anyway, I don't have time for travelling.'

'Thank you, Mr Fearon. That's all for now.'

Mel switched off the recording and turned to Grenville.

'We would like to interview you under caution, as well, sir. Would now be convenient?'

'No, it wouldn't, DC Cotton,' he replied, glaring at her. 'In fact, you would be wasting your time. My responses to your questions would be the same as my brother's, so, if you want to interview me again, you will have to arrest me. And I really wouldn't advise that.'

The two brothers stalked out of the interview room without waiting for an escort. Sally and Mel looked at each other and, almost simultaneously, made the same remark.

'Twats!'

Chapter Thirty-Eight

'Have you found something?' Mel asked Robbie, anxiously, as they sat down in the Cat and Cushion.

'Yes, I have. I've pulled the video apart and I've found a couple of things. Firstly, the date it was recorded doesn't match the time stamp on it. It was recorded much later than it appears, at a time when Tom was in hospital. The newspaper was genuine, but they could have got hold of a back number. That's irrefutable evidence of his innocence.

'The other thing is the lighting. They tried very hard to match the colours, but the images of Tom's face were taken under different lighting conditions from those used when the body his face was attached to was filmed. The skin tones are different. The girl was filmed under the same conditions as the body. What was happening, sickening as it is, really did happen. But it wasn't Tom doing it.'

'That's brilliant, Robbie. You're an absolute genius. So, what do we do now?'

'Well, that's the problem. I used hacking tools to get access to the video on the police server. It was totally illegal, and if it was found that I'd done it, I would be sacked and jailed, even though it was in a good cause.'

Mel looked heartbroken.

'I have an idea, though,' Robbie continued. 'I have some friends in a hacking group in Leicester. They could use what I've found and put it on the internet, redacting any illegal images and identifying features. They could use it to show how deep fake videos can be identified. I could then come across it and draw it to the attention of the local investigation team and the CPS. With any luck, they would realise what had happened and drop the charges.'

'How about your friends? Won't they get into trouble?'

'They are extremely good at covering their tracks. The places they have been, you wouldn't believe, and they've never been caught yet. And I trust them completely.'

'OK. Then let's hope to fuck it works. I can't bear to think of what Tom's going through.'

'Neither can I, Mel. There's one other thing, a positive.'

'Yes?'

'Once it's been proved that the video is a fake, we can try and find out where it came from. I suspect no-one's bothering much at the moment, but it would be good to track down who made it and do something nasty to them. We might also be able to identify the girl.'

'You do mean arrest them, don't you?' Mel smiled.

'Of course. I'm not going to throw any laptops around again, am I?'

Mel smiled fondly at him, thanked him effusively and

left the pub, feeling positive for the first time since Tom's arrest. In her preoccupied state she didn't notice the black SUV that followed her steps to the pub car park and stayed two cars behind her as she drove home.

Chapter Thirty-Nine

Day 15

'YOU'LL NEVER BELIEVE THIS, SALLY,' said Mel, excitedly. 'I've just come back from the Magistrates. Abas Sayyid told the court that he would be entering a plea of not guilty.'

'What?' Sally nearly dropped her coffee. 'He admitted it, under caution, in the presence of his solicitor. His statement will be entered in evidence.'

'That's right. And Galloway has told him to find another brief, as he can't support a not guilty plea, given what Abas has told him.'

'Bloody hell. Doesn't he realise he'll get a longer sentence if it goes to a full trial?'

'Well, he must do. It's ridiculous.'

Sally looked thoughtful for a minute then slowly responded.

'I think I might know why he's doing it. He's gay, right?'

'I guessed so, from what he said about protecting his friend. Go on.'

'Well, in Afghanistan homosexuality is illegal. If he was sent back, he would face torture and execution. They'd probably kill me if I went there, too,' she grinned, wryly. 'Also, I think he wants his day in court, to tell people what it was really like at the centre. He is one fucking brave guy.'

'Christ,' replied Mel, 'you mean he'd rather spend years in a British prison than go back home, because of his sexuality? That's bloody heartbreaking.'

''Fraid so, Mel. 'Fraid so.'

'Sorry, Jack. Addy's idea won't work. The hole in the road,' said Chidgey, gloomily.

'Why the hell not?'

'The Council says we can't go digging holes without proper training and insurance. The water company isn't keen, either. We could use their contractors but they might talk, and the OCG could find out.'

'Shit. We really do need eyes on those premises. Is there anything else we can do in the street that wouldn't look out of place?'

'Well, we can't park a burger van there, that's for sure. It's just a back street. Send someone down there to have a look, would you? Not Martin or Trevor, in case they're recognised.'

'I'll go myself, in my own car. There must be something, for fuck's sake.'

Five miles away, in a building set back from the main road, two men were focussing on a laptop. The screen flickered into life and a Zoom meeting started. Both men flinched slightly when the man with the cold, grey eyes began to speak.

'You have one minute to convince me I should still be paying you. Starting now.'

Fisnik Hasani began to speak.

'The first house is running well and making money. The girls the police took have been replaced and punters are coming in. Two more houses are being set up. The computer operations are generating income and we have taken over the distribution of heroin on the Eastside housing estate. That is the biggest market in the town. We have started supplying cocaine. We are taxing shops again but had to burn one to teach the owner a lesson. He is now compliant. The bomb at the police station was a success and the cops are working from other buildings, inefficiently. Reprisals are underway on individuals. Unfortunately, the drug cop spotted his bomb and it was neutralised. We will try again. The computer cop has been arrested and will go to jail. We are working on the others, and they will suffer soon.'

'That is...satisfactory,' said the grey-eyed man. 'What are the cops doing? Have they interfered?'

'Not so far. We will put a bug in their offices when we get a chance. We have identified an employee we can use as an informer and will turn him shortly. Some photos of Nikolla's work should be enough, but we may give him some money. A suspicious car drove past the house but it has not been back. We are watching for it and will take action if necessary.'

'Competition?'

'None. There was some local resistance to the drugs takeover, but we dealt with it. No-one dares to challenge us. We have a reputation,' Fisnik said, proudly.

'Keep it that way. You have a business target. The income from our Mexton operation must return to the level it was before the police meddled. You have three months to achieve this, or I will need a very good reason not to take action against you. You know what happened to Kreshnik Osmani.'

'I do. It will not be necessary. You have my word.'

The grey-eyed man shut down the call without further comment.

'Fuck,' said Fisnik, switching from Albanian to English. 'We need a drink.'

He reached for a bottle of rakia and two glasses. The two men drank deeply, each dreading the consequences of failure, the thought of Nikolla's particular set of skills at the forefronts of their minds.

'There's a possibility, guv,' said Jack, pushing open DI Chidgey's office door.

The DI started in his seat, as if he'd just woken up.

'Sorry. Yes, Jack. What've you got?'

'There's a street light in Jubilee Terrace that seems to be permanently on. It's just down the road from number 37 and on the opposite side of the road. I suspect the sensor on the top is covered in bird shit, so it thinks it's night-time all day. If we can get the Council to clean it, and let us put a camera there at the same time, we might get a result.'

'That's great. I'll make a phone call. We should get authorisation by tomorrow morning. Well done, Jack. I was, er, having a think when you came in. We really need to get a shift on with these Albanians before they attack us again. I gather Tom Ferris is claiming he was set up by them. I hope that's true.'

'I'm sure it is, guv. He's a decent bloke. I'll go and find a volunteer to go up in the cherry-picker and fit the camera.'

Jack left Chidgey's office in a pensive mood. Was the DI OK? His clothes were clean but rather shabby, and he could have paid a bit more attention to his shaving. There was also a faint odour of cider about him, sometimes. Perhaps he lived on his own? Was he widowed? Still, it was none of his business, as long as the man did his job. As long as he actually did.

Chapter Forty

WHAT WAS the matter with those bloody parrots, thought Mel, dragging herself from a dream that featured Tom, herself, and a Costa Rican beach. And no clothing. Rubbing her eyes, she pushed her feet into slippers and stumbled to the top of the stairs, wondering why the birds were making such a racket. What was that smell? Why was there a cold draught coming up from the hall? Instantly, she switched into police officer mode and ran down the stairs.

The front door was wide open and a balaclava-clad male was pouring a liquid over the floor. Petrol. She took a flying leap off the bottom stair and landed in the pool of accelerant. The would-be arsonist stumbled back and pulled a cigarette lighter from his pocket. Before he could use it, Mel kicked him hard in the groin, wincing as her slippers offered little protection. As he doubled over, she knocked the lighter out of his hand and tried to grab his arm. But the shiny soles of her slippers skidded on the wet laminate floor and she fell backwards, twisting before she hit the ground. She managed to grasp an ankle, scratching it as her opponent pulled free. He twisted and kicked her in the head. She rocked back, stunned, and watched despairingly as the man picked up the lighter, fumbling with the wheel. A spark appeared, but no flame. He tried again, but before he could get the lighter to work, a car raced up the road, headlights flared, there was a crash and her neighbour's car alarm split the night.

The attacker muttered something, undoubtedly obscene, in a foreign language and limped down the path to where a black SUV was waiting, its engine running. Mel rushed out into the road and managed to catch the registration number as it drove off. Then she looked around to try and make sense of what she'd heard. Her heart jumped in her chest and all thoughts of her petrol-soaked pyjamas fled.

'Tom! What are you doing here? We're not supposed to meet. But it's a bloody good job you came along when you did.'

'It wasn't a coincidence. I put a motion-sensitive camera in the hall and rigged it to send an alarm to my laptop whenever it picked up movements. I got here as fast as I could. God, I've missed you. Quick. Get inside. The neighbour's coming out. I'll talk to him and apologise. He'll do his nut but I'll promise him he'll be compensated for the inconvenience as well as the damage. He doesn't know I'm not supposed to be here.'

The neighbour pacified, Tom returned to the house and hugged Mel as if she'd just returned from the dead.

'You must call this in. It's those fucking Albanians again. But I was never here. Will they get any forensics?'

'The bastard dropped his lighter and I scratched his ankle. There should be skin cells and blood for DNA.

Maybe prints. I'll just say he was spooked by a passing car. No need to mention the car alarm – which, I presume, was deliberate.'

'It was. Look, I'd better go, before anyone else sees me. A lucky escape, but now they know where we live, you'd better find somewhere else to stay for the time being.'

'What about the parrots?'

'I'll move back in. They already think they've got me, so I should be reasonably safe. But you take care. Maximum care.'

'I will. Of course. Now scram!'

They kissed, at length, and Tom vanished into the night as Mel phoned the station to report the attack. Her heart ached to see him go, but she knew it wouldn't be too long before he was cleared. In the meantime, she had to change out of her flammable clothes and wait for her colleagues and SOCOs to arrive. She longed for a shower but knew she had to wait until fingernail scrapings had been taken. Still, there was nothing to stop her using the other hand to pour herself a large brandy. Maybe two.

His sore testicles were the least of Vjosa Dibra's worries. He had failed, and Oktapod didn't tolerate failure. His record had been good so far. Perhaps he would be given another chance. He desperately racked his brains for a way of redeeming himself and saw his chance when he came across a parked police car, the officers inside taking a coffee break in the middle of their night shift. He pulled a pistol from the glove box, drew up behind the vehicle and fired six rounds, wildly, at the back window. As he drove away, he clipped the car's wing mirror, not noticing the impact above the roar of his engine. Heading back to base, he hoped with all his heart that this would be sufficient atonement for his failure. After all, two cops instead of one had to be better. Didn't it?'

Chapter Forty-One

Day 16

'ANOTHER LIFE LOST, MEL?' teased Jack, obviously relieved, at the morning briefing. 'You seem to have more than the usual nine. Lucky again, I suppose.'

'Oh, it was my consummate self-defence skills, mate, not luck. Though it's a good job a car came by before the petrol went up.'

Jack smiled and DI Chidgey called the team to order.

'I think most of you know Mel's house was targeted by an arsonist last night and she escaped without any serious harm. PCs Dawnay and Halligan were not so lucky. They were shot last night, shortly afterwards, in a stationary police car.'

A shocked silence fell.

'Were they killed?' asked Addy.

'Fortunately not,' replied the DI. 'Halligan was hit in the fleshy part of his ear. A ricochet off a door pillar got under

Dawnay's stab vest and injured his shoulder. They're both in hospital for check-ups but aren't likely to be there long.'

'Fuck,' swore Martin. 'I presume it was the same person?'

'Undoubtedly. It's highly unlikely that there were two maniacs attacking police officers in Mexton on the same night.'

'Do we have any evidence?' asked Trevor.

'Fortunately, yes. Mel got the number of the vehicle driven by the arsonist. The plates were fake, but we should be able to track it using ANPR. We may get some idea of where the OCG is holed up. The vehicle scraped the police car mirror and left paint residues, so if we can find it, there'll be a link, as well as gunshot residues inside it. Also, Mel got some skin and blood from her attacker, and that's being fast-tracked for DNA as we speak.'

'Where are you living, Mel?' asked Martin. 'You can't stay at home, surely?'

'You'd be safe in a nice warm cell in the custody suite,' joked Trevor.

'I'm staying with a friend, thank you,' she replied, tartly. 'Need to know, and all that. I nip back to feed the parrots and keep them company for a while, but I daren't sleep there.'

'When you've finished,' interrupted DI Chidgey, 'we've got crimes to solve. We are installing a camera on top of a street light in Jubilee Terrace later this morning. We'll need people to monitor recordings, on a shift basis, so we can see who's going in and out and identify vehicles used by the OCG. There may come a point when we'll need to watch in real time, so let Jack know when you can help.'

'Did the lab get anything from the lighter in Stefan's shop?' asked Addy.

'Yes. DNA from the wheel confirmed the identification we made from Interpol's photo. Zamir Prifti. A genuinely nasty character.'

'How about surveillance on the pool hall, guv? Is it worth a go?' asked Martin. 'We might be able to identify and track vehicles.'

'I had thought of that,' replied the DI, irritably. 'It would be, if we had the resources, but we don't.'

'What about SO15? It looks as though all they're doing is sitting on their arses. So far, all they've done is tell us about the bomb that nearly killed us.'

'That's hardly fair, Martin,' said DS Angela Wilson, SO15's liaison with the team. 'We've been working through thousands of bits of info, intelligence reports, surveillance footage and intercepted emails. I'm sorry we haven't found anything yet, but we are trying.'

'OK, Angela, I apologise. But can you help us with this?'

'I'll talk to Steve. See what we can do.'

'Thank you, DS Wilson,' said Chidgey. 'Now does anyone else have any bright ideas?'

'Does the drug squad have anyone undercover on the Eastside who could identify the new dealers and get vehicle numbers or names?' asked Trevor.

'They wouldn't tell us if they did. Any undercover officer would come from a different force, and whether or not they have one in place would be strictly on a need-to-know basis. But I've asked Derek Palmer if his usual informants can keep an eye open.'

'I suppose we don't have any phones to track,' suggested Mel. 'Do you have anything, Angela?

'No, Mel. I'm afraid not,' she replied.

'The gang member we found dead in the wheelie bin had nothing on him,' Jack reminded the team. 'Until we can make an arrest, we have no phone number and no chance of tracking anyone to the OCG's headquarters. Basically, we're fucked.'

'How about Mr Paweski's shops?' asked Addy. 'Could we stake them out and arrest the extortionists?"

'I've spoken to him,' replied Mel. 'He's seriously thinking about getting his mates together and doing some vigilante stuff. I strongly advised him against it and suggested he kept paying until we take down the gang. If we arrest someone, the OCG might torch another of his shops or even kill him.'

'I think you're right, given what we know about these buggers,' said the DI. 'Run through how it works, will you? How do they get the money?'

'Stefan could be in any one of his shops, so if they turn up where he isn't, someone directs them to where he is. They also warn him the gang's on its way. He hands over the money when they arrive, and they go. If it doesn't seem enough, they threaten him and say they want more the next time.'

'All right. How far apart are his shops?'

'They're all within three miles of each other.'

'When do they usually collect?'

'It seems to vary. Usually, it's Sunday night. His tills tend to fill up over the weekend. He does a lot of contactless sales, but many people still pay cash. He keeps extra money with him, in case there's not enough in the tills to meet the gang's demands. But he said they're coming back for more this evening.'

Chidgey thought for a moment.

'How's this for a plan? We can't stake out all his shops, but we could have a mobile unmarked car driving around tonight. If they go to the wrong shop, he can phone us to say where he is when the suspects are mobile. He can have a phone, with a text giving his location, ready to send in case they turn up at the right one. As soon as he sees them approach, he can send the text without them noticing. I take it he's got more CCTV now?'

Mel nodded. 'Yes, and we've put some of our own in place as well.'

'So, what's the idea, guv? We arrest them? I thought that wasn't an option,' said Martin.

'No,' replied Chidgey, 'and we're not going to follow them, either. We'd need more cars to do that without being spotted. I'll get authority to plant a tracker on their vehicle, and, with a bit of luck, it'll lead us to their HQ. So, I need a volunteer to plant the device in a way that won't attract attention. Any offers?'

Mel thought for a moment.

'Anyone bending down to tie their shoelace beside the car would look too bloody obvious. I've an idea forming. I'll come and see you, guv, when I've thought it through. But I can do it. I started some surveillance training before the... incident. I hope to resume it when things calm down a bit.'

Most of the team smiled, but Jack looked worried.

Chapter Forty-Two

THE ELDERLY WOMAN picked her way across the uneven paving stones near Stefan's shop, her gait suggesting she was slightly the worse for drink. She carried a bag for life, the tatty state of which suggested it should really be in the plastic bag equivalent of a care home. As she approached the black SUV, she tripped, the bag tore and half a dozen cooking apples rolled into the street.

'Me crumble,' she muttered to herself. 'There goes me crumble.'

The driver of the vehicle watched her impassively in his wing mirror, clearly not intending to help. The woman clumsily rounded up her apples from the pavement and gutter, and as she did so, she slipped a tracking device into the wheel arch of the SUV.

'Thanks for bleedin' nothing,' she snapped at the driver, as she drew abreast of the front of the car. He didn't respond.

She continued along the street in the same uncertain

manner, until she turned the corner into a side road. Then she straightened up and sprinted to the unmarked police car that was waiting for her.

'That go OK?' queried Jack Vaughan.

'Like a dream,' replied Mel, pulling off a grey wig, glasses and an ancient overcoat. 'Like a dream.'

Fisnik hated boy racers. He liked the power of the SUV they let him drive, and enjoyed cruising at speed, but had no interest in driving in a way that would attract attention. He didn't need to prove himself by overtaking everything in sight and cutting up slower cars. The young man in the souped up Corsa was particularly annoying, trying to overtake on bends and pulling up close behind him with flashing lights and screeching horn. Fisnik had had enough, so immediately after the next bend, he slammed on his brakes, expecting the youngster to pull up sharp. Fisnik would then have a forceful word with him.

This tactic was not entirely successful. The Corsa driver was using his mobile phone and failed to brake in time. His nearside wing hit the offside rear of the SUV and the Corsa spun across the road, colliding with a lamppost. The bonnet sprang up and steam poured from a wrecked radiator. The driver, dazed from the impact and the exploding airbags, stumbled out of the wrecked car, clenched his fists and began to approach Fisnik, who had got out of his vehicle to inspect the damage. He had second thoughts when he saw Fisnik's bulk, and the expression on his face, and contented himself with screams of abuse.

'You drive like fucking idiot,' said Fisnik, ignoring the young man's insults. 'You lucky I don't break your fucking neck.'

'What about the insurance? Who's going to pay for my car?'

'You are, you piece of shit. You tell insurance company or police, I come and find you. You won't like it. Now fuck off, little boy.'

Fisnik looked briefly at the damage to his car. It wasn't too bad and there were at least two garages in the town who would repair it for free, with a little persuasion. As he drove off, he didn't notice the remains of the tracker, crushed and scattered across the middle of the road.

'We've lost the bloody signal,' Trevor shouted. 'Look at this.' He pointed to a trace on a computer screen. 'It was working fine until it went round this bend just the other side of Camberton. Then it died.'

'Is there anything out there that could interfere with the transmitter?' asked Jack. 'Power lines or something?'

'No. Nothing. It's farmland with a few houses once you leave the village. They must have found it, or it dropped off and got run over.'

'Well, I fixed it properly,' bridled Mel, 'and it certainly wasn't visible, unless you crawled under the car.'

'An RTC?' suggested Martin.

'Could be,' replied Jack. 'I'll ask Traffic to take a look for any signs. Meanwhile, it looks like we've been wasting our sodding time.'

'Not entirely,' said Mel, thoughtfully. 'You know that road, don't you, Jack?'

'Too bloody right,' he said. 'Hard to forget some bastard firing a shotgun at you. What are you suggesting?'

'Do you think they could be using that farmhouse? The one where three of the gang died? I mean, they wouldn't expect us to look there, would they? Not after what happened.'

'I did look, online,' said Trevor. 'Not long after the... attack.' He couldn't bring himself to say 'bomb'. 'There's planning permission in place to convert the building into a health spa and luxury retreat.'

'I presume they won't put the building's bloody history in the brochures,' chuckled Mel. 'Might be worth taking a look at the place, anyway.'

'OK, Mel,' replied Jack. 'Nip out there with Sally when you've got a moment. That's it for tonight. See you all in the morning.'

Chapter Forty-Three

Day 17

Musgrave Farmhouse was surrounded, at a distance, by a chain-link fence topped with razor wire. Boards bearing the name of a local security company were fixed to the fence at intervals, advising readers that CCTV was in operation. The ground in front of the building had been cleared of trees and bushes, leaving no cover for anyone to approach it unobserved. A temporary hut stood inside a gate and a couple of empty skips were placed beside it. There was no sign of any building activity, but when the detectives got out of the unmarked police car, a burly man in a hi-vis jacket emerged from the hut.

'What you want?' he said. 'This is building site. No visitors without appointment.'

'It's all right, sir,' replied Mel, as the two officers showed their warrant cards. 'We're just following up a line of inquiry. When will the work start, do you know?'

'You need to ask the boss. He's not here. I think he can't get the workers.'

'Do you have an address?'

The man shrugged, went back into the hut and returned with a business card.

'You call him, he will meet you. I have to get on.'

What, exactly, the man had to get on with was far from obvious.

'Thank you, sir,' said Sally. 'By the way, can I ask where you're from?'

'Wroclaw, in Poland. I am here legally. You want me to prove it?'

'No, no. I'm sure everything's all right. Just curious. My brother-in-law is from Wroclaw. Janos Kowalska. I don't suppose you know the family?'

The man shrugged.

'No. Wroclaw is a big city.'

'We won't take up any more of your time, sir,' said Mel. 'We'll get in touch with your boss. Good day.'

The man didn't respond and returned to his hut.

'What was that all about, Sally?' asked Mel when they were seated in the car.

'He's no more Polish than I am. Kowalska is a female name. If I had a Polish brother-in-law, which I don't, his name would be Kowalski. He didn't know that.'

'Who's a smarty-knickers, then!' grinned Mel. 'But that was definitely an eastern European accent. Did you notice that bulge on his hip, under his jacket?'

'Firearm, do you think?'

'Could have been a radio or something. Or a pistol stuck in his belt. I'm not sure I want to find out at the moment.

OK. Here's a test for you. Take a look at the road leading up to the gate. What do you see?'

'Tyre tracks, loads of them, in the mud. They look like cars, maybe a light van or an SUV.'

'Good. What don't you see?'

Sally thought for a moment.

'Tracks from heavy vehicles. Lorries and what have you.'

'Exactly. Those skips must have been there a while, and there's no evidence of trucks delivering building materials, excavators or other building plant. Sometimes, it's not what you see, it's what you don't see that matters.'

'Yeah, yeah. The dog that didn't bark in the night. I know the story. So, this is a front, then.'

'That's what it looks like to me. We'd better get back to the station and let the boss know.'

Chapter Forty-Four

'SOMETHING'S GOING ON, guv, but it's not building.' Mel concluded her account of their visit to the farmhouse. 'The guy at the gate looked like a heavy rather than a builder, and he may have been armed. So, what do you want us to do?'

DI Chidgey looked pensive and pulled at his rather grubby shirt collar.

'It might be worth talking to the name on the card. Gavin Simmonds, was it?

Mel nodded.

'See if you can find out anything more about the so-called spa. Also, someone should check the Land Registry to see who owns it.'

'It's an offshore company, guv,' said Trevor. 'I looked it up while Mel and Sally were out of the office. They bought it a few months ago. There's no details of the directors or what they do.'

'So do we think it's the OCG's HQ?' asked Addy.

'Quite possibly,' replied Chidgey, 'but it's too early to

say with certainty. It definitely looks as though there's a connection, though. Good work, folks. I'll let DI Morton and Mr Farlowe know what you've found.'

'Can we get surveillance on the farmhouse?' asked Martin.

'Difficult,' replied Mel. 'The building is some distance from the road, so even if we could get a camera set up on public land, it wouldn't pick up who was getting out of cars or entering the premises. Anyway, I doubt we can set up a camera on the road without it being noticed. We certainly can't have people lurking in a car and taking photos.'

'Shit,' said Chidgey. 'It's a pity we can't hack in to the slippery fuckers' own CCTV, like Lisbeth Salander.'

'A bit fairytale, that, isn't it?' said Addy.

Mel looked thoughtful.

'How about a drone?' suggested Trevor.

'It's too quiet out there,' replied Jack. 'They'd hear it. It might work if they were next to a motorway, but not in such a rural area.'

'Are there any crime scene photos from the shooting?' asked Martin.

'There should be,' replied Jack. 'Look on the system and print off any you can find. It would be useful to put them on the board.'

'OK,' summarised the DI. 'We've identified a protection racket, a knocking shop and, probably, a computer fraud operation linked to the OCG. What we don't have is any evidence connecting them with the bombing, apart from the dead lad with explosives traces on him. We know there's a bomber still operating in the area, from the attack on DS Palmer and the booby trap in the old warehouse, but we can't tie it all together in a way that would convince a jury. Before I finish this secondment and DI Thorpe returns, I want these bastards arrested. So crack on. And there's a bottle of Scotch for the first person to find a viable bombing suspect.'

'So, what do you reckon to DI Chidgey, then, Jack, now he's been here a while?' asked Mel, as they queued for the coffee machine.

Jack pursed his lips and thought before venturing an opinion.

'He seems as rough as a bucket of scrumpy, but there's a lot more to him than that. He's clearly on the ball, although I think he's fond of the pub. It doesn't seem to affect his judgement though. I think he's all right. Funny, I get the impression he's lonely.'

'I wondered that, too. He's not said much about his personal circumstances, but I suppose he wouldn't.'

'I've an old mate in the Avon and Somerset force. I'll see if he knows anything about the DI. Our pub quiz team is challenging one of theirs, so that'd be a good opportunity to chat.'

'Blimey. On tour, are you?'

'Not quite,' Jack smiled, 'but our landlord used to run the pub my mate drinks in, near Bristol, so we thought it would be fun. And Sarah's the designated driver.'

'Poor woman...'

Before Mel could elaborate, the subject of their discussion came up to them.

'You two have got a bit of a reputation in my force,' Chidgey said. 'Nicking that armed poisoner in the old bogs in Weston went down really well. They're calling you the kami-khazi twins.'

'Thanks, guv, but his weapon was a replica,' said Mel, slightly embarrassed.

'Yes, but you didn't know that. So, all credit to you. It's hard enough getting appreciation in this job, so don't knock it.'

Jack and Mel smiled and let the DI get to the coffee machine before them, both noticing the cidery odour about him.

'How're you doing, Reg?' asked Sally, placing the obligatory bunch of grapes on the table beside her former colleague's hospital bed.

'Not too bad,' he replied. 'The bullet just grazed the top of my shoulder bone and did some damage to the muscles. It will be a while before I can use my arm again and I'll need physio. A couple of inches lower and it would have smashed up nerves, bone and blood vessels. Serious damage, not like on the films where the shot guy is back in the office three days later, with just a sling and a grin.'

Sally smiled.

'You know,' Reg continued, 'this is the first time I've been really injured on the job. I've had a few bruises while arresting people, or policing football matches and so on, but I'd thought I'd retire with a clean slate, as it were. So many colleagues have been badly hurt or killed, and I thought I was the lucky one.'

'So will you come back?'

'I think that depends on Occupational Health and how long I take to recover. I've only a few months more to do, so I guess it's in the balance.'

'I'll miss you when you go, Reg.'

'Hang on! I'm not planning on pushing up daisies in the near future. I'll still keep in touch. But, thanks, Sally. Appreciated. Now, you'd better get out there and catch those villains.'

Sally said goodbye and walked slowly down the hospital corridor, brooding. She knew the job could be dangerous, but it always brought the risks home to her when a colleague was injured or killed. So far, she'd been lucky, but at the moment, Mexton didn't seem a very safe place to be a police officer.

Chapter Forty-Five

MEL AND SALLY were shown into Gavin Simmonds' flashy office, having finally secured an appointment for the late afternoon. Sleekly suited, with thinning sandy hair and immaculate dentistry, Simmonds exuded enthusiasm, although there was a certain wariness in his eyes. Another man, thin-faced, tall and also expensively dressed, was present, and Simmonds introduced him as soon as he had shaken hands, moistly, with the detectives.

'This is Mr Chawte. I'm sure you don't mind him being present.'

'Not at all, sir,' replied Mel, 'but this isn't a formal interview. We just need some information about the spa project you're involved in. You are, I believe, the CEO of Mexton Beauty Developments?'

'That's quite correct, officer, and Mr Chawte is the company solicitor. What do you need to know?'

'What are you proposing to do with the premises? We

were out there earlier today and very little seemed to be happening.'

'Our plans are ambitious, DC Cotton. We want to build a health spa that will attract people from across the whole county, if not the country. To do that, we have to get everything absolutely right. We are still working with architects and suppliers to establish a beacon of excellence in the optional health care field. Going forward, we will seek the endorsement of major influencers in this area. Once we have realised our vision and actualised our inspiration, we will be producing online material and brochures. I'll put you on the mailing list, if you like.'

'Thank you, sir. The gentleman we spoke to on site suggested that nothing was happening because you couldn't get the workers you need.'

The two men exchanged glances.

'Good as Brexit has been for the country,' continued Simmonds, 'there have been one or two minor difficulties with labour. We expect to overcome them shortly, and site preparation can begin. So, we are where we are.'

Difficult to be where you're not, thought Mel, saying nothing.

'Tell me, why are you interested? Two pretty ladies like you don't need any major enhancements, but I'm sure we could offer you a few tweaks – with a blue light discount, of course.'

Mel almost choked and Sally responded in her stead.

'The premises concerned, sir, were the site of an armed siege last year that resulted in three fatalities. Given the building's history, I wonder whether your punters, sorry, customers, would be prepared to stay there?'

'We prefer the term "clients", and we have no knowledge of the events you describe,' interjected Chawte, icily. 'I hope you will not be spreading malicious rumours about our project, officers. If you do, you can be assured of the fact that you will answer for them in court.'

'That is not our intention, sir,' said Mel, equally coldly. 'But you will appreciate that we are curious about the fate of a building that was used by a criminal gang.'

'Of course,' said Simmonds, trying to lighten the tone. 'You have your job to do and we are happy to help. As far as I know, the property was purchased from the estate of a farmer who died a couple of years ago. It took some time to sort out probate, I believe, and I have no idea what it was used for in the meantime. You would, of course, be welcome to look around the old building at some point, but I'm afraid that ongoing building works make that impossible for the time being. Health and safety, you know.' He put on a rueful smile.

'I don't think that will be necessary, sir, but thank you,' replied Mel. 'We won't take up any more of your time. If you would like to send a copy of your brochure to Mexton police station, I will take a look at it.'

Simmonds smiled as he showed the detectives out. Chawte looked angry.

'Christ, what a pair of wankers,' exploded Sally, when they were safely out of earshot.

'Too bloody right,' said Mel. 'To use his management speak, I was itching for an energetic foot/bollocks interface, going forward. But I controlled myself. Pretty ladies indeed. He's a fucking dinosaur. One thing, though – that slimy lawyer was lying.'

'How so?'

'He said he knew nothing about the shootings at the farmhouse, but he was the solicitor for one of the Albanian gang members. No way didn't he know.'

Sally whistled.

'So, what do you think's going on?'

'I think the spa thing is a front. I think the gang is using the farmhouse as some kind of headquarters, believing that we wouldn't look at it again. The so-called building site provides security. If they do go ahead with any kind of development, I wouldn't be surprised to find it was a money-laundering scheme for the profits from their other operations. I don't know a lot about financial crimes, but I've been told that quite a few of the businesses in Mexton centre – phone shops, vape bars, foreign barbers – can't possibly make a profit. There's too many of them. So, some of them, at least, are laundering money. A big development like this spa could do it much more efficiently. Anyway, that's for the experts to assess.'

'What about Simmonds? He didn't look Albanian.'

'I think he's just a front man. They must have some kind of hold over him. Financial, blackmail or fear – or all three. A smarmy English voice, spouting the jargon du jour, wouldn't attract suspicion. Anyway, we'll type up our notes and report back at the morning briefing tomorrow. I'll pick up a bottle of wine on the way back to yours. Show my appreciation for you putting me up.'

'You're always welcome, Mel,' said Sally, smiling as she put the car into gear.

Chapter Forty-Six

Tom Ferris signed in at the makeshift police station, in accordance with his bail conditions, and was about to leave when he heard a voice behind him.

'DC Ferris. Come with us, please.'

He turned to see DCI Mark Christopher, a senior officer in child protection, and a woman he didn't know, waiting for him.

'I haven't been called DC Ferris since my arrest,' he said. 'What's going on?'

'You'll find out,' said the DCI, smiling. The woman beside him remained impassive.

Tom was led to a small room at the back of the station. The woman keyed a code into the lock and opened the door. Tables loaded with computers, laptops in evidence bags and DVDs stretched along one wall, and there was an open laptop on a desk. Christopher gestured to Tom to sit down.

'What is this?' he asked, nervously. 'Who is your colleague?'

'This is DI Cara Blaine,' replied the DCI. 'She's from the NCA and specialises in computer crime.'

'Oh. Yes. I've heard of you, DI Blaine, but we've not met.'

The DI smiled briefly.

'We've brought you here because there is an anomaly with the evidence against you,' she said. 'You are welcome to have a Federation rep and a solicitor present, but this isn't a formal interview. To be honest, I don't think you'll need one.'

'It's OK,' Tom said. 'Carry on.'

Christopher typed a password into the laptop and turned it so that Tom could see the screen.

'This was posted on the internet last night. Press play when you're ready.'

Tom did so, with trepidation. A black and yellow design, mimicking a series of popular instruction books, appeared with the title 'Deep fake for beginners', followed by a video clip of a disguised magician pulling a pair of handcuffs out of a hat. A slightly distorted voice explained how deep fake videos could be constructed and then went on to show an edited version of the sequence that led to Tom's arrest.

Tom froze and pressed pause.

'What the fuck's going on?' he asked.

'Carry on, said the DCI, smiling. Tom complied.

This time, there were no indecent images of the girl. Anything illegal had been cut out or obscured. But the commentator went into great detail about how the video was faked, pointing out the date anomaly, the difference in skin tones and other inconsistencies. Tom wasn't named, and no details of where the deep fake came from were given, but it was obviously the crucial one. The clip ended with a photo of a tropical pheasant, its feathers spread with dozens of eyes photoshopped onto its plumage, and the caption 'Argus: Eyes everywhere'.

'What do you know about this, DC Ferris?' asked Blaine.

'Absolutely nothing. I've never seen it before. And who the hell's Argus?'

'Argus is a hacking group we've been trying to trace for some time. They style themselves white hat hackers, and it's true, they've uncovered some nasty people and pointed us to evidence against them. But they also cause mischief. They frequently hack the *Daily Mail* online edition, posting witty captions or changing text and images in the sidebar of shame.'

Tom couldn't help grinning. Someone had shown him images of the Cabinet in clown outfits, several famous billionaires reimagined as highwaymen and the Home Secretary of the day distorted to look like Cruella de Vil from the Disney cartoon. The *Mail* had been furious, Tom recalled, but couldn't stop the attacks.

'You may find it funny, DC Ferris,' the DI said, sharply, 'but what they do is illegal, as you well know. However, they seem to have done you a favour here. This confirms what several of your colleagues have said. You were fitted up.'

Tom sighed with relief. The tension and fear left him, and he almost crumpled in his chair. He gathered his thoughts for a moment and then spoke.

'I'm grateful for this. I really am. But why didn't you simply tell my solicitor and get me released?'

'For two reasons,' replied Blaine. 'Firstly, we want to

know who would do this. The original images clearly showed serious offences being committed, even though it wasn't you in the video. So, we want to go after them. Secondly, we want to know who the Argus people are and how they got hold of highly restricted police material. First off, who would want to frame you?'

'Most of my work at the moment is dealing with cyber scams based in other countries. I've also done some work on child pornography, although I prefer to leave that to experts. I do lend a hand on occasions. Most of these criminals are small scale. I suppose there are two possible groups. A while ago I helped take down a local group of paedophiles with right-wing connections. They are all in jail or dead. They wouldn't be clever enough to do something like this, certainly not from a prison cell. So that leaves the Albanians.'

The two other officers exchanged glances.

'As you are probably aware, there has been a sustained campaign against Mexton police, following a series of arrests last year that focused on an Albanian OCG. You obviously know about the bombing, when I lost my hand, but my fiancée has been attacked, a bomb was left for a drug squad officer and two uniformed officers have been shot at. I helped with the computer fraud aspects of the operation against the gang, so I suspect that's why I was targeted.'

'That makes sense,' said Christopher. 'I know that there's a vast amount of hacking and scamming going on, by people based in eastern and central Europe.'

Tom nodded his agreement.

'How about this Argus group?' asked Blaine. 'How could they have accessed the video?'

'No idea, to both,' said Tom. 'I'd never heard of them until today and I don't deal with hacking as a rule. Perhaps they found the video on the net? Have you attempted to trace its provenance?'

'We are working on it. I have to ask you, formally, do you know who gave the Argus group that video?'

'I have no knowledge of how they gained access to that video,' said Tom, equally formally. But there was a tickle of suspicion at the back of his mind that he would never share with the NCA.

'You'll be pleased to know that we've already spoken to the CPS and the charges against you have been dropped,' said Christopher. 'Your line manager has been informed and you may return to work as soon as you like. You will appreciate that, given the evidence, we had no option but to pursue the matter. I will make it absolutely plain to everyone concerned that you are completely cleared of any wrongdoing. I hope you won't feel bitter, but I will understand if you do. I've heard nothing but good things about you, Tom, and I hope I'll hear more in the future.'

He stood and shook Tom's hand. Blaine nodded and smiled slightly.

'You're free to go, but can you liaise with the NCA over tracking this video? You may have some insight into how and where it came to be made.

'Yes. Yes, I will. Thank you, sir.'

Tom nodded to the two officers and left the room, a mixture of joy and anger energising his step. He couldn't wait to see Mel again – and to track down the bastards who had tried to destroy him.

Tom was greeted with smiles and a round of applause when he entered the incident room in search of Mel. Obviously pleased with his reception, he murmured his thanks but refrained from mentioning his suspicions about who proved he'd been fitted up. As he passed the whiteboard, on the way to the coffee machine, he stopped short.

'Where were these photos taken?' he called out.

'Musgrave Farmhouse,' replied Addy. 'Where the Albanian shootings happened. Why? You look like a ghost.'

'That clock,' Tom said. 'There was one just like it where that phoney video was filmed.' He studied the photos carefully. 'And that wallpaper. It's the same. So, it was definitely those OCG bastards who went after me.'

He shuddered and pulled out his phone to pass on the information to DI Blaine. Just as he finished the call, Mel entered the room, rushed over to him and embraced him fiercely.'

'Oi! Get a room, you two,' someone called, and DI Chidgey, emerging from his office, smiled.

'Go on. Piss off and go home early. You've got some catching up to do,' he said.

Mel and Tom needed no further encouragement.

Chapter Forty-Seven

JUST AS MEL got into her car, she answered her phone to an angry Stefan Paweski.

'Did you get those scum who took my money? Did that bloody tracker in the bag work? What about last night? Why can't you stop them?'

'We haven't arrested anyone yet, Stefan, and I'm sorry. We did track them to some premises they use, that we didn't know about, and we identified the man who did the talking. We still don't know where their headquarters are, because last night's tracker failed for some reason, but we have suspicions. Until we find out for sure, we can't move against them.'

'That's not bloody good enough. I need protection, and if you can't provide it, I'll have to do it myself.'

'Please be careful, Stefan. I've told you that you're allowed to use reasonable force to defend yourself and your property. You are not, repeat not, allowed to batter someone half to death because they threaten you. And you certainly cannot carry baseball bats or other weapons in the street.'

'Fuck that,' Stefan shouted. 'My business is at risk and I'm not allowed to protect it? What kind of country is this?'

A rather more peaceful one than Albania, was what she wanted to say, but she contented herself with more advice.

'There is another consideration, Stefan. This gang is particularly ruthless. If you escalate things and attack their members, they will retaliate. Possibly lethally, in order to show other victims what happens when people disobey. We will get them, I promise you, but please try to keep your head down in the meantime.'

'OK,' he replied, grudgingly. 'One month. Then my friends will help.'

He hung up without saying goodbye, leaving Mel desperately worried about his safety. She had taken to this shopkeeper and admired his bravery. She really didn't want to come across him on a mortuary dissection table.

Mel unfolded herself from Tom's arms and climbed out of bed, the evening sun throwing beams of light through the gap in the curtains. She emerged from the bathroom and suddenly swore.

'Oh, shit. I'm sorry, love. I forgot. I've invited Robbie out for a meal tonight. There's something I needed to talk to him about. I'm so sorry. I didn't expect you to be back.'

Tom looked slightly disappointed, then smiled.

'Trying to make me jealous, are you?'

'Yes. With our gay best friend.'

She threw a pillow at him.

'Should I cancel?' she asked.

'No. I need to thank him for clearing me. Unofficially, of course. It's all good. Get him round here. I don't feel like going to a restaurant.'

Mel smiled.

'I won't have time to cook. I'll order a takeaway.'

'That's fine. So how much time have we got?' he grinned.

'Purely theoretically,' said Mel to Robbie as she passed round glasses of beer, 'is it possible to hack into a private CCTV system?'

'Yes and no,' Robbie replied. 'It depends on how it's set up. Why do you want to know?'

'It's Musgrave Farmhouse, on the Ryegate road, out beyond Camberton. We think the OCG is using it as its headquarters. We can't carry out surveillance, as we would be spotted, and it's not practical to put one of our own cameras there. What did you mean by yes and no?'

'If it's an old-style wired system – truly closed-circuit – then there's no way to get into it without making a physical connection to the wiring. If it's a wireless system, with a connection to the internet, then it's much more feasible, technically. You could hack into a live feed and also interrogate any storage device, if you know what you're doing. Mind you, you'd need a pretty high-level authorisation to do so.'

'That would be problematical. We only have suspicions

about the building. No real evidence, just some vehicle movements and an indication that the video used against Tom was filmed there.'

'Are you looking for some unofficial help?'

'Robbie! Would I do such a thing?' Mel pretended to be offended. 'We can't have people like those Argus folk getting involved in an anti-terrorist operation, can we?'

'No. Of course not. But there may be more local help available.'

'I see. Well, I wouldn't want anyone getting into trouble. Another beer?'

Chapter Forty-Eight

Day 18

'OK, folks. What have we got from the camera on the lamppost?' DI Chidgey yawned and scratched his chin, the noise of his nails, rasping though the stubble, just audible to the detectives seated nearest to him.

'The good news,' replied Addy, 'is that the OCG doesn't seem to have spotted the camera. The results aren't so good.'

'Well, come on, then.'

'The SUV Mel planted the tracker on comes and goes most days. For a while, there was damage evident to the offside rear of the vehicle, but it's now been repaired.'

'That must be how the tracker was knocked off,' commented Mel. 'Perhaps they didn't notice it, after all.'

'Carry on, Addy,' said Chidgey, not responding to Mel's comment.

'We have a list of punters arriving by car, which we got

by tracing their plates, but no sign of any females leaving or entering.'

'How about other males?'

'There's a couple of individuals who come and go regularly. It looks like they live there – they bring shopping in. Unfortunately, we can't get clear images of their faces. The camera's too high up, and they usually wear baseball caps, so we can only go by clothing. One male did look up when the guys were fixing the light and placing the camera. We ran the image through the facial recognition software and got a hit. He's one of the men involved in the protection racket, name of Zamir Prifti.

'Well, confirming the link between the two criminal activities is useful, I suppose,' said Chidgey. 'It would be good to identify someone senior in the OCG, though. So far, I think we've only seen a few footsoldiers.

'What about this bomb-maker who's supposed to be in the country? Anything more from MI5 or SO15?' asked Martin.

'Nothing much, I'm afraid,' replied Angela Wilson. 'We've been watching ports and airports and there's no sign of him leaving. As far as we're concerned, he's a definite threat. He's been suspected of bombings in Paris, Amsterdam, Warsaw and Tallinn, but there's never been enough evidence to arrest him. Interpol have given us a slightly clearer photograph of him, which I've circulated.'

'Thanks, Angela,' replied Chidgey. 'I'll make sure all uniformed patrols get it. One more thing. Who the bloody hell sent me this DVD?' he asked, glaring at the team. 'It's in the box for an old film, *The Conversation*, but there's no writing on the disc. Why would anyone think I'd want it?'

'Have you played it, guv?' asked Trevor.

'No, I haven't. I thought it might have a virus, so I got Amira to check it. It's clean. I'll play it now.'

Chidgey slotted the disc into his laptop, which was linked to the whiteboard. The screen flickered into life and the split screen images of a farmhouse, a road and several sections of fencing appeared. Various vehicles came and went, and individuals were seen getting into and out of them. The time stamps on the videos suggested they were taken up to a week previously.

'Where the fuck is this?' he demanded.

'It's Musgrave Farmhouse, guv,' replied Sally. 'The pictures must be from their CCTV system.'

'Then how did we get it? I don't remember getting authorisation to seize footage. I may be getting on a bit, but I'm not that bloody forgetful.'

'It isn't seized,' said Jack, 'it's hacked. And someone's taking the piss, because that film's all about surveillance, but with microphones and cameras.'

'That's bloody great. It's illegally obtained, so we can't use it as evidence. It's fucking useless.'

'Not completely,' said Mel. 'We can watch it and see who's on it. It may give us leads we can follow up and collect some usable evidence later.'

'I'm not even sure we can do that. Suppose we nick some bastard on the basis of images on the disc. Even if we find him with a pistol in his pocket, the defence will want to know why we grabbed him. Some shitty lawyer might claim the arrest was unlawful and the arsehole could get off. Sorry, we might as well bin it.'

'For fuck's sake, sir,' shouted Mel. 'We've been blown

up, officers have been killed, I've been attacked twice, my fiancé's been maimed and you're pissing about over evidence that could identify who's behind it. What would you do in Avon and Somerset? Let us all get blown up? If you won't watch the disc, I will. Give it to me.'

She stood up and made to approach the laptop.

Already florid, Chidgey's complexion developed the hue of an angry beetroot.

'I'm closing the briefing. Mel, my office.'

'Sir. Look!'

Angela Wilson spoke up, urgently.

'That face. Can you run it back a few seconds?'

Chidgey did so, grudgingly, and froze the image.

'It looks like that photo of the bomb maker. He's here in Mexton. It's probably the most important piece of intel we've had. With your permission, I'll take the disc and share it with MI5. If they provide you with information, which you then act on, we can use the national security argument to rebuff any challenges as to how it was obtained.'

'Devious cow,' muttered the DI, as he ejected the recording. Angela appeared not to hear him.

'Here it is. Enjoy. And if you find out who sent it, let me know and I'll nick them. It's forensically clean – no prints or DNA – so it's a clever bastard behind it. And as for you, Mel,' he turned to her, 'get out of my sight and go and do something useful.'

Chapter Forty-Nine

Jack caught up with Chidgey as he reached his office. He stepped inside and closed the door.

'Can you go easy on Mel, Geoff? She's still suffering from PTSD, following a sword attack before all this started. The bomb and nearly being shot haven't helped. Angry outbursts are often part of the condition. She's been having counselling, which, she reckons, helps. I'm surprised she's not off on the sick, but she's a fighter and a bloody good detective.'

'Nevertheless, I will not have a junior officer challenging me in such an unrestrained way, in front of the rest of the team. It won't bloody do.'

'I know. I'll have a very strong word with her. I'm sure she'll apologise off her own bat. Can you leave it there?'

'I suppose so. But if she does anything like that again, she'll be on a disciplinary charge.'

'Thanks. I'll make sure she doesn't.'

'You do that. Now let me get on with sorting out the overtime claims.'

Jack left the DI's office without saying anything more and beckoned to Mel, who was waiting anxiously beside her desk.

'Come with me and don't say a word,' he commanded, and led her out of the building to a nearby coffee shop. He ordered drinks, and after they arrived, he started speaking.

'What the bloody hell was that all about? You lost it in there. It's OK to present a contrary argument, and you can even have a go at me. But you do not, repeat not, challenge a DI like you did, especially in front of the team. If you have a problem with his decisions, raise it in private. I know the team was all on your side, and most felt exactly the same, but he's the boss. Now you can speak.'

'I'm sorry, Jack. I just couldn't bear the thought of valuable evidence being ignored, after everything that's happened. I'll apologise to Mr Chidgey first thing tomorrow. Am I really in the shit?'

'I think I've managed to pull you out. This time. Look, I know what you've been through and I've explained to the boss about your PTSD. But for God's sake be careful around him. He's not a happy bunny, by all accounts.'

'Thanks, Jack. I really appreciate it. But what have you found out about him?'

'He had a decent career with Avon and Somerset, putting away some really serious criminals. Two years ago, his wife died, and after that, he coasted for a while, according to my mate in his force. He transferred to Mexton a few months ago, possibly thinking a change of scene would restore his enthusiasm. His secondment to our team will probably be his last job before his retirement, which he's not looking forward to, as he lives alone and has no children. If anything, coming here has bucked him up and he's determined to get a result. He wasn't being deliberately obstructive; he was just looking at the letter of the law.'

'I know, but...'

'Never mind. It's sorted, and we've got a valuable lead. Exactly what we'll do with it, I don't know. DI Chidgey does want to know where the disc came from, though. It's Cheap Goat, isn't it? The same person who sent us those hacked emails during the right-wing paedophile case?'

'I...I can't say, Jack.'

'And would I be right in thinking that Cheap Goat is also skilled at hurling laptops at gunmen?' His voice was stern, but he was smiling slightly.

Mel blushed.

'You may think that, Jack, but I couldn't possibly comment.'

'You said that the last time. Well, if, by any chance, you should encounter said animal, perhaps you would point out that the DI is anxious for him to move on to pastures new? Pastures that involve very limited exercise and lousy food.'

'I will. If I should encounter him – by chance, of course.'

'Right. Now finish your coffee and go and catch a murderer.'

Mel walked back to the office feeling both ashamed about her outburst and grateful to Jack for interceding on her behalf. She would apologise to the DI, as agreed, and perhaps seek help from her counsellor, although she knew the service the force used was overwhelmed, because of the bombing. Chidgey's determination to track down who produced the disc was worrying, though. She couldn't bear the thought of Robbie losing the job he loved, and going to prison. If he did, it would be her fault for encouraging him to hack the farmhouse's CCTV system. She wouldn't involve him in anything illegal again. She hoped.

Peter Fearon looked up from his desk at the figure standing in front of him, with a jolt of surprise.

'I didn't expect to see you again,' he said, nervously.

'Well, I thought it was time we caught up,' the figure replied. 'There's something you need to know. The police are asking questions about his death.'

'I know. They've been to see me. I didn't say anything. They accepted my alibi.'

'Good. And if they come back?'

The question hung in the air.

'I'll still say nothing. There's no proof, is there?'

'No. None. And we need to keep it that way.'

The figure leaned on Peter's desk.

'Anyway, here's a little present. I know you like a toot or two. I'll leave it with you. You look a little pale, so enjoy it. Be good.'

A small plastic bag containing a whitish powder

appeared in the figure's gloved hand and Peter seized it avidly. By the time he'd tipped out some of the powder onto the cover of a book, the figure had vanished. He rolled up a ten-pound-note, fumbling with the slippery plastic, and snorted a line. The hit from the cocaine gave him a brief burst of euphoria, but, within minutes, he realised that something was wrong. He began to feel dizzy, his pulse hammered in his ears and he started to wheeze. His breathing became worse and he groped desperately for his Epipen. But where was it? He was sure it was on his desk. Frantically, he staggered to his feet and headed for the jacket hanging on the back of his office door. Had he left it there? But before he could reach it, he vomited, collapsed, and within minutes, he was dead.

The figure slipped out of the back entrance to the history department, avoiding the camera in reception, and dropped Peter Fearon's Epipen, swiped from his desk during the conversation, into a waste bin. A job well done.

'I've tracked down that old girlfriend of Alan Fearon's, Mel,' said Sally. 'Saffron Flowers, birth name Tina Bennet. She was a very famous model in the sixties, apparently. She lives on the south coast, not too far away. Worth a visit?'

'You bet. She may have some useful background or even a name or two. I'll clear it with Jack and we'll nip down there tomorrow. Can you phone her and make an appointment? Then we'll have another chat with Peter Fearon.'

Sally nodded and reached for the phone.

Chapter Fifty

MEL KNOCKED on Peter's Fearon's office door, intending to ask him a few more questions. Getting no reply, she pushed it open. It moved about half a metre then hit an obstruction. She stuck her head round the door and froze when she saw the historian face down on the carpet.

'Call a paramedic, Sally. Fearon's either dead or very ill,' Mel shouted, easing herself through the gap.

She crouched, felt for a pulse in Fearon's neck and shook her head.

'He's dead. Better phone DI Chidgey as well. It looks as though this could be a crime scene, so you'd better stay outside. Ask for a uniform to control the scene.'

Mel stood up and looked around the office. It was just as untidy as on the previous occasion they'd visited, but there were no obvious signs of a struggle. She noticed a smell of vomit around the corpse, almost masking an artificial scent of aftershave or perfume. A small plastic bag on the desk caught her attention, and she could see, without moving any closer, that it contained some whitish powder.

'Could be he's taken cocaine,' she called to Sally, 'but a little bit of blow isn't usually fatal, surely. When you speak to the DI, suggest the pathologist takes a look. Perhaps there's something else there. Go back to the office. I'll hang on here until the SOCOs arrive.

Two hours later, Dr Durbridge stood up from examining Peter Fearon's corpse and polished his glasses on his sleeve.

'Your suspicions may be right, DC Cotton. I don't think this was simply a cocaine overdose. It looks like he went into anaphylactic shock and couldn't breathe. Initial signs suggest asphyxiation, but I'll be able to confirm this when I get him on the table. I would suggest you get the contents of that bag analysed as soon as possible. Do you know if the victim had any allergies?'

'No, doctor,' Mel replied, 'but we can ask his relatives. They should know.'

'Well, please let me know what you find.'

'Will do. Once the SOCOs have finished, the undertaker will bring him to you. Thank you.'

As Mel headed back to the station, leaving PC Halligan guarding the scene and the SOCOs busily at work, her mind was racing. What was a respectable historian doing taking cocaine? Perhaps there was more to Peter Fearon than they realised. What was in the drug that killed him? Was it just a contaminated batch, mixed with fentanyl or something? She had seen no reports of lethally cut cocaine on the force's bulletin system. The other possibility, which was seeming increasingly likely to her, was that someone had deliberately added something toxic to it. So, who the hell would want to kill Peter Fearon?

On an impulse, she turned the car around, phoned Jack on the hands-free to let him know where she was going, and headed for Davvi's office. A frozen-faced receptionist reluctantly phoned her boss and told Mel that Davvi could spare her five minutes. She pointed to a seat in the foyer and said that Davvi would be down shortly. After a half-hour wait, which Mel was sure was deliberate, the irritated entrepreneur came out of the lift and stalked over to her.

'What do you want this time?'

'I'm afraid I have some bad news, Mr Fearon. Your uncle has been found dead in his office.'

'So? I hardly knew him, so I don't really feel much grief. How did he die, as a matter of interest?'

'I can't say. The pathologist will be carrying out a post-mortem tomorrow. But, may I ask you: did he regularly take cocaine or any other recreational drug?'

'How would I know? I haven't seen him since my mother's funeral and he didn't look like some drug-crazed hippie then. He's a historian, for God's sake, not a Canary Wharf banker.'

'OK. Thank you. Did he have any allergies?'

'That I can answer. Nuts. He was a bloody nuisance at

Christmas, when we used to meet up, with other people eating nuts. Anybody would think people were spraying ricin around the place. Is that all?'

'Yes, thank you, Mr Fearon. I'm sorry for your loss.' Not that he was, she thought to herself. 'We'll be in touch when his body is released and someone can arrange a funeral.'

'Well, tell Grenville. I'm too busy. Good day.'

Davvi turned on his heel and marched back to the lifts without a goodbye or any other acknowledgement of Mel's presence.

Mel checked her watch and decided there was still time to talk to Grenville Fearon. She phoned Sally, asked her to tell Jack what she planned, and suggested that she gave Nicola and Sarah Fearon the news.

'We may need to interview them formally at some stage,' she said, 'but it's worth having a quick chat now. Are you OK with that?'

'Well, I've delivered the death message on quite a few occasions,' replied Sally, 'in more tragic circumstances than this. I'm sure I'll cope.'

'I'm sure you will.'

As she hung up, Mel reflected on how well Sally was shaping up as a detective. She was pleased to be working with her and knew she would go far. She would certainly argue for Sally's secondment to CID to be made permanent.

'I'm sorry, but I've got some bad news for you, Mr Fearon,' said Mel, as Grenville Fearon showed her into his office. 'Your uncle has been found dead in suspicious circumstances.'

Grenville's flushed face blanched.

'When? How?'

'He was discovered this afternoon, in his office. The cause of death hasn't been established, but there was a suggestion that he had taken cocaine. Do you know if he was a user?'

Grenville switched into professional mode and straightened up in his seat.

'I have no knowledge of any illegal use of drugs by my uncle. Indeed, it is some time since I last saw him, so I do not know how he occupies his time outside his university duties. I'm sorry to hear he is dead, but I'm afraid I cannot shed any light on the matter. Is that all?'

'Not quite, Mr Fearon. Can you think of anyone who might have a grudge against him?'

'No. As I have indicated, I did not know him well. I wouldn't have thought history was a field inspiring murder. Most of the bloodshed historians deal with is in the past.'

He attempted a thin smile.

'One more thing,' interjected Sally. 'Did Peter Fearon have any allergies?'

Grenville thought for a moment.

'Yes, he did. Prawns or nuts or something. He had a row with the caterers at our mother's funeral, as I recall. Is that relevant?'

'We're not sure at the moment, sir,' replied Mel. 'It's just something the pathologist asked about.'

Grenville grunted as the two detectives left. He thought for a few minutes, looked up a phone number and dialled it.

Chapter Fifty-One

Nicola Fearon, dressed up to the nines, looked at Sally with disdain, as though the plainly dressed police officer had gate-crashed a society ball in ripped jeans and a hoody.

'What do you want now? Should I call my solicitor?'

'I'm sure that won't be necessary. There's something I'd like to talk to you about. I'm afraid Peter Fearon was found dead this afternoon. I'm sorry to give you bad news.'

Nicola shrugged.

'I know. Grenville's just phoned me. I can't say he's any great loss. What did historians ever do for anyone? Do they generate any wealth? Almost as bad as sociologists. I suppose it's sad, but I didn't really know him.'

'So you wouldn't know of anyone who hated him enough to kill him?'

'Kill him? Do you thing he was murdered?'

Nicola seemed mildly alarmed.

'We don't know yet, but the circumstances are suspicious.'

'Oh. Well, in answer to your question, no I don't. Sarah disliked him, though. She had a big argument with him, at our mother's funeral, about how historians have glossed over the – quote – iniquities – unquote – of the British Empire. All this woke shit. But I seem to remember him pointing out that his field was the Russian Revolution and its effects on Europe. Perhaps he pissed off the KGB and they came after him with Novichok.'

'Well, we're not following that particular line of inquiry, at the moment. Did you hear anything else of interest at the funeral?'

'No. Now I need to go. I'm hosting a party for some of our wealthier clients. If you have any further questions, contact Grenville. He is still my solicitor.'

Sarah Fearon seemed almost grateful to be called away to talk to Sally, when she joined her in the foyer of the Social Care offices.

'Meetings, bloody meetings. It's a wonder we ever get any work done,' she smiled. 'How can I help you?'

'I'm sorry to bring you bad news,' Sally began.

'If it's about Uncle Peter, I already know,' interrupted Sarah. 'It's a shame. He was a pretty harmless guy, by all accounts, and I believe you think he was murdered?'

'His death is being treated as suspicious,' said Sally, 'but we haven't had the results of the post mortem yet. There was a suspicion that he had taken cocaine. Would that surprise you?'

Sarah shrugged.

'A lot of people seem to take it these days. It's become quite cheap. But he was on the arts side, so I would have thought cannabis would have been more his line. Sorry, mustn't fall for stereotypes.'

'Can you think of anyone who would want to harm him?'

'No, I can't. He always seemed a pretty inoffensive bloke. Historians don't usually make deadly enemies.'

'I gather you had a row with him after your mother's funeral.'

'Oh. Yes. A spirited discussion, I would call it. We disagreed over the role of historians in massaging the facts about past British imperial crimes. He explained that his field was Russia and we called a truce. Poor bloke, he had a bad time of it that day, what with me having a go and the caterers trying to poison him, as he claimed. Some of the food had nuts in it and they couldn't tell him which. I felt sorry for him and invited him for a drink later.'

'Did he accept?'

'Not at the time, but we met for coffee a few times and continued our discussions, this time on a more amicable basis. I quite liked him and I was sorry when Grenville told me he was dead.'

'Thank you, Ms Fearon. We'll let you get back to your meeting,' smiled Sally.

Sarah looked at her watch ruefully.

'Thanks for the brief respite, anyway.'

'At last. A real human being!' said Sally, as she reported her conversations to Mel, back at the police station. 'Sarah actually seemed to care.'

'Yes. A nice change. They're not exactly a model family, are they? No-one, apart from Sarah, has given a toss about the death of their uncle. I've got aunts and uncles, and I don't see them often, but I know I'll be upset when they die. By the way, do you know anything about perfume?'

'Not really my field,' replied Sally. 'I don't use it, and neither does Helen. Why?'

'Nothing really. Something's niggling me. I wondered what Sarah had on. We'd better track down Trevor. He's sent me a text saying he's found something interesting.'

'Follow the trail of biscuit crumbs,' said Sally, which made Mel smile.

Chapter Fifty-Two

Day 19

Saffron Flowers coughed volcanically, the heavy amber beads of her necklace rattling as her shoulders shook. She brushed back her long grey hair, a few streaks of blonde still visible, and looked at the detectives with curiosity.

'So, what do you want to know about Johnny, then?'

'Did he have any enemies, Ms Flowers?' asked Sally.

'Apart from me, you mean? Not that I know of.'

'You parted badly?'

'You could say that. We were together for about three years. Got our pictures in *Melody Maker* and the *New Musical Express*. There was even a mention of us in *Oz* magazine when we did that legalisation of cannabis benefit concert. We were quite a couple – him the hip musician and me the glamorous model.'

She pointed to a slightly dog-eared poster on the wall of the seedy flat, sandwiched between adverts for events at

The Roundhouse and Alexandra Palace. The woman pictured was clearly Saffron. She had flowers in her hair, a picture of a marijuana leaf on her cheek and very little clothing. The image was stunning.

'Why did you break up?' asked Mel.

'Johnny never had any problems getting women to drop their knickers. I thought he was settled with me, and although we allowed each other a bit of latitude, he promised he would always come back. It was the time of free love, you know, but I can't help feeling the guys got a better deal. Anyway, he started wittering on about eastern religions and cosmic truth and all that stuff. Next thing I knew, he'd shacked up with a so-called priestess from a sect I'd never heard of and was being soaked for money. I was out on my arse and my career took a hit as a result. I was no longer hot property. He pushed me out of the place we were sharing – I wasn't spiritually pure enough, apparently – and I ended up in a squat in Notting Hill. It was bloody derelict, and although I didn't know it at the time, it was riddled with asbestos and the room I crashed in was full of the dust. Hence this bloody cough.'

Her shoulders heaved again as another bout took hold.

'So, yes, I hated him. I held him responsible for the decline of my career. Cosmic fucking truth doesn't pay the rent, does it? I managed a few modelling jobs over the years, but I was a bit too old for Page 3, and, anyway, my tits were too small for *Sun* readers. I got a few other jobs, in shops and bars, when my looks had gone – poorly paid and mind numbing, but at least I survived. Hardly a rock star lifestyle, though.'

She grinned savagely and indicated her faded wallpaper, shabby furniture and threadbare carpet.

'Worst of all, if he hadn't thrown me out, I wouldn't have this disease. But if you're asking me if I killed him, I have a question for you. Do I look like a killer? Do you think I could afford a hitman? You said he died about eight years ago. Even then I was physically weak and far from wealthy. So don't be bloody silly.'

Sally glanced at Mel and spoke.

'We're not considering you as a suspect, Ms Flowers. We just need to know if there is anyone in his background who would have borne a grudge. How about that priestess you mentioned?'

'That didn't last more than a few months. Eventually he realised that giving money to a company based in Croydon wasn't a path to spiritual enlightenment and that the priestess was about as genuine as a seven quid note. But the bastard never sought me out afterwards.'

A tear appeared in her eye and she reached for a tissue.

'So, in answer to your question, I don't know anyone who hated him enough to kill him. As far as I know, he never killed anyone, shagged a fourteen-year-old or impregnated a gangster's daughter. Any repercussions would have happened much sooner, if he had. I'd look to the family, if I were you. An odd lot, by all accounts. Now, if you'll excuse me, I'll gaze at my posters, play some vinyl and remember happier times.'

Mel and Sally thanked Saffron for her help and left the dingy premises, both pondering on the impermanence of fame and beauty.

Chapter Fifty-Three

Day 20

'So what have you found, Trevor?' asked Mel, sipping her coffee and grabbing a biscuit from Trevor's packet, after a morning briefing at which little was reported.

'I've been looking through the photos of punters outside the brothel in Jubilee Terrace,' he replied. 'Most of them had their faces obscured, but one was bare-headed and the camera picked up a better image. He seemed familiar, and when I looked at the whiteboard again, I recognised him. It's Peter Fearon.'

Mel whistled.

'So, he wasn't just a boring academic with a taste for cocaine. He was unmarried, so perhaps that's where he got his jollies.'

'Do you think that's where he got the coke?' asked Sally, perching on Trevor's desk. 'We know the OCG supplies drugs as well as sex.'

'What? A special deal? Blow with every blow job, ten percent discount? I suppose it's possible, but I'd have expected more deaths if there's a mucky batch going around. No, the more I think about, it the more I think it was someone who knew him and knew he was allergic to nuts. In other words, a family member or a close friend. Possibly the same person who killed Alan, possibly not.

'Poison!' Mel exclaimed.

'What are you talking about?' asked Trevor. 'The Mexton Borgia's inside and will be for life.'

'Not that kind of poison. The perfume Poison, though why anyone would want to call it that beats me. It's what Sarah was wearing when I first met her, and I think I caught a whiff of it in Peter Fearon's office.'

'You don't suspect her, do you?' asked Sally. 'She seems so decent.'

'Well Harold Shipman seemed pretty decent to his patients, until he killed them. We have to suspect everyone, however pleasant.'

'But that stuff's not exactly exclusive, is it? I've seen it in dozens of shops. I'll bet some of Peter Fearon's colleagues have used it. Maybe Nicola, as well.'

'True. It's not proof. But it does suggest that a woman wearing Poison was in Peter's room not long before we found him. I still think the other members of the family are more murderous, but I've certainly not discounted Sarah.'

'Oi! Miss Marple!' called Jack, who had heard part of the conversation. 'Phone call for you. It's Stefan Paweski.'

Mel walked back to her desk and picked up the phone with a heavy heart.

'How can I help, Stefan. Has anything else happened?'

'Those bastards are demanding more money. They're coming back on Thursday and they want twenty-five percent. I can't afford to pay and you are letting them get away with it. Your stupid tracker didn't work and they are still out there. What are you going to do about it?'

'Look, I'm really sorry. I can't tell you very much, but I can say that their protection racket is only part of a much larger picture. We want to stop all these people's activities at the same time. If we act against the people who are attacking you, we could compromise the whole operation.'

'I don't care about your fucking operation. My livelihood is at stake. Next collection day I will have my compatriots in all my shops and these bastards will regret they ever came for me. And don't worry, we won't patrol the streets with weapons.'

'Stefan, please. I really don't want you to get into trouble. You're incredibly brave and...'

Stefan cut the call.

Chapter Fifty-Four

Day 21

Amira Khan, the IT specialist, approached Mel's desk with a puzzled expression on her face.

'What's up, Amira? Something wrong?' Mel asked.

'Not exactly. I've been looking at Peter Fearon's laptop to see if he had been receiving threatening emails, as you asked. You told me he didn't use social media and didn't get on with technology.'

'Well, that's what he told me.'

'He was lying. He had Tor installed on his machine and had a significant presence on Twitter and Facebook, under a series of aliases. He also participated anonymously in several chat rooms.'

'So, what's the significance of Tor?'

'It's the onion router. It means he could get onto the dark web, look at stuff and buy things without being traced. Criminals, illegal porn users and terrorists use it. If you want a good bomb recipe without the Security Service knowing what you're doing, or need to buy bits of a pistol for reassembly in the UK, this is the router you need.'

'What was he doing with it, then?'

'That's the problem. His searches can't be traced. Maybe GCHQ could get something off his laptop, but they wouldn't consider a history professor in Mexton a threat to national security.'

'Bollocks! How about the chat rooms? I presume he didn't just gossip about his colleagues at the university?'

'Not unless they're interested in leather and bondage.'

Mel burst out laughing.

'Really? I would never have suspected him of being so adventurous.'

Amira chuckled.

'Everyone needs a hobby, I suppose. Anyway, there's nothing illegal about what he looked at online, but there were several references in the conversations to pornography sites. Leatherladiesstripping.com seems to come up a lot. I've refrained from visiting it, but Mr Fearon had been on it quite a lot.'

'So just a bit odd, then. Nothing seriously dodgy.'

'Apart from a discussion about snuff movies. Videos showing people actually being killed. Some of the participants have referred to sites on the dark web where these can be viewed.'

'Was Peter Fearon looking at them?'

'Not as far as I can see, but, as I said, I can't trace what he did via Tor. He did once write a paper on executions in Tsarist Russia, for a history journal, but that could have just been part of his academic work.'

'Anything else?'

'There were a few recommendations in the chat rooms for establishments where men can act out their fantasies. I've got some email addresses I can pass on to you, if that would help.'

'Yes, thanks, Amira. That's great. I'll ask Trevor to pose as a punter and find out where they are. This is really useful for building up a picture of our victim.'

'My pleasure,' Amira replied, heading back to her office, which some of the less PC detectives called the Geekery.

'Have you found out anything useful about Sarah?' Mel asked Sally.

'Not a lot. Her only arrest is for that public order offence during the environmental demo, and she has no serious driving offences on record. Her finances seem sound at the moment, but they have been less stable in the past. She was heavily in debt for a number of years, until the inheritance.'

'So, she did stand to gain from Alan's death.'

'It looks like it. I've tried to trace her expenditure, and it seems as though she had a gambling habit. There are large credit card payments to bookmakers and online gambling sites.'

'They're a bloody menace, aren't they?'

Sally nodded and continued.

'From ten years ago until recently, she was certainly spending more than she could earn as a social worker, so she must have been getting extra cash elsewhere. I've no idea where, and neither does HMRC. Should we have a chat with her?'

'Not yet,' replied Mel, thoughtfully. 'I don't want her to know we're looking at her. Was this what Nicola meant by not so squeaky-clean, do you think?'

'Well, it's not that scandalous, surely. It wouldn't put her job at risk, unless she was pinching the coffee money or fiddling her expenses, and her recent spending suggests she's not gambling any more. Perhaps she had help to quit?'

'Could be. So how else could she have been supplementing her income?' Mel mused. 'I don't see her working in a bar or driving an Uber.'

'Stocks and shares? Does she own any property she lets out?'

'Not that we've found. It would have to be something she could lose her job over, or at least be ashamed about, but not so risky that she could be arrested. That rules out dealing drugs or most types of fraud.'

The two detectives studied the whiteboard. The photograph of Peter Fearon leaving the brothel caught their attention. They looked at each other and, simultaneously, said, 'The game!'

'Hang on, though,' said Sally. 'I can't see her hanging around on street corners offering blokes a good time.'

'No,' Mel replied,' but she could have been working through an escort agency. There are several in Mexton that offer company, with extras if clients are prepared to pay for them.'

'OK, but she meets a lot of people in her work. What if someone recognised her on a website?'

'We've only seen her in her working clothes, which are

practical and slightly dowdy. She wears no make-up to work and hardly any jewellery. But she's got a good figure and nice hair. If she was glammed-up a bit, she'd be a lot more attractive, especially ten years ago. And, of course, she'd use an alias. If she did meet someone she knew in the course of the work, chances are they would keep quiet about it, too. I'll ask Trevor to do us a favour and look through the escort agencies' websites in case she's still on one. He's the king of the keyboard around here. Sarah probably doesn't need to do it any more, now she's got Alan's money, but there may still be some online presence. She said she donated a lot of money to green charities, but perhaps she used some of it to pay for rehab.'

'He'll enjoy that,' Sally chuckled. 'Better write him a note for his wife, in case she finds out.'

Mel laughed.

'Come and get some coffee while we think about Sarah Fearon providing some extremely social services.'

'Why do I always get the sleazy jobs?' said Trevor, pretending to moan. 'DI Thorpe had me going through all those videos of blokes doing blackmailable things last year, and I've just spent two hours looking at working girls on websites.'

'Do you want to go and take a cold shower?' Mel teased.

'Sod off,' he replied, smiling. 'Anyway, I've found something. This agency, Mexton Magic Encounters, hasn't updated its website for a couple of years, and, towards the end of the list, there's this page.'

He turned his laptop so Mel and Sally could see the screen. They studied the image of a scantily clad, voluptuous woman holding a glass of champagne. Her face was partly obscured by a diamante-encrusted mask, and the caption read, 'Meet Madame Mystery for an evening you'll never forget'.

'That's her, isn't it?' said Sally.

Mel nodded.

'I contacted the agency, posing as a punter,' continued Trevor, 'and a woman told me that Madame Mystery had retired. She apologised for the out-of-date website and offered me the services of Sophisticated Sophie or Elegant Allegra instead.'

'Which you declined,' grinned Mel.

'Of course. But the woman certainly indicated that more was on offer than philosophical discussions about the state of the world.'

'Thanks, Trevor, that's great. I really appreciate your help and I'll buy you a big tin of biscuits at Christmas. I think we'll have a chat with Mexton Magic Encounters and see what they can tell us about Madame Mystery.'

Chapter Fifty-Five

'ARE you ladies looking for gentlemen companions?' began the proprietor of the escort agency.

Her sales pitch stopped abruptly when Sally and Mel produced their warrant cards.

'All our ladies and gentlemen are self-employed,' the woman resumed, 'and we offer an introduction service only. Should they enter into a private arrangement with clients subsequently, that is entirely their business.'

She recited the words as if she had done so many times.

'A pimp by any other name would smell as bad, eh?' muttered Sally. 'I bet you take commission.'

The woman glared at her.

'You gave a rather different impression to my colleague when he phoned you earlier,' said Mel. 'But we're not from the vice squad. We're investigating a murder. What can you tell us about Madame Mystery?'

'Our files are confidential...' the woman began.

'Bollocks,' said Mel. 'We can get a warrant to impound them within the hour,' she bluffed, 'and we'll stay here until it arrives to make sure you don't delete anything.'

The woman gave the detectives a poisonous glare and then sighed.

'I suppose it's not a problem. This woman came to us about ten years ago. She said she needed to make extra money because she had some gambling debts and her job didn't pay enough to cover them. She wouldn't say what she did. She looked as if she would scrub up well, so I suggested some make-up she could use, the type of lingerie that would suit her figure and so on. She was frightened of being recognised, so we came up with the Madame Mystery idea – a brand, if you like. We agreed that she should keep her mask on at all times and that she wouldn't be expected to appear in public with her clients. Surprisingly, it worked really well. Quite a few gentlemen liked the idea of not seeing the face of who was...entertaining...them. She did pretty well, but about a year ago, she stopped abruptly. Presumably, she'd cleared her debts.'

'Did she tell you her name?'

'No. She told me almost nothing about herself. She was obviously educated, rather reserved at first, but clearly desperate. She could only work at the weekends, but that wasn't a problem. We have quite a few ladies with day jobs on our books.'

'Did she have any problems with clients?'

'Not really. On a few occasions, she had to cancel at short notice, because something had come up at work, but she always rearranged the appointment. Once, a client tried to get her to do something she didn't want to do – she wouldn't say what – and got a bit rough. She hit him in the face with a champagne bottle and broke his nose. We banned him.'

Mel looked startled.

'Did she assault anyone else?'

'Not unless they asked her to. Funny, she didn't look the sort of person to belt a bloke with the Bolly, but you never know. Anyway, it was self-defence.'

Sally grimaced.

'Was this her?' asked Mel, showing the woman a photo of Sarah Fearon.

'Yes,' the woman replied, studying the picture. 'Ditch those clothes, turn the clock back a few years, add a bit of lippy and mascara, and that's Madame Mystery.'

'Well, that was interesting,' said Sally, as they walked back to the car.

'Thinking of some part-time work, are you?' joked Mel.

'I don't think Helen would approve,' Sally grinned. 'But we now know how Sarah paid her debts, and that she stopped the escort work once she got Alan's money.'

'We do, and, also, we know that she can become violent if pushed. Not that I blame her.'

'Wasn't Alan Fearon killed with a champagne bottle?'

'All Dr Durbridge said was that he'd been hit with a blunt instrument of some kind. He wouldn't speculate as to the type. There were no glass fragments in the skull, and anyway, the bottle wouldn't have broken. But you're right. Two of his children did mention a bottle of champagne in the room where they confronted him. Davvi and Sarah, I think.'

Chapter Fifty-Six

Day 22

'So WHAT HAVE we got on Peter Fearon's murder?' asked DI Chidgey when the team settled down for the morning briefing. 'We're calling it Operation Wisteria, by the way.'

'Amira's been through his laptop,' replied Mel, 'and it seems he had some slightly sleazy interests – leather and that sort of thing, with a possible interest in snuff movies. There were some encrypted files that she's working on, but she's found nothing illegal so far. He was seen leaving the brothel in Jubilee Terrace, but we assume he was there just as a punter. I can't see him being involved with the OCG. Has the PM report come back?'

'Yes. Dr Durbridge suggested we had the cocaine sample examined and the lab found a significant quantity of peanut powder mixed in with the drug. Nobody cuts coke with nuts, so it was put there deliberately, by someone who knew of his allergy.'

'In other words, his family,' interjected Addy.

'Exactly. But why would the buggers want to kill him?'

'Perhaps he knew something incriminating. Maybe they thought he might talk, now we're investigating Alan Fearon's death,' suggested Martin. 'Whoever killed Alan must have killed Peter.'

'OK. Check all their alibis for around the time of Peter's death. Did anyone see who visited him in his office?'

'No. The department was quiet. Most people were at meetings and there were no students in that part of the building. It's probable that the killer came and went via a back entrance, since no-one unusual was seen at reception. SOCO's found an unused Epipen, in a rubbish bin near this entrance, and it's being examined for Alan's DNA. The prints on it were too smudged to be of use.'

'So the killer took it to prevent him saving himself. Sneaky bastard,' said Chidgey. 'What's all this about a perfume, Mel? Was he a cross-dresser or something?'

'No, guv,' Mel replied, wearily. 'I smelt a scent in his office that I think is called Poison. It's pretty common. Sarah Fearon uses it, so does the receptionist at Alan's university. I think I smelt it in Nicola's office, too. If it was the killer's, and if the killer has to be a family member, then we're looking at Nicola or Sarah. And, no, boss, it wasn't Grenville's. He uses one of those aftershaves that can paralyse a bison at twenty paces.'

The team laughed.

'Never underestimate the power of smell,' said Chidgey, reflectively. 'Remind me to tell you how we caught the Muckspreader Murderer back in 2009. Anyway, do we have anything else?'

'I have a few ideas,' said Mel, 'but I want to think them through before sharing them. Peter Fearon's murder has confirmed one of my suspicions, but I need to check a couple of things. If I'm right, we'll need to arrest all the Fearon siblings simultaneously.'

'Oh, Gawd,' moaned Jack. 'You're not going all Hercule Poirot, are you? Gathering the suspects together and revealing the identity of the killer in front of everyone?'

'Not exactly, Jack. I am aware of PACE. But I want to make sure they're not alerted to the arrest of one of their number. Once we've checked their alibis for the time of Peter's murder, we can move.'

'OK,' said Chidgey. 'You get on with checking whatever it is. The rest of you, talk to the Fearons and find out where they were when Peter was killed. I want a full explanation of your ideas before we do anything, Mel. We don't want to look like prats. Right. Off you go.'

Mel spent the next couple of hours telephoning airlines and making copious notes. Addy, Trevor, Sally and Martin each contacted one of the Fearons and took statements from them concerning their whereabouts when Peter probably died, then Trevor busied himself going through Peter Fearon's finances. After collecting the results of her colleagues' enquiries she took a large swallow of coffee, wishing it was something stronger. Although she was sure of her facts, and the likelihood of her conclusions, she was still nervous. After all, she was only a DC, and a relatively new one at that. DCs don't normally present the solution to a murder to their senior officer but, since she had been kept mostly at arm's length from Operation Fieldmouse, she had thought of little else apart from Alan Fearon's murder and Tom's nightmare situation. She straightened her jacket, crossed her fingers and joined Jack in Chidgey's office.

Chapter Fifty-Seven

The DI invited her to sit and regarded her through slightly bloodshot eyes.

'Get on with it, then,' he said.

Jack, sitting in the other chair, smiled encouragingly.

'I believe we have enough evidence to arrest the Fearons for conspiracy to murder their father and perverting the course of justice.'

'What, all of them?' asked Jack.

'For the moment,' replied Mel. 'I have my suspicions as to who struck the fatal blow, but we'll need to get confirmation from the interviews, which is why we don't want them to know about their siblings' arrests. So what do we actually know about the night of the row? We know that all four visited their father and at least three of them attempted to persuade him to share his winnings. They all needed money – Davvi and Nicola wanted to expand their businesses, and Sarah was in debt to the bookies but claimed she didn't want his money, which we know wasn't true. Grenville just likes money. At some point there was a row. My neighbour heard it, and Sarah, who said she was in the garden at the time, also reported it. We don't know who said what, or what exactly happened, but it's possible he was struck with a champagne bottle that fractured his skull. He was never seen again.'

'But he went to Australia,' interrupted Jack. 'There are flight and hotel records.'

'No, he didn't,' replied Mel. 'There was a reasonable family resemblance between Peter and Alan back in those days. I saw a photo of him at the conference he attended in Budapest. I did some checking on flights. Peter's return flight from Hungary arrived at Gatwick three hours before Alan's flight was due to depart for Melbourne. Grenville was picked up speeding out of Mexton, in the direction of the airport. He claimed he was visiting a client but hasn't been able to prove it.'

'So you're saying it was Peter who flew to Australia, not Alan. Why the hell would he do that?' Chidgey demanded.

'Two possible reasons. Grenville, or one of the others, knew about his sexual peculiarities and threatened to expose him to the university and on social media if he didn't do as he was told. Also, Trevor found a series of significant sums appearing in Peter's bank account over the succeeding few years. They weren't large enough to attract suspicions of money laundering, but they added up to sixty thousand in total. So, I believe Grenville grabbed Alan's passport, ticket and Australian tourist visa, met Peter off his plane and forced him to impersonate his brother. The passport photos would have looked sufficiently similar to fool the authorities. He stayed down under for a few days, then flew back using his own documents. I checked, and he came back on a Qantas flight to Heathrow on the twenty-first of June.'

'Well, that solves a mystery,' said Jack. 'But what was going on while Grenville was doing all that?'

'The others left after Fearon was dead, although Sarah said she left while he was alive and the others were still there. No-one else mentioned that, and we'll need to explore it in the interviews. Later on, my neighbour heard a car returning but couldn't get a description or the plate as he wasn't facing the street. I reckon that the remaining conspirators had returned to clean up the crime scene, remove the murder weapon and bury the body. This would have taken some time, and would have made a certain amount of noise, but my neighbour at the back wouldn't have heard, as he fell asleep shortly after he heard the car. There's just a shop next door and a park on the other side. They then returned to their lives and waited patiently for Alan Fearon to be declared dead, safe in the knowledge that they would eventually inherit large sums.'

'OK,' said Chidgey, 'we can arrest them for conspiracy to murder, preventing the lawful and decent burial of a dead body and perverting the course of justice, but who struck the fatal blow?'

'I have my suspicions, but we'll need to get them confirmed during the interviews. Once they're in custody, I'm sure at least one of them will crack.'

'Good enough for me. Invite them to come to the station voluntarily, first, and arrest them if they refuse. Make the most of the custody clock. I'll borrow a few uniforms for you and we'll pick them up in an hour.'

Chapter Fifty-Eight

MEL AND SALLY were outside Davvi's office building, twenty minutes before the scheduled arrest time, when they saw his car speeding out of the underground car park.

'Where the hell's he going?' muttered Mel. 'Has he been tipped off about the arrests?'

'Well, something's spooked him,' Sally replied. 'Do you want me to follow him?'

'Go for it, but try not to let him clock us.'

Sally swung the unmarked police car into a gap in the traffic, four vehicles behind Davvi. The traffic flowed smoothly until they came to a set of temporary traffic lights, bracketing roadworks, which turned red a few moments before Davvi reached them. He ignored the red light, shot through in a cloud of exhaust fumes and disappeared. Mel looked at Sally, nodded and switched on the flashing blue lights concealed on the car. As they moved off they heard a screech of skidding tyres and the crunch of vehicles colliding. Sally eased forward, as the cars in front pulled in to let her past, and put her foot down with blues and twos going. A hundred metres further on, the source of the noise was obvious. Davvi's sports car was jammed under the front of a utility truck, which, Sally presumed, had also jumped the lights from the opposite direction. The truck's illegally fitted bull bars had ripped the car's bonnet off and crumpled it against the smashed windscreen. Davvi was invisible, hidden by the deployed air bag.

Sally leaped out of the car while Mel called for backup and an ambulance. She wrenched at the driver's door but it wouldn't budge, so she ran round to the other side. The other door gave slightly, and she managed to get the tip of her baton into the gap between door and frame. As she heaved on it, the door opened, with a dull grinding sound, and Sally saw Davvi, his face covered in blood, slumped on his seat with his unused seat belt dangling.

'Mr Fearon. Davvi. It's DC Erskine. Hold on, an ambulance is on its way.'

Davvi mumbled something incoherently and then shouted, as if he'd suddenly remembered something.

'She's coming for us. She's fucking coming for...' He lapsed into unconsciousness.

'So, it is a woman behind it,' said Sally as the traffic unit took charge of the scene and an ambulance carried Davvi to hospital.

'Looks like it. I'll call Jack and see how the other arrests have gone.'

Mel phoned the DS, listened for a few seconds and swore.

'Bollocks! Sarah and Nicola are both in the wind and the team that was supposed to pick up Grenville got caught up in a demonstration on the way. We're pretty close, so we'll get him. Jack's put out an alert for the women and tagged their cars for the ANPR cameras. Put the blue lights on and shift!'

Within ten minutes, the police car pulled up outside Grenville Fearon's office. The door to the building was open and there was no-one in reception, the staff, presumably, having left for the day. Peculiar noises were coming from the solicitor's office. Mel looked at Sally, nodded, and rushed for the door.

Chapter Fifty-Nine

Five minutes earlier

'Hello, Grenville,' the woman said, stepping into his office and closing the door behind her.

'Why are you here? I thought we weren't supposed to meet until the fuss has died down.'

'Don't worry. The police haven't a clue. And why shouldn't we meet? You could be giving me legal advice.'

She moved towards him, unbuttoning her blouse and slipping off her bra.

'What...what are you doing?'

'I thought you deserved a treat,' she said. 'You've been so helpful, sorting everything out for us.'

'But...but...you're my sister.'

'Probably. But we don't know for sure we've got the same father. And, anyway, you can't deny you've lusted after me ever since I was fourteen.'

Grenville's expression was a peculiar mix of puzzlement and desire, but his groin decided the matter.

'Now get those trousers off and lie down.'

Grenville complied, still looking slightly uncertain until the woman hitched up her skirt and straddled him. She leaned forward, her breasts grazing his expensive fitted shirt, and pulled a plastic bag from her waistband.

'Relax,' she said. 'This'll make it more fun.'

Before Grenville could object, she slipped the bag over his head and twisted it tightly around his neck. Uncertainty turned to fear, which turned to panic, as Grenville realised that this was not a seduction. He thrashed and struggled, his face turning purple, but his skinny and unfit body couldn't shift the sturdy woman astride him. Each attempted breath sucked the bag into his mouth, and his legs kicked in a futile attempt to dislodge his attacker.

'Get off him!' Mel's voice cut through Grenville's grunts and wheezes. 'You're under arrest.'

Nicola Fearon rolled off her brother with an expression of contempt. Grenville lay still until Sally pulled the bag off his head and checked that he could breathe. He jerked, coughed as he regained consciousness and promptly threw up.

'Another minute and I'd have finished the pathetic little prick off,' spat Nicola. 'He really thought I was up for it, the moron.'

Mel handed Nicola her bra and blouse and, when she was dressed, informed her that she was under arrest for attempted murder, recited the caution and handcuffed her. Grenville struggled into his trousers, embarrassment competing with fear for the upper hand.

'She...she...tried to kill me. She's my bloody sister and she tried to seduce me and kill me.'

'I think we need to have a chat about that, Mr Fearon,' said Mel. 'But we'll wait until Nicola's been taken to the station. Sally's phoned for a car. Are you OK? Can you breathe properly? I'm happy to drive you to the hospital. Would you like a glass of water?'

'No. It's OK,' Grenville said, collapsing into his office chair and retrieving a bottle of whisky from his desk drawer. 'You got here just in time, I reckon.'

He poured a large measure of Scotch into a coffee cup and drained it in two gulps.

'I would strongly advise you to get yourself checked over, said Mel. 'Your throat could swell up later and stop you breathing.'

'OK. OK. I will. Now stop fussing. Is this a formal interview?'

'Not at the moment, but we would like you to come down to the station to make a statement. If you feel unwell, we can get a doctor to take a look at you. Is that OK? We'll give you a few minutes to recover.'

'I suppose so. I just need to visit the lavatory and I need to make a couple of confidential work calls.'

Before Mel could answer, two uniformed PCs arrived and escorted Nicola to a waiting police car. Grenville returned after ten minutes, picked up his jacket and followed the detectives to their car.

Chapter Sixty

'WHAT THE FUCK'S GOING ON?' asked Mel, as she arrived at the custody suite with Sally. 'Why's Nicola Fearon at the desk collecting her belongings?'

'No idea, Mel,' her colleague replied. 'Why don't we ask her?'

The two detectives hurried over to their erstwhile prisoner.

'Ms Fearon. Why are you leaving? You were arrested on suspicion of attempted murder.'

Nicola turned round with a saccharine smile that sat awkwardly on her pinched face.

'My sweet brother telephoned your Detective Chief Inspector and confirmed that it was just a prank. I had no intention of harming him, as he knew. I think he was just a bit confused by your arrival. I've spoken to him and apologised for shocking him. We used to play tricks on each other as kids, but I guess this went a little too far.'

'Do you seriously expect us to believe that, Ms Fearon?'

said Mel. 'It looked very much as though you were trying to kill him. And you said something about finishing him off.'

'Well, I was joking. I'm sure you can construe a non-lethal interpretation of the term "finishing him off". And appearances can be deceptive, Detective Constable, can't they? Take yourself, for instance. You look pretty plain, but your figure's OK. A bit of make-up and you would have plenty of interest if I put you on our dating site. You could certainly supplement your police pay.'

Mel struggled to maintain a professional demeanour.

'There is another matter, Ms Fearon. We would like to talk to you again about your father's death. Are you prepared to remain here for interview, voluntarily?'

'Not a fucking chance,' snarled Nicola. 'I've had quite enough of this police harassment and I'm going home.'

'In that case,' replied Mel, 'Nicola Claire Fearon, I am arresting you on suspicion of conspiracy to commit murder. You do not have to say anything...'

As Mel recited the caution, Nicola's face whitened and she lashed out at Mel, her long fingernails missing the detective's eyes by millimetres. Sally grabbed Nicola's wrist, spun her around and handcuffed her hands behind her back. Two uniformed officers escorted her back to the custody sergeant, who authorised her detention when Mel explained the grounds for Nicola's arrest. She was led to the cells, swearing and complaining of police harassment.

'What do you make of that?' asked Sally, when Nicola Fearon was well clear of the area.

'I didn't know whether to laugh or throw up,' replied Mel. 'That was as clear a case of assault, and probably attempted murder, as I've ever seen. And Grenville was terrified when we rescued him.'

'So why should he want to get her off the hook?'

'She must have some kind of hold over him. He's a director of her company. Perhaps she found out about some professional misconduct. Perhaps they're both involved in something illegal. Maybe she thought he would grass her up for murder. I don't know.'

'It's bound to have something to do with Alan Fearon's death,' said Sally.

'More than likely. Presumably he's deeply involved in the conspiracy, but maybe there's something else. Could he have killed Peter?'

'Not unless he was wearing Poison. We think it's a woman, remember?

'Yes, of course. Probably. We'd better go and have a chat with Grenville. I asked a uniform to put him in an interview room and give him a cup of tea. We won't tell him Nicola's been arrested for murder.'

Mel switched on the recording equipment in Interview Room 2, recited the caution and introduced the people present.

'Can you confirm, Mr Fearon, that you do not wish to have a lawyer present?' she began.

'I'm a lawyer, as you know full well, and I don't need anyone else, thank you very much.'

'OK. And your throat is not troubling you?'

'The only thing troubling me is this irritating attention from the police. I've told you that Nicola was only playing a prank on me and meant no harm. I feel embarrassed about being found in that position but I do not want any action taken against her. Is that clear?'

'Perfectly clear, Mr Fearon. But we want to talk to you about another matter.'

She nodded to Sally, who opened a folder and addressed Grenville.

'In your previous statement, you told us that when you were stopped for speeding, on the night we believe your father died, you were rushing to meet a client who needed your help. You also said you couldn't remember the client's name. Do you stand by that statement?'

'Yes, I do.' Grenville glared at the detectives.

'What type of client would need your services so late in the evening, Mr Fearon? You don't handle criminal cases, so you wouldn't be needed by someone who had been arrested. I'm not a lawyer, but I can't imagine someone needing face-to-face advice on a trust or a conveyance so urgently. Would you like to comment?'

'No, I wouldn't. As I said, I don't remember the details.'

'Are you aware,' asked Mel, 'that the road you took is the route from Mexton to Gatwick Airport?

'Possibly.' Grenville began to look uncomfortable. 'What, precisely, is the relevance of that?'

'It's relevant because, had you been going to Gatwick, you would have met your uncle's flight, shortly after it landed.'

'I still fail to see the relevance.'

'Let me show you this document,' said Sally. 'For the recording, it lists selected arrivals and departures at Gatwick Airport on the night of the seventeenth of June 2013. Do you see anything of interest there, Mr Fearon?'

'No. I'm not a bloody plane spotter. Look, how much longer is this nonsense going on? I'm tired and I'd like to go home. I'm here voluntarily and I can leave when I want.'

'Of course you can. But the point of interest is that this flight from Budapest, which your uncle was on, arrived three hours before the departure of the flight to Melbourne on which your father was booked.'

'So? What of it? You know Dad took that flight and I can't imagine his brother hung around an airport in the middle of the night just to chat with him. What are you getting at?'

'What we are getting at,' said Mel, 'is the fact that your father never left the country.'

Grenville paled.

'Nonsense. We even traced the hotel he stayed at before we could have him declared dead. How he ended up back in Mexton, no-one knows.'

'A Mr Fearon did take the flight and stay at the hotel. We confirmed this. But it wasn't Alan Fearon. I suggest to you that you were involved in Alan Fearon's murder, in some capacity or other. You collected your father's travel documents and raced to the airport in order to meet Peter Fearon, after his flight landed, and persuaded him, by blackmail and/or promise of payment, to impersonate his brother. They looked sufficiently alike for this to work. Peter then returned, on his own passport, a few days later. Would you like to comment?'

'No, I fucking wouldn't, other than to say this is a complete fabrication. You've been reading too many thrillers, young lady. I've had enough of this nonsense and I'm leaving.'

'I'm afraid you're not,' said Sally. 'Grenville Fearon, I'm arresting you on suspicion of conspiracy to murder, preventing the lawful and decent burial of a dead body and perverting the course of justice.'

She repeated the caution and the two detectives led their captive to the custody suite for processing.

Sarah Fearon stepped out of the community centre, looked cautiously around and headed for her car, parked a couple of streets away. Good, she thought. No-one she knew had seen her. She had just clipped on her seatbelt and was about to start the car, when a grey saloon pulled in front of her, preventing her from moving. She wound down her window, but before she could remonstrate with the driver, he stepped out of the car, holding out a warrant card.

'Sarah Fearon?'

She nodded.

'I'm DC Martin Rowse. We'd like to talk to you further about your father's death and certain other matters. Are you prepared to come to the police station voluntarily? If not, I'm afraid I'll have to arrest you.'

'Well...yes...I suppose so. I'll follow you in my car.'

'That won't be necessary, Ms Fearon. You'll ride with me, and my colleague, DC Adeyemo, will follow in your car. Can you give him your keys, please, and come with me?'

A nervous Sarah followed Martin, realising that the other detective was right behind her, blocking any possible escape route.

'What do you want to talk to me about? Surely you don't need another statement?'

'All will be clear when we get to the station, Ms Fearon. It's best if you don't say anything until we get there. If you need to call your solicitor on the way, please feel free.'

Sarah shook her head and remained silent for the half-hour journey.

Chapter Sixty-One

'How DID you get on with Grenville Fearon?' asked Jack, as the two women approached the coffee machine.

'He's denying everything, as we expected,' replied Mel. 'He's definitely involved with the cover-up, but I doubt he struck the fatal blow. I don't know whether he was involved in planning the murder – or whether it was premeditated or just a conclusion to a row that turned violent. We'll talk to Nicola next, though we really need to arrest Sarah. Any sightings?'

'Not so far. She could be guilty or she could have dropped out of sight for perfectly innocent reasons. All we know is she left her office in a hurry and wouldn't say where she was going.'

'Hmm. I know it's a cliché in fiction, the nice guy turns out to be the killer, but it looks bloody suspicious to me.'

'Yeah. I suppose so. Good luck with Nicola – I'll watch on the monitors.'

Nicola radiated hostility as she sat facing the two detectives in the interview room.

'I'm afraid it is not possible for your brother to act as your legal representative at the moment, but we can offer you the services of the duty solicitor,' said Mel, once the formalities had been concluded.

'Not bloody likely. I don't need some second-rate brief to tell me to go "No comment", and that's all you're getting from me.'

'As you wish, Ms Fearon, but we have certain information we wish to lay before you, and I suggest you take the opportunity to challenge it should you disagree.'

Nicola simply scowled.

'Firstly,' began Sally, 'we believe that Alan Fearon was murdered on the night of the seventeenth of June 2013 by one or more of his children. Do you have anything to say about that?'

'No comment.'

'Secondly, we believe that Peter Fearon was intercepted by your brother, Grenville, at Gatwick Airport on his return from Budapest, and was persuaded or compelled to impersonate Alan. He used his brother's documents to travel to Australia and returned, a few days later, under his own name.'

Nicola fidgeted.

'No comment.'

'Did you attempt to kill Grenville in case he admitted this?'

Nicola started to speak but reverted to 'No comment'.

'Did you return to 42 Craven Street late in the evening of your father's death?'

'No comment.'

'Once we identified Alan's remains and started investigating,' said Mel, 'the killer or killers became nervous. The weakest element in the conspiracy was Peter Fearon, who didn't actually kill anyone. He had to be disposed of. We know he was murdered by someone who added peanut powder to his cocaine, almost certainly a family member who knew of his allergy and removed his Epipen, so he couldn't save himself.'

The muscles in Nicola's face tensed visibly and her skin whitened beneath her make-up.

'No comment,' she spat.

'Furthermore,' continued Mel, 'we believe that a woman was responsible. There was a strong smell of perfume in Peter Fearon's office, the same perfume you're wearing. Poison. SOCOs also recovered a hair from Peter's desk, and this is being processed as we speak. Once we know whose DNA it matches, we will seek the CPS's authority to charge that person with the murder of Peter Fearon.'

Nicola crumpled in her seat then drew herself up and straightened her shoulders.

'I would like to speak to my solicitor now. In Grenville's absence, it will have to be Tom Locke of Lambert, Crewse and Locke. Kindly inform him he is needed.'

Nicola remained mute while Mel suspended the interview and escorted her back to the custody sergeant.

'So, what's your take on that, Sally?' asked Mel, once they were back in the incident room. 'Guilty or not guilty?'

'She was certainly rattled when you mentioned the hair.'

'Yes, she was. Trouble is, it didn't have a root, so the lab will only get mitochondrial DNA. It won't be possible to differentiate between Sarah and Nicola.'

'Oh. Still, I think she was definitely involved in Alan's death, though whether she killed him herself I don't know. I don't believe that scene with Grenville was a prank, and perhaps we can persuade him to change his story. She's obviously ruthless, so she could have been tying up loose ends, even if she's not Alan's killer.

'Purely speculating,' continued Sally, 'perhaps Sarah killed Peter and Nicola killed Alan. Which means all four of them are involved in the conspiracy and Sarah isn't as decent as she seems.'

'Could be. As I said to Jack, Sarah's behaviour was suspicious and there's a gap in her day that could coincide with the time of Peter's death. We're looking out for her car, and it won't be long before we find her. Can you contact the hospital and find out when Davvi is likely to be fit for interview? I'll let DI Chidgey know what we've got from these two.'

'OK. Hang on a bit. I've just had a text. Martin and Addy are bringing Sarah Fearon in. Her parked car was spotted by a police motorcyclist, apparently, and they were waiting for her to return to it. Time for a quick coffee before we have a chat.'

Chapter Sixty-Two

'YOU'RE a difficult person to track down, Ms Fearon,' said Mel, once the formalities had been completed and Sarah had declined the services of a solicitor.

'You left your office in a hurry, shortly before my colleagues came to talk to you this afternoon, and told no-one where you were going. Can you see why it seems a little suspicious?

'Firstly,' replied Sarah, stiffly, 'I had no idea you wanted to talk to me again, and, secondly, I had a private matter to attend to. That's why I told no-one and switched my phone off.'

'Can you tell us the nature of this matter?'

'I'd rather not.'

'OK, we'll come back to that. On the day your uncle was killed, there is a gap in your work diary, provided to us by your manager, which coincides with the window for Peter's time of death. Was that a private matter, too?'

'Yes, it was.'

Sarah looked uneasy.

'Returning to the time when you last saw your father,' said Sally, 'can you confirm he was alive when you left him?'

'Yes, of course. I've already told you that. Twice. I also told you that I left before the others did.'

'None of them mentioned that.'

'I suppose they were too busy arguing. I tried to phone Dad later, to wish him a safe journey, but his phone was off.'

'Would it surprise you to know that he never went to Australia?'

'Of course.' Sarah looked puzzled. 'Why do you think that? We know he went there.'

'We believe that Peter Fearon was forced, by Grenville, to impersonate your father and take the flight instead of him, using Alan's documents. He came back to the UK using his own passport a few days later.'

'So are you saying that Grenville killed Dad and made Uncle Peter cover it up?'

'Not quite, Ms Fearon. We believe that Alan Fearon was killed by more than one of his children because he refused to share his lottery winnings. Grenville organised the cover-up while others buried his body and cleaned up the crime scene. We are still trying to work out exactly who was involved. Can you help us?'

'No, I can't. As I said, I left him alive. I suppose I wouldn't put it past the others to do something like that. They're all pretty grasping, after all, but I had nothing to do with any murder.'

'Getting back to your uncle's death,' said Mel, 'he had to have been killed by a family member who knew about his allergy. His Epipen was removed to prevent him treating the anaphylactic shock. We believe he was killed by one of the conspirators, in case he confessed to covering up his brother's death. We also have evidence that suggests a woman was involved. SOCOs recovered a hair from Peter's desk and we will be looking for a match with his children's DNA.'

'Look,' said Sarah, angrily. 'I had nothing to do with my uncle's death. I rather liked him. And I had no motive for killing Dad. The others needed his money but I didn't.'

'I'm afraid that's not strictly true, is it, Sarah?' Mel said, gently. 'We know about your gambling habit and the measures you took to feed it. Your father's money helped you get away from degrading part-time work. The perfume I smelt in Peter's office, when I found him dead, was the same as the one you're wearing now. And if we find a match between the hair we found and yours, we will be seeking CPS approval to charge you, unless you can give us a good reason not to.'

Sarah put her head in her hands and started to sob, silently. After a minute, she wiped her eyes on her sleeve and looked at Sally.

'Can I take a break, please? I need to make a decision. And can I have a drink of water?'

'Interview suspended at 18.30,' said Mel, switching off the recording equipment and following Sally out of the room.

When the detectives returned, Sarah was sitting up straight and had a determined expression on her face. Mel re-started the equipment and reminded Sarah that she was still under caution. Sipping slowly at a plastic cup of water, Sarah began to speak.

'It's true that I found Dad's money useful. I hated having to sell myself and I hated my gambling addiction even more. I did give money to environmental organisations, as I told you, but not as much as I implied. I'm sorry. In fact, I used a lot of it to clear my debts and pay for rehab.'

She paused and drank more water.

'The stress of discovering that Dad had been murdered made me want to gamble again. I had an overwhelming urge to go online and bet. I'm a member of Gamblers Anonymous, and on the day Uncle Peter died, I had an emergency meeting with my sponsor, who helped me overcome this urge, at least temporarily. Today, I attended an afternoon meeting of the group, at the community centre, which is where I'd been when your colleagues found me. I left the office a bit early and walked in the park for a while, well away from betting shops, until the meeting started. Obviously, I couldn't tell my colleagues where I was going, on either occasion. I will give you contact details and written permission to talk to my sponsor, if you need to confirm this. Satisfied?'

'Thank you, Ms Fearon. That would be most helpful.' Mel looked thoughtful and handed her a pen and paper. Would you mind waiting here while we check this out? We'll be as quick as we can.'

'All right. I suppose I don't have much choice, do I?'

'Well, not really. But we would be grateful if you would remain voluntarily. It would save an awful lot of paperwork. Can I get you a coffee?'

'White, two sugars please. And you'll find my sponsor at home at the moment.'

An hour later, her alibis confirmed, Sarah was stopped by Mel as she was leaving the police station.

'I've arranged a lift home for you, in an unmarked car. I'm sorry this has been traumatic for you, but I'm sure you understand why we acted as we did.'

Sarah nodded.

'I can now tell you,' continued Mel, 'that Nicola and Grenville have been arrested on suspicion of conspiracy to murder your father and committing a number of other offences. We have yet to talk to Davvi, as he was injured trying to leave Mexton. If you can think of anything about that night that could help us – anything you noticed or overheard – please get in touch.'

'I will, DC Cotton. I don't owe the others anything and I'd be glad to see the killer, or killers, behind bars. Good night.'

Chapter Sixty-Three

Day 23

MEL AND SALLY caught up with Davvi in the hospital car park.

'Good morning, Mr Fearon,' greeted Mel. 'The nurse told us you were being discharged. How are you feeling?'

'Er...all right, thanks. A few bruises and aches. No major damage, although they kept me in overnight in case I had concussion. Which I don't. Why are you here?'

'We'd like to invite you to come to the station to answer some questions about your father's death.'

Davvi's face contorted.

'Then I'd like to invite you to take a flying fuck at a rolling doughnut. I've had enough of this police harassment and I'll make sure it's all over the internet. So, piss off.'

'I wouldn't advise that, Mr Fearon. I'm arresting you on suspicion of conspiracy to murder, preventing the lawful and decent disposal of a dead body and perverting the course of justice. 'You do not have to say anything...'

Davvi struggled as Sally handcuffed him and Mel finished the caution. Throughout the short journey to police HQ his expression slowly changed from anger to fear. He maintained a sullen silence until the detectives led him to the custody suite, where he finally spoke.

'Call Grenville. He's my solicitor and I want him here.'

'I'm afraid he is unable to represent you, Mr Fearon. He is here, but he's in custody, under suspicion of committing the same offences as you are. I can also tell you that Nicola is under arrest and Sarah has been helping us with our enquiries. Would you like us to contact the duty solicitor?'

Davvi's legs appeared to give way. He swayed and managed to catch hold of the counter, just preventing himself from falling.

'Oh fuck, oh fuck, oh fuck,' he whispered, as tears began to flow. 'I knew it would all come back. I should never have gone along with it.'

'Please don't say anything more, Mr Fearon,' said Mel, urgently. 'We need to record an interview with you. Now do you need a solicitor?'

'It won't make any difference,' replied Davvi, dejectedly. 'Let's just get it over with.'

Sally led Davvi into the interview room and fetched him a drink of water. Mel switched on the recording equipment, repeated the caution and asked Davvi to confirm that he did not require a solicitor.

'Can you start,' she began, 'by telling us what happened on the night of the seventeenth of June 2013?'

Davvi composed himself and began to speak, haltingly at first, and then with more confidence.

'Dad called us all round to the house, saying he had something important to tell us. We had heard about his lottery win and we assumed that he was planning to share it with us. Instead, he sat there gloating and told us that we were a bunch of chancers and parasites and that the last thing he would do would be to give us money. He itemised all our so-called faults, pointing out that we had hardly contacted him since Mum died and had never supported him when he had little money. Even Sarah, who had kept in touch, was slagged off for her gambling. His announcement was that he was going to Australia that night and was going to live it up, spending his winnings and travelling.

'Things got heated. Sarah wandered out into the garden, crying, while the rest of us tried to persuade him to change his mind. Sarah left and the row continued. At one point I told him his music was crap and it wasn't surprising his career had collapsed. That hit a raw nerve and he punched me in the face. I staggered back, and as my vision cleared, I saw Nicola, a murderous expression on her face, pick up a bottle of champagne from an ice bucket and smash Dad on the side of the head with it. He dropped to the floor, unconscious.'

'Was he dead?' asked Sally.

'Not at that point. He still had a pulse and was breathing, weakly. I collapsed on a chair while Grenville and Nicola huddled together, whispering. Then Grenville picked up a cushion from the sofa and held it over Dad's face while Nicola held his head steady. I tried to intervene, but Grenville said we would all go to prison if he woke up. I didn't know if that was true but I went along with them. I wish I'd done something...oh God, I think I'm going to be sick.'

Sally rushed out of the room and fetched a waste paper bin, which Davvi held in front of him, just managing to control his nausea. Mel resumed the interview.

'What happened next?'

'We drank the champagne while we tried to work out what to do. I wanted to call the police and say that Nicola was defending me and didn't mean to kill him. Grenville said that was stupid as the pathologist would realise he'd been suffocated as well as hit on the head. Grenville spotted his travel documents on the sideboard and had the idea of forcing Peter to impersonate Dad. He wouldn't say what hold he had over him. He found out that Peter was at a conference, and was due to arrive at Gatwick late that night, and checked the timings of the flights. He shot off to the airport and Nicola and I went back to my place to collect a shovel and cleaning products. We went back to the house later on and buried him. It was mostly me – Nicola didn't want to chip her precious fingernails, but she did at least clear up the mess in the house. It took ages as we were trying not to make a noise. Then we took the cushion and the champagne bottle and left. Nicola went round the following day to tell Dad's neighbour that he'd gone to Australia.'

Davvi put his head in his hands, stifled a sob then straightened up.

'I didn't kill him. It wasn't a conspiracy, just Nicola and Grenville acting in the heat of the moment. We knew Peter was a weak link from the start, but when I heard he'd been killed I guessed I could be next, as my crimes weren't as serious as the others, and they might have thought I'd confess. I kept thinking about it and tried to phone Nicola yesterday, but couldn't get through. She's absolutely ruthless and I thought she was coming after me, so that's why I ran. I didn't know you were looking for me. Please believe me.'

Mel thought for a moment and then nodded to Sally.

'That's all for the moment, Mr Fearon. We'll need to talk to you again later. We will be consulting the CPS to decide which charges to bring. For the moment, you remain under arrest, and I would seriously advise you to consult a solicitor.'

She terminated the interview and led Davvi back to the custody sergeant.

'Right,' she said to Sally, once Davvi had been taken away. 'Coffee and a chat with DI Chidgey. I think we'll be in the pub tonight.'

Chapter Sixty-Four

'So WHAT DID the CPS go with, boss?' asked Martin, as the DI placed a tray of glasses on their table.

'Murder, perverting the course of justice and preventing the lawful and decent disposal of a dead body for Nicola and Grenville, but just the last two for Davvi. Nicola will also be charged with Peter Fearon's murder and supplying Class A. She's confessed to those, but is claiming she wasn't involved with Alan's murder. I don't think the jury will believe her. So, well done Mel!'

The others raised their glasses in salute.

'You mentioned that Nicola was more likely than Sarah,' said Jack. 'Why was that?'

'Well, they both had motives, wanting money, and Sarah had been involved in a fracas at an environmental demo, so she was definitely a possible. She also hit a punter, who cut up rough, when she was on the game. But Nicola was psychologically violent to her employees and once threw coffee at one of them. She radiated ruthlessness, so I was inclined to favour her.'

'So, you're developing a copper's instinct, are you?' laughed Trevor.

'Perhaps I inherited it. You know both my...Fuck.'

Mel's answer was interrupted by three rifle bullets smashing through the window behind them, shattering the tempered glass into fragments and leaving a gaping hole. Jack, sitting in front of the window, slumped forwards and DI Chidgey roared as a line of blood erupted from the side of his face. The detectives dived for the floor as the gunman switched to fully automatic fire. A hail of bullets raked the room, hitting the barman in the head, wounding a customer sitting on a stool by the bar, smashing bottles and light fittings and peppering customers with fragments of glass from the window. As soon as the firing stopped, Addy rushed to the door, in time to see a black SUV leaving a trail of smoking rubber as it sped away from the pub. The sounds of screaming from terrified and wounded patrons filled the pub, completely drowning out Eric Clapton singing *I shot the sheriff* on the music system, while the detectives looked aghast at Jack, sprawled across the table, apparently unconscious.

Chapter Sixty-Five

Day 23/24

IT TOOK all night and much of the following day to process the Cat and Cushion. Jack and the wounded customer were whisked off to hospital, and a private ambulance took the shot barman to the mortuary, once a paramedic had confirmed death. DI Chidgey refused to go to hospital but accepted first aid treatment from a paramedic, despite being warned that he could need stitches. Cordons were set up in the street, and uniformed officers recorded the names of everyone in the pub before they left so that they could be interviewed later. SOCOs searched for bullets in the pub and spent cartridge cases outside, photographing the scene exhaustively. By lunchtime they had left, an emergency glazier had been called to repair the window and the pub was shut, with no opening date in view. DCI Farlowe, on the scene within half an hour of the shooting, sent the detectives home after they had given brief statements, instructing them firmly not to come into work until a briefing at three o'clock.

'Any news on Jack?' asked Martin, before DCI Farlowe could open the briefing formally.

'He should be all right,' replied the DCI. He wasn't hit by a bullet as such but by a section of the window frame that hit him on the side of the head and briefly stunned him. The worst aspect was a large splinter of wood that got stuck in his neck, missing his carotid artery by a couple of millimetres. The paramedics spotted this and took extra care when moving him, and a surgeon removed it safely. The hospital's sending him home today and he'll be back at work soon.'

Sighs of relief went round the room and one officer muttered, 'There but for the grace.'

'DI Chidgey will be back tomorrow. He finally agreed to get the cut on his face looked at so he's gone to A&E. He'll be fine.'

'So do we have anything on the shooter?' asked Mel.

'Addy got the reg of the black SUV leaving the scene. It belongs to a Land Rover owned by a farmer in Shropshire. The plates had been changed, obviously.'

'Makes a change from a pink Fiat, I suppose,' muttered Martin.

'Is that all, guv?' Trevor asked.

'Not quite. The weapon used was probably an AK-47 or a clone of one. The first shots were in a burst of three and the rest were fully automatic, which an AK-47 is capable of. Also, the spent cartridges and recovered bullets are compatible with that make of rifle. A birdwatcher reported someone apparently carrying such a weapon about ten days ago. I asked Gerry, one of the civilian investigators, to check the database for any local sightings and that was what he found. The operator who took the call didn't take it seriously, which is why it wasn't flagged up to us, but Gerry checked the grid reference where it was seen. You won't be surprised to hear that it was in a field next to Musgrave Farmhouse.'

'So, we can raid the bastards,' urged Mel.

'Not yet,' replied Farlowe, 'but it gives us grounds for proper surveillance and we needn't rely on those hacked videos, which, of course, I know nothing about. So, we need boots on the ground looking for witnesses, CCTV, ANPR and so on for last night. Uniforms are talking to local businesses and residents, but we need to be looking at the rest.

'How much longer are you going to keep on doing this, Martin?'

Alice Rowse poured her husband a cup of coffee and held his hands, trying to still the trembling in his arms.

'You're shit scared after that bomb, you were nearly killed twice by that drugs gang a few years ago and now you've been machine-gunned. Your colleagues are being attacked left, right and centre. When will it bloody stop? I can't raise little Chloe on my own and she loves her dad. She's not going to be satisfied with annual visits to your fucking gravestone.'

Tears spilled from Martin's eyes and he leaned forward to hug his wife, ignoring the coffee spilling on his shirt.

'I don't know, love. I thought CID would be safer than uniformed policing. A chance to use my brain instead of my muscles. I never expected to be stabbed, blown up or shot at.'

He attempted a smile.

'Remember when you said these old sports cars were dangerous because they didn't have airbags? I said they were perfectly safe, but I hadn't reckoned on someone trying to kill me by fixing the brakes.'

'It's not funny, Martin. I'm scared shitless every time you walk out that door. I don't know if you'll be coming back.' She started to sob. 'Is there anything else you can do, for Christ's sake?'

'We have talked about this, love. All my skills are in policing, especially as a detective. And it may seem selfish, but I really value and respect my colleagues, even the DCI, who's a bit weird. I can't think of anything else to do.'

'Well, I can,' said Alice, shoving a printout across the table. 'Mexton Investigations. It's a private detective agency, just setting up, and they're recruiting. Ex-police officers welcome, it says. Why don't you contact them?'

'But I don't fancy spending hours sitting in a car, watching for husbands going over the side or arseholes playing football when they're claiming disability benefits.'

'Yes, but none of them is going to leave me a widow and Chloe fatherless.'

'All right, all right,' Martin said, seeing the steely resolve in his wife's eyes. 'I'll drop them an email. Now, have we got anything stronger than coffee, 'cos I really need it?'

Chapter Sixty-Six

Day 25

'Guv.' An anxious Mel knocked on DI Chidgey's door.

'Come in, Mel. What is it?'

'It's Stefan Paweski. The gang's changed the collection day again. It's tomorrow and he's getting his mates to stake out his shops and fight back. I'm really worried this will escalate and he'll end up charged with assault, or worse.'

'So what do you want us to do? Arrest him?'

Chidgey seemed slightly distracted and rubbed at the dressings covering the cut on his face.

'Of course not. Is there any way we could nick these guys without compromising the whole operation? The protection racket isn't linked to Jubilee Terrace, and the OCG wouldn't know we'd identified the premises.'

'Oi dunno, Mel,' replied Chidgey, his Somerset accent broader than ever. 'The NCA is keen to pick them up in one co-ordinated sweep. And Mr Farlowe agrees.'

'Yes, but this guy is really suffering. He's a decent bloke and he's co-operated with us all along the line. He's lost a lot of money, which he can't afford. He doesn't deserve to be abandoned and left to face GBH charges – or lethal force from the gang.'

Chidgey sniffed, wiped sweat from his brow with a crumpled piece of kitchen towel and thought for a moment.

'I'm sympathetic. I really am. Tell 'ee what I'll do. I'll talk to the DCI. See what we can do. Be good to nick some of these fuckers.' His voice began to drift and he looked as though he was about to fall asleep.

'Leave it with me, DC Collins.'

'Thanks, guv. I'll wait to hear from you and I'll let Stefan know we're trying to do something.'

What the hell was the matter with him, thought Mel as she left the DI's office. Was he pissed? Why did he get my name wrong? And why did he sound like a reject from The Wurzels? She couldn't smell cider on him, for a change, but he was clearly not right. She'd better have a word with Jack when he got back.

After Mel had left, DI Chidgey swallowed half a glass of water and a couple of paracetamol, hauled himself to his feet and stumbled towards the DCI's office, which he entered without knocking.

'What is it, Geoff? You look awful.'

'Feeling a bit rough, that's all. Look, we've got to do something about these protection fuckers. Nick 'em and soon. We'll 'ave a war on the bloody streets if we don't. We knows where they're to, so let's not bugger about.'

'Sorry, Geoff. We can't do anything without the NCA agreeing. They're involved too, and we want to get all these offenders at once.'

'Fuck the NCA.' Chidgey's voice rose sharply. 'They're not 'aving their livelihoods destroyed. Just 'ave the shits menacing Paweski. We don't need to raid the farm. It's separate. We're supposed to be keeping the Queen's fucking peace, ent we?'

Chidgey started breathing heavily and Farlowe recoiled.

'Geoff. Sit down. You shouldn't be in work. You've obviously been affected by the shooting more than you think. I'll talk to the NCA and see if we can do something for Mr Paweski. Now go home and don't go to the pub on the way. In fact, I'll get someone to take you.'

Farlowe spotted Sally Erskine walking past his office and called her over.

'Can you take DI Chidgey home, please? Make sure he's OK?'

'Yes, guv.'

Sally took the DI's arm and led him back to his office, where he collected his coat and mobile phone.

'Do you want these?' she asked, handing him an unopened box of antibiotics.

'Spose so,' Chidgey replied, stuffing them in his pocket. 'Load of rubbish, really.'

As they left the building, Chidgey's gait became more

and more uncertain. He had just managed to make it to the car park when he fell to the ground. Realising that an ambulance could be hours away, Sally grabbed hold of the driver of a traffic car, who was just going on shift.

'Get us to the hospital. Now. Blues and twos. The DI's collapsed.'

The bemused officer helped her to get the unresponsive detective into the car, and within seconds, the vehicle was roaring out of the car park as if in hot pursuit of bank robbers.

'Galloping infection,' pronounced the A&E Registrar. 'It's a good job you brought him in when you did. We've stabilised him, pumped him full of antibiotics and he should be OK. But why on earth didn't he get that wound seen to properly when it happened? My SHO remembers him coming in a while after it happened, and it looked pretty nasty, but we cleaned it up and dressed it. And he clearly hasn't been taking his antibiotics – the box is still full.'

'I can't really say, doctor,' replied Sally. 'A few of us think he's been neglecting himself, but we don't know much about his personal life. I think my sergeant has spoken to him a bit, but he's off sick following the shooting.'

'Well he could have died. Do try and impress on him the need to take his medication and look after himself. Does he have any next of kin who can keep an eye on him?'

'I think he has a sister in Bath. We'll get in touch with her.'

'Please do that. I'll ask the nurses to let you know when he's likely to be discharged.'

'Thank you, doctor,' said Sally, wondering how they were going to cope with yet another officer off sick. At least DCI Farlowe was still fit and well.

'I'm sorry to tell you that DI Chidgey is ill,' said DCI Farlowe, as he addressed the detectives in the incident room before he left for home. 'He developed a serious infection in the wound he sustained in the pub shooting. I'm not sure how long he'll be off. I have one bit of good news for you, however. Before he went to the hospital, DI Chidgey persuaded me that we should arrest the extortionists attacking Mr Paweski. The NCA wasn't happy but acknowledged that it's gone on too long. It's happening tomorrow night, but I must emphasise that no-one must give any indication that we know about Jubilee Terrace or Musgrave Farmhouse. Am I clear?'

The detectives nodded and Mel smiled.

Chapter Sixty-Seven

DCI Farlowe parked his Alvis in the drive of his detached house, lining the wheels up neatly with the edging stones that delineated his manicured lawn. He double checked that all the car doors were locked and approached the house, keys in hand. He began to feel uneasy. Something wasn't right. There were scuff marks on the gravel in front of the door, but he hadn't been expecting a delivery, and the postie always left his letters in the mailbox by the gate. The brass keyhole cover wasn't quite in position, and the side gate to the back garden looked slightly open.

Someone had tried to get in. That was clear. But had they succeeded? He pulled out his phone and composed a text. Cautiously, he approached his front door, his finger hovering over the send button. Was he being paranoid? He didn't want to call out a team for no good reason – the force was too overstretched. But, so far, he was the only prominent member of the team who had not been attacked by the

Albanian OCG. Perhaps it was his turn. Perhaps he was in serious danger.

He got his answer when the door began to open and he glimpsed a pistol in a man's tattooed hand. He just managed to type another three letters and press send before the door opened fully and the intruder stepped out, clubbing him on the side of the head and stamping on his dropped phone.

Dazed, Farlowe felt himself being manhandled through the hall and dragged into the kitchen. His assailant, all muscles and tattoos, bound his wrists with plastic ties and secured him to a chair with gaffer tape. As his head cleared, he became aware of a second, smaller, man in the room, a man of whom the bulky gunman seemed to be scared.

'Good evening, Mr Policeman,' the smaller man said, expertly slicing through Farlowe's waistcoat and shirt with a wicked, gleaming blade. 'My name is Nikolla and we are going to have a talk.'

Martin Rowse was heading for the gents when his phone pinged with an incoming text. Debating whether or not to answer it, he made up his mind when he saw the DCI's name and the subject. He knocked on the door of DSup Gorman's office and burst in, prompting an irritated glare from the senior officer.

'Guv. The DCI. He's in deep shit and he needs armed response.'

'What? What's happened? This had better be good. Where is he?'

'At home. He's sent a text. There's an intruder. And the last thing in the message was "ARU".'

'OK. He wouldn't ask for firearms unless it was critical. Get a couple of cars round there but tell them to go hold back until armed support arrives. And hope to God they won't be too late.'

Chapter Sixty-Eight

Farlowe stared at the two men holding him captive. The larger one stood impassively to one side, his arms folded, while Nikolla started spreading a collection of tools, kitchen implements and household chemicals on the kitchen table in front of him. Farlowe felt sick with fear. His terror intensified as Nikolla explained how he was going to use the various items in front of him.

'What the hell do you think you're doing? This isn't bloody Albania.'

'Retribution and a warning,' replied Nikolla, smiling pleasantly. 'You and your colleagues have caused my employers a great deal of trouble and they have asked me to ensure that it doesn't happen again.'

'Don't be stupid. The more you attack us, the harder we'll go after you. You'll have the whole country's police forces on your trail. Ordinary criminals will inform on you and Interpol will be on full alert.'

Nikolla shrugged and continued arranging his equipment.

'Interpol is useless. They don't even know who my employers are. The few officials that do are bribed, compromised or too terrified to do anything. And you British police are so soft, you don't even carry guns.'

Farlowe didn't reply.

'So, over the next half an hour, you are going to tell me exactly what you and your colleagues know about Oktapod – yes, I see you recognise the name – and what your plans are. Then I will kill you. How long it takes, and how painful it is, is completely up to you. You may have seen what I did to Kreshnik Osmani, so you know what to expect. Farlowe did, and screamed as the first cut drew a line of fire across his chest.

An armed response vehicle pulled up outside Farlowe's home within fifteen minutes of the DCI's text. Officers crept up the drive, avoiding the noisy gravel, and took cover behind the shrubs that decorated the garden, carbines at the ready. Two more eased the side gate open and worked their way around the back of the house, keeping below the level of the windows. When all were in position, Sergeant Terry Carter, the Operational Firearms Commander, switched on his megaphone.

'Armed police. Come to the door with your hands on your heads. Leave any weapons behind. Do exactly as you are told by the officers waiting and no-one will get hurt.'

There was no noise from the house and Carter repeated

his message. Two minutes later there was the sound of two shots from the back garden, one louder than the other, followed by a scream. Carter's radio crackled with a message. The front door slowly opened and Nikolla stepped out, supporting a half-conscious DCI Farlowe. Blood was running down Farlowe's chest, from a series of cuts, and his trousers were saturated. The knife at his throat glinted in the evening sunlight and the eyes of its holder gleamed.

'If you value your colleague's life, you will give me the keys to a car and let me drive away. You will not follow or track me. If I see or hear any police activity before I get to my destination, he will die. Horribly.'

'Throw the knife away, get down on the ground and put your hands on your head,' shouted Carter. 'Do it now.'

Nikolla didn't move, except to draw the knife across Farlowe's throat, leaving a thin line of blood.

Carter repeated his command twice, and when there was no response, he spoke quietly into his radio.

'Alpha seventy-four, use your judgement.'

There was a flash and a puff of smoke from behind a lavender bush. Nikolla staggered as a round from a police carbine hit him in the side of the chest, wrecking his heart. The knife and DCI Farlowe hit the ground at about the same time, and officers rushed to their fallen colleague's aid. When the scene had been declared safe, paramedics ran from the ambulance parked outside the house and checked him for vital signs.

'His pulse is weak but he's alive. He's obviously lost a lot of blood, so we'll get a drip into him and blue-light him to A&E. The second one's dead.'

'There's another one at the back of the house,' said Carter. 'Have you got time to confirm life's extinct?'

'Better not. Your colleague's the priority and time's vital. I'll radio for someone else.'

With that, the two paramedics stretchered the DCI to the ambulance and drove away, with lights flashing and sirens howling.

'So, what exactly happened at the back?' Carter asked an armed PC who emerged from the path at the side of the house.

'The suspect burst out of the back door with a pistol. He hit me in the chest with a single round, and I returned fire, hitting him in the thigh. I didn't have time to aim for his chest. He bled out from an artery. I tried to stop the blood flow but he died within minutes.'

'Are you OK?'

'My body armour stopped the round, but I'll have a bruise.'

'OK. Get it checked out. You know the ropes. Go back to the station with the rest of the unit and follow the usual post-incident procedures. I'll notify the IOPC.'

'Will do, Sarge. Lucky he didn't go for a head shot.'

'As always, mate. As always.'

Chapter Sixty-Nine

Day 26

Detective Superintendent Gorman called the team to attention and began the morning briefing.

'As some of you know, DCI Farlowe was attacked at home last night by two members of the Albanian gang. One was just a foot-soldier, name of Mergim Kola, but the other, from what the DCI managed to tell us, was called Nikolla. He was the man who tortured a Kreshnik Osmani to death last year.'

Several members of the team shuddered, recalling the photos of Nikolla's work.

'He had started work on the DCI but was interrupted when backup arrived. Stupidly, he attempted to hold Mr Farlowe hostage, for an escape attempt, but was killed by an armed officer. Kola was shot when he discharged a pistol at another officer and died at the scene.'

'So what about the DCI?' interrupted Addy.

'He'll be fine. He lost a lot of blood, but the wounds were not too deep. He'll be off work for a while, and will have some more scars, but the medics say he'll make a full recovery. So, I'm now the SIO for Operation Fieldmouse until DI Chidgey returns, but DS Vaughan is back this afternoon and will be looking after things from day to day, reporting directly to me. He will be co-ordinating the operation to arrest those individuals preying on Mr Paweski. I have been in contact with our colleagues in the NCA, and you will be pleased to know that things are being put in place for a series of raids on the OCG. It won't be too long before we take them. In the meantime, please continue to take extreme care with your personal safety.'

Chapter Seventy

'We're on,' shouted Jack. 'Stefan's called in. They'll be at his shop on The Parade in ten minutes. Notify the mobile units. Mel, Addy, you're with me.'

The detectives rushed down to the car park and jumped into an unmarked vehicle, speeding out into the road with lights and sirens going, switching them off as they drew near to the target.

'ETA four minutes,' called Jack into his Airwave. 'Tactical Firearms Commander please stand by.'

When they arrived at The Parade, there was no sign of the Albanians' vehicle. Two unmarked cars were parked fifty metres from Stefan's shop, one up the road and one down, with their lights out. Jack's vehicle parked opposite, while the ARV sat in a side street, its engine running. Three minutes later a black SUV pulled up outside Stefan's shop. Two men got out while the driver remained, occasionally revving the engine. After thirty seconds, Jack's phone buzzed with a text from Stefan and he switched on his headlights. The two cars parked on the same side as the SUV shot forward, blocking the target vehicle back and front, and the ARV swung out of the side road and pulled up alongside, officers spilling out with weapons at the ready. The driver of the SUV wrenched on the steering wheel and tried to mount the pavement, but a parking meter blocked his way and the police vehicles effectively clamped him in place. Swearing in several languages, the Albanians obeyed the AFOs' commands to lie on the ground. Before they did so, the driver looked around and eyeballed the officers present.

'You're fucking dead,' he spat. 'All of you.'

'A good result,' said Jack, sipping his pint in the nearly empty Cat and Cushion, sitting well away from the previously broken window. 'That's three of the bastards off the streets tonight, and we'll argue that they shouldn't be bailed as they're likely to reoffend. We've got enough evidence from the cameras in Stefan's shops, and his testimony, to put them away. He's a brave guy. The Makarov pistol in the car was a bonus. When prints come back, we'll get someone for possession.'

'So what happens now, Jack?' asked Mel. 'Is the OCG going to come back at us?'

'They might. So, keep on being careful. Stefan will be stepping up security at his shops, and we'll be keeping an eye on them in case anyone tries to torch them – or him. But we expect to move against the OCG soon.'

'About bloody time,' muttered Trevor.

'Yes, I know. But we can't go off at half cock. With any

luck, tonight's work will have thrown them and they'll be working out what to do. So, we'll maintain surveillance on the knocking shop, the snooker club and the farm. The Border Force has been alerted to look out for any more suspicious Albanian nationals coming into the country, but they tell us that some criminals have been slipping in pretending to be refugees. Interpol is on the alert, as well. You don't look happy, Martin. What's up?'

'Something's niggling me. That barman over there. He's new, isn't he?'

'I've not seen him before,' said Trevor. 'Why?'

'I think I have. Possibly near the brothel. And he seems to be taking an interest in us. He keeps looking over and fiddling with his phone, as if he's taking pictures.'

'All right,' said Mel. 'I'll go and chat him up. Keep an eye on my drink.'

Mel sauntered up to the bar, leaned on the bullet-chipped counter and asked for a packet of crisps.

'You're new, aren't you?' she asked, smiling, as the young man served her. 'How do you like working here?'

'It's OK,' he said. 'Better than a burger place. I don't smell when I finish work.'

Mel smiled again.

'Can I ask where you're from? Your accent isn't local.'

'I'm from Romania. I came here before your Brexit. Why you ask?'

'Oh. I just wondered. You sound like a couple of Albanian gentlemen I once arrested. I'm a police officer, but I expect you know...'

Before she could finish the sentence, the man hurled a tray of glasses at her and dashed through a doorway behind the bar. Mel vaulted over the counter and followed him down a narrow corridor, jumping over a mop and bucket that he tipped into her path. Her quarry crashed against a fire exit, frantically banging on the bar to release the door. He tumbled out, the alarm shrieked, and he tripped over a crate in the untidy yard. He stumbled to his feet, shoved his hand in his pocket and pulled out a flick knife.

The click of the blade unfolding chilled Mel and she froze, her limbs locking rigid as a wave of terror washed over her. She was two metres from him, and she wished desperately she'd had a baton or pepper spray with her. Then her police training kicked in. She unfroze, looked around the badly lit yard for a weapon and seized a broom propped against a wall.

'Put the knife down,' she yelled, swinging the broom back and forth between them.

'Fuck off, police bitch.'

He slashed at her, missing by a metre, and Mel cracked him across his left shin with the broom. He cursed in Albanian and charged, his knife held low. The broom fell from Mel's hand as she stumbled backwards, the knife slicing through the fabric of her jacket. She twisted as the weapon went past and swung her elbow hard into her assailant's face, breaking his nose. He screamed and charged again. Mel dodged behind a pile of barrels, tipping the top vessel onto the ground. The attacker fell over it, then made a peculiar coughing sound. Mel picked up the broom again and approached, cautiously. In the light from an anaemic street lamp shining over the pub garden wall, she could just make out the hilt of the flick knife protruding from the Albanian's chest.

'Oh, fuck,' she muttered as she heard her colleagues emerging from the fire door.

'What's happening Mel? And where did you get the broom? Hogwarts?' asked Sally, then stopped short when she saw the injured man. 'Is he dead?'

'I don't know.'

'He's alive,' Jack shouted. 'Call an ambulance. And tell the landlord he can't use his yard for a bit. It's a potential crime scene.'

'He'll not like that. Are you trying to get us banned?' said Mel, her voice shaky as she tried to forget the sight of the knife sweeping towards her stomach.

'You know it's procedure, Mel. In case he dies. But what about you? Are you OK?'

'OK, I suppose. You know how I feel about blades. But where the hell were you lot?'

'Sorry. We're not all as athletic as you,' Sally apologised. 'Trevor's still got his arm in a sling, Martin and Addy were sitting on the wrong side of the table, and I tripped over Jack. We looked a right bunch of wallies.'

'What I would like now is a large brandy and a lift home,' grunted Mel. 'I'll dictate my statement into my phone and WhatsApp it to you. I'll type it up in the office tomorrow. OK?'

'Sorry Mel,' replied Jack, his voice full of concern. 'You know you have to write your statement before you go off duty. I'll give you a lift to the station and then take you home. You're definitely on minus lives now, aren't you?'

'Almost, Jack, but not quite. Now, that brandy.'

Jack led her back into the bar, provided the drink, and

waited while she phoned Tom, to warn him she would be late home.

'Another knife, then.' Tom took Mel in his arms and hugged her tightly.

'Yes. Another stupid young twat. This time it nearly killed him. I barely touched him and he fell on it.'

'At least you didn't beat the shit out of him.'

'No. Not this time. I'll give a statement, but they probably won't even involve the IOPC. I still keep thinking about that sword flashing towards my neck. It's not as bad as it was, and the counselling helps, but I reckon I'll always have a thing about blades. Just part of the job, I suppose.'

'Do you want to change police roles?'

'No. Not yet. I enjoy this one, even though it has its dangers. I couldn't bear being stuck in an office all day. I'm not ready to be a sergeant, either. Maybe in a few years. If I live that long.'

'Well, I think you'll make a bloody good DS. Now, I've cooked a vegetable vindaloo and opened a couple of Cobras, so let's eat. Try and take your mind off knife-wielding Albanians.'

Given the ferocity of Tom's legendary curries, Mel thought it would probably work. At least for a while.

Chapter Seventy-One

THIS WAS one of the woman's easier tasks. Getting into the premises presented no problems – a simple lock, no alarm and no-one watching the snooker and pool hall, in a run-down part of town. Finding out that the building had mains gas was a bonus, since she didn't have to haul a cylinder of propane down the steep and narrow steps. She surveyed the building, quickly and efficiently, until she came across a disused kitchen area where, presumably, rudimentary food had been prepared for patrons of the former nightclub. Her eyes lit on a rusty grill, and a few minutes tinkering with a wrench, padded to avoid scratch marks, yielded a satisfying hiss of escaping gas. All that remained was to place a couple of lighted candles at the far end of the main lounge and get well clear before the flammable cloud reached them.

The explosion was heard half way across Mexton. The front of the building was blown out and Swarbrick Street was impassable, blocked by debris. Half the roof slid off and flames licked around the rafters, with sporadic blazes elsewhere. A torrent of water from a burst main carried a filthy tide of debris down the gutter, blocking drains and causing minor floods. There wasn't an intact window within fifty metres, but, to her satisfaction, there were no serious injuries reported. No-one was in the street at that time of the night, and the premises were all non-residential. The job done, she submitted her invoice for pest control services and looked forward to the payment landing in her Swiss bank account.

Chapter Seventy-Two

Day 27

'A BUSY NIGHT,' said Jack, at the start of the morning briefing. 'There's been an explosion at the OCG's pool hall. Some of you may have heard it. The place was destroyed during the early hours.'

'I'm not sorry to see the back of that dive,' said Martin, fingering his scar and recalling how he had nearly lost his life there, when it was the Maldon Club. 'Is it suspicious?'

'The fire service initially thought it was gas, but the army bomb disposal folks will be taking a look at it when it's safe to enter, just in case it was used to store explosives. Any forensics we might have got, if we raided it, were completely buggered.'

'Could they have done it themselves? Covering their tracks?' asked Addy.

'Maybe. But why now? All we've done is stopped them squeezing Stefan Paweski. As far as they know, we don't know what else they're up to and no more raids are planned. Anyway, once the soldier boys have finished, Peter Dalgliesh, the fire investigator, will examine the site. He's promised to let us know if he finds anything suspicious, in advance of his formal report. He's a good bloke. If there's anything iffy, he'll find it.

'Now, the business at the pub,' he continued. 'Well done, Mel. That was a useful collar. The lad was filming and recording us. We also found a bug in his pocket, which, I presume, he was going to plant in our usual corner, and some interesting contacts on his phone.'

'It was Martin who spotted him,' Mel replied. 'I didn't expect him to do a runner and pull a knife. How's he doing, by the way?'

'He nearly bled out, but the paramedics got to him in time. He's had surgery and is in the hospital under guard, with absolutely no visitors permitted. We don't expect him to talk, but at least we can stop him reporting back to the OCG. The pub landlord said he'd only started that night, and had offered to work cash-in-hand, so he didn't ask for references.

'I suppose we're not getting anything from the scrotes we arrested,' said Addy.

'No. Nothing. They went "no comment" even before their brief arrived. He argued for bail at the magistrates but it was refused.'

'Who was the solicitor, as a matter of interest?' asked Trevor.

'Vernon Chawte,' replied Jack 'Why?'

'He seems to be the go-to brief for all sorts of unpleasant characters. I suspect the OCG has him on a retainer.'

'OK. Look into him. You never know what might turn up. You won't get a client list but have a look at some court records and see who he's defended. The NCA might be interested in what you find, as well.'

'Already done, guv,' said Trevor. 'He seems to have made a career out of defending various low lifes. Not just the Albanians we dealt with last year, but drug dealers, pimps and minor thugs. Some serious players, too. He's pretty good at arguing for reduced sentences and has tripped up officers giving evidence on more than one occasion, letting some nasty people walk free.'

'A credit to his profession, then,' commented Jack.

Trevor grinned wryly.

'There's something else,' continued Jack. 'The latest bug sweep found a couple more devices in the toilets. One in the men's and one in the women's. This means that the OCG still has an insider, possibly planted in the maintenance company or the cleaning firm. Theoretically, everyone should be checked before they work here, but there are ways around this if you have the resources. Which the OCG does. So, we've been authorised to ask a behavioural psychologist to help screen all non-police staff entering the building. He's new to the area, so no-one will recognise him, and he'll watch people as they come into work. If necessary, he'll mingle with them, carrying a clipboard and asking innocent questions. His cover is that he's doing some financial auditing. His name is Dr Chris Milverton. Don't take any notice of him while he's working.'

The detectives nodded, although some of them looked sceptical.

'Right. Some actions on Operation Fieldmouse. We

need the surveillance on the OCG reviewed and the contacts on the barman's phone identified. Trace the phone's movements and those of the contacts, if possible. I'll sort out the authorisations. Check his call history. Does he have a vehicle? If so, where has it been? Look at ANPR. Search his premises. The address he gave the landlord is probably false, but check it anyway. We will strike soon, but we need as much information on these people as possible before we do. I'll allocate the tasks shortly. Please report back to me and I'll update DSup Gorman. Thank you, everyone.'

With that, the team dispersed, the anticipation of finally arresting the people behind the bombing that had taken so many colleagues' lives spurring them on.

Chapter Seventy-Three

JACK CALLED the team together shortly after lunch.

'DI Morton would like a word with us all,' he announced. 'Come to the front, Steve.'

'Thanks, everyone. I thought you should know that I and my colleagues in SO15 have concluded that the explosion at the police station was not the result of ideological terrorism. It was purely a criminal act, and given the presence of a known bomb-maker in the country, it was undoubtedly the Albanians. I'm sure this isn't news to you. As a result, the SO15 officers temporarily stationed here will be returning to London, although DS Wilson will be staying behind to lend a hand and liaise with me should it be necessary. I can't stress how much I admire your dedication and tenacity in the face of this outrageous attack. It's been a pleasure working with you, and I wish you all the best. You'll catch these bastards, I'm sure you will.'

If Morton was expecting applause, he was disappointed.

A few people smiled weakly, some grunted and others sighed.

'Thanks, Steve,' said Jack. 'We appreciate the work SO15 has done, and thanks for leaving us Angela. Safe journey home. Now, back to the OCG. Detective Superintendent Gorman has been talking to the NCA and it looks as though we'll be able to do warrants pretty soon. Obviously, we won't be looking at the pool hall, but we will do the farmhouse and Jubilee Terrace. We'll have armed support and people from the NCA Modern Slavery and Human Trafficking Unit to support the women in the brothel. We have a list of vehicles regularly used by the OCG so we'll be on the lookout for them, and ports and airports will be notified in case vehicles, or individuals, attempt to leave the country.

So, stay patient for a few days longer and carry on building up the evidence. Thanks, everyone.'

'Well thanks for fucking nothing,' said Martin, as he and Mel queued for the coffee machine. 'They tell us what we know already and then bugger off, patting us on the head and leaving us to it.'

'You mean SO15?' said Mel. 'I think you're being a bit unfair. Their job is terrorism, ideologues and politicos with bombs and guns, not vengeful crooks. There must be loads of other shit they're supposed to be dealing with. They've helped a lot with processing information, and we're approaching the end of the investigation, so I understand why they're pulling out. We can manage without them, I'm sure.'

Martin just grunted and made his coffee.

PC Halligan stood in the doorway of the solicitor's office, at the top of a three-storey building, and stared morosely at the corpse in front of him. He had been looking forward to going off shift a bit early, when Control had asked him to attend a possibly suspicious death in the business quarter of Mexton. He'd been waiting for CID for nearly an hour and was seriously fed up, so he was less than polite when Jack and Addy arrived.

'What took you so long?' he grumbled. 'Some of us have got homes to go to. The paramedic was here ages ago and pronounced death. Can I knock off now?'

'When I say so,' replied Jack. 'If this is a crime scene you'll bloody well stay here until someone relieves you. Now what have we got?'

PC Halligan straightened up and gave his report, not completely concealing his annoyance.

'Apparently, the cleaners come in on Sundays so they can give the place a good going-over without disturbing the lawyers. One of them found this bloke here and called an ambulance. She also called us, because she saw a bottle of pills and an empty whisky bottle on the desk in front of him.'

'This bloke. Have the decency to give him a name.'

'Sorry, Sarge. He's Vernon Chawte. A solicitor. As you can probably tell from the offices.'

'But isn't that...' began Addy, ignoring the hint of sarcasm in Halligan's voice.

'Yes, it is. Brief to various undesirables and company solicitor for the firm that owns Musgrave Farm. OK.' Jack thought for a moment. 'Obviously, this looks like suicide, and we wouldn't normally spend a lot of time on it. But, given that it's Vernon Chawte, I'm suspicious, particularly as he's in the office at the weekend. I think we should treat this as a crime scene. We'll stay out here, just in case. Get some tape and a clipboard from the car, PC Halligan, and seal off the room. We'll need to cordon off the whole building, so check if there's anyone else on the premises. If so, take their details and send them home. Addy and I will talk to the cleaner who found him, when you've got this room taped off. Meanwhile, I'll let DSup Gorman know.'

An hour later, the building was empty, apart from a team of SOCOs and a uniformed officer who had relieved PC Halligan. After a couple of hours photographing, evidence gathering and sampling, the Crime Scene Manager declared that they had finished and the undertakers removed the body. The office remained sealed, pending the DSup's visit in the morning, and, from the outside at least, things returned to normal.

Five miles away, in the kitchen at Musgrave Farm, Vjosa Dibra removed a wide-stemmed plastic funnel from a paper bag in his pocket and threw it on the open fire. It melted and caught fire, oily smoke and yellow flame leaping up the chimney, while the smell of burning plastic filled the room.

'It's done,' he said, in Albanian. 'No problem.'

Chapter Seventy-Four

Day 28

DI Chidgey entered the incident room, neatly shaved and wearing a freshly pressed suit. Several team members called out, 'Welcome back, boss.' He smiled, rapped on the desk to call the team to order and spoke clearly and crisply.

'As some of you know, I developed a massive infection as a result of the injury I sustained during the pub shooting. I went a bit doo-lally, as I didn't bother to take my antibiotics and it made me delirious. It's thanks to Acting DC Erskine's quick thinking that I'm here today. So you know who to blame.'

The team laughed. Chidgey was about to continue the briefing when his phone rang.

'DI Chidgey? It's Dr Durbridge. I found something during Mr Chawte's examination yesterday that concerns me.'

Chidgey put his phone on speaker so others in the incident room could hear.

'As you suspected,' the pathologist continued, 'Mr Chawte died of an overdose of diazepam mixed with whisky, sometime yesterday afternoon. It's a common means of attempted, and successful, suicide and can be treated if the patient is hospitalised in time. But I have my doubts that this was suicide.'

'Why's that, doctor?' the DI interjected.

'There were some circular lesions in the man's oesophagus that looked as though someone had forced a tube or something similar into his throat. There was also some slight bruising to his neck and face, which suggests that his head had been held.'

'So, he was murdered!'

'Well, let's just say that my findings are consistent with someone having forced him to ingest the drug and the alcohol. Whether you treat it as murder is up to you.'

'Thank you, doctor. Helpful as usual. And thanks for working on a Sunday. I'll brief my colleagues accordingly.'

The DI switched off his phone, turned to the waiting officers and frowned.

'Chawte was murdered. Whoever did it made a crude attempt to pass it off as suicide. Why the bloody hell would anyone kill him? Jack, can you organise a team to search his home and collect any electronics, documents and so on? We can't touch his work stuff, as it's protected by legal privilege, but we can look at his personal phone and computer, if he has one.

'OK. We'd better see if he's been picked up on any

CCTV near the office, but if he's the killer, he would have covered his face.'

'Chawte obviously pissed someone off. Perhaps he was skimming money from the OCG?' suggested Martin.

'Maybe,' said Trevor, thoughtfully. 'But maybe they're cleaning house. Getting rid of loose ends before moving on to something else. I bet the front man for the health spa will be next. I'm sure they'll get rid of him mindfully and holistically.'

The team chuckled.

'You could be right, Trev,' said Jack. 'But if they're moving on or changing tack, we'd better take them soon.'

'Well the good news, Jack,' said Chidgey, 'is that we're planning to strike on Friday morning, but, for Christ's sake, don't mention it to anyone. In the meantime, keep on Chawte. We need to know everything about the bugger and who he dealt with.'

Mel joined Jack in the queue for the coffee machine, looking thoughtful.

'DI Chidgey's smartened himself up a bit. Any idea why?' she asked.

'I think taking over officially from the DCI while he recovers has given him an extra impetus. He was certainly respected in Avon and Somerset a few years back. Perhaps he's regained his old form.'

'Hmm. If DI Thorpe doesn't come back from maternity leave, will you go for her old job? Surely you're qualified and experienced enough?'

'I am, but I won't. I'm not interested in all the paperwork and management stuff. I prefer to keep up with what's happening on the front line and nicking the odd villain myself. Why, are you after my job?' he joked.

'God, no. I've not been here long enough. I'll probably study for the sergeant's exams in a couple of years, but I want to get my personal life sorted out first. The house needs work and we're supposed to be getting married, but I've still no idea when. By the way, do you fancy being best man? Tom wanted me to ask you.'

'I'd be honoured, Mel,' he beamed. 'Thank you for asking. Now come on, the machine's free.'

This one should be fun, she thought. The vehicle's electronics were comparatively easy to hack, using apps she'd found via Tor, and all she had to do was wait for a suitable opportunity. One where only her targets would be harmed. Her chance came when she saw the SUV approaching the Eastside estate, no doubt carrying drugs for distribution to the low-level dealers who now worked for the Albanians. Her fingers flickered over the laptop keys as the car began to turn at the roundabout on the main road. The vehicle stopped, its hazard lights flashed and the windscreen wipers started up on maximum, even though there was no rain. The occupants tried frantically to open the doors, which remained locked despite their efforts.

Traffic built up behind the stalled SUV and a cacophony of car horns, from blocked vehicles, drowned out the incessant bleeping from the OCG's ride. Within fifteen minutes a police car arrived and attempted to move the SUV along, to no avail. PC Halligan rapped on the driver's side window but the occupants merely gestured, indicating that they were powerless.

Before Halligan could respond, his radio crackled.

'Stand back, stand back. Occupants may be armed. ARV dispatched.'

Halligan started and backed away, terrified. The men in the SUV redoubled their efforts to get out but remained trapped. Ten minutes later, armed officers surrounded the vehicle and forced open the doors, arresting those inside. As they did so, the windscreen wipers and horns stopped working and the remaining doors unlocked.

'What the bloody hell's happening?' PC Halligan asked the Operational Firearms Commander, when the driver and passenger had been bundled into a police van.

'Control got a tip-off that a vehicle containing drugs and armed suspects was immobilised on the edge of the Eastside. The caller didn't give a name and the voice was distorted. So, we were deployed, in case it was kosher. We've recovered a couple of pistols and a holdall of baggies – probably heroin. A good result.'

Halligan nodded and returned to his car, relieved that the experts had handled the situation. No-one noticed the small drone, thirty metres above, that sped from the scene once the police van had pulled away.

Chapter Seventy-Five

Day 29

Dr Chris Milverton sat at a small desk in a corner of reception, positioned so that he had a clear view of everyone as they filed into the temporary police station to start work. Ostensibly, he was working at a laptop and on a pile of papers strewn over the desk in front of him. His badge, clipped to a visitor's coloured lanyard, declared he was from Mexton Accounting Services. Given that the building was still far from fit for purpose, since converting old council offices into a functioning police station had proved difficult and people had to work as and where they could, no-one took any notice of him, hunched over his machine. In reality, he was watching everyone entering, and his screen displayed CCTV images from behind the reception desk, rather than spreadsheets. He was watching for behaviours, actions and expressions that didn't quite fit. He could screen out those with hangovers, flu or simple exhaustion and was looking particularly for nervousness or, perhaps, fear. If the OCG had planted a mole amongst the staff, they would probably have been coerced.

He spotted a likely suspect after an hour's observation. A young man in the overalls of the maintenance company, whose pale face and twitchy demeanour suggested he had something serious on his mind. Either that, or he was on some kind of controlled substance. Milverton picked up his phone and dialled the CID office, alerting them to his suspicions. Addy confirmed he would meet the suspect, who would then be interviewed. The psychologist continued watching.

Gary Bristow nearly threw up when Addy and Trevor stopped him as he stepped into the corridor outside the CID office, carrying his box of tools.'

'Can we have a word, Gary?' said Addy. 'It won't take a moment.'

Gary nodded and let himself be led to an interview room.

'What's this ab...ab...about?' he stammered. 'I've done nothin' wrong.'

'We have a few questions for you. You're not under arrest but we will caution you,' replied Trevor. 'You can have a solicitor present if you feel you need one.'

Gary shook his head, beads of sweat flying off his forehead, and listened to the caution.

'How long have you been working here, Gary?' asked Trevor.

'Umm...a couple of weeks. Why?'

'So you're confident about what you have to do, where to go, and so on?' Trevor ignored Gary's question.

'Yeah. No problem. I'm fine.'

'It's just that you seem nervous, especially now we're talking to you. It's as if there's something on your mind. Would you like to say anything about that?'

Gary gulped and his complexion turned even paler.

'Are you married, Gary?' asked Addy. 'Any children?'

'Not married, but me and my partner have a baby.'

Gary looked as if he was about to cry.

Addy looked at Trevor, who took up the thread.

'It's just that we have reason to believe that someone in the station is providing an Organised Crime Group, the ones who blew up the old station, with sensitive information about police operations. Also, we keep finding listening devices on the premises that we believe this group is having planted. Can you tell us anything about that?'

For a second, Gary looked as though he'd been punched in the stomach by Mike Tyson. Then he howled and howled for a full three minutes. He pulled a small box, with a short wire attached, from his pocket and slammed it on the desk.

'The bastards made me. They watched me coming to work and grabbed me on the way home. They said they would rape Marie and strangle little Lisa if I didn't help them. I had to. I had to. What would you have done?'

He looked imploringly at the two detectives.

'OK, Gary,' said Addy. 'We can protect you and your family. But you have to help us. For the moment, we are arresting you on suspicion of misconduct in public office and we're detaining you. I will need to discuss this with someone more senior, but I would strongly advise you to obtain the services of a solicitor.'

Trevor recited the caution again and the two officers escorted Gary to an empty room, where he would wait until he could be transferred to the custody suite. A uniformed PC was stationed outside, but as he left, Trevor put his hand on Gary's shoulder.

'I'm sure we can sort something out and protect your family,' he said. But, inside, he wondered whether Gary, Marie and Lisa would ever be safe.

'Thank you, Dr Milverton,' said DI Chidgey, shaking the psychologist's hand vigorously in his office. 'The guy you suspected has confessed, and I'm glad he's the only one. He was under extreme duress and I hope we don't have to prosecute the poor bugger. Send us your bill – I can't promise it will be paid quickly, but it will be paid.'

'My pleasure, Detective Inspector. Anything I can do in the future, please let me know.'

'We will, doctor. We will.'

Chapter Seventy-Six

Chidgey escorted Dr Milverton back to reception and wished him farewell. Then he returned to the incident room where the team was waiting.

'Well we've got the bug and we've got the bugger,' he beamed. 'I never knew a psychologist could be so useful. Of course, they'll try again, but we'll be watching for them.'

'Guv,' said Martin, slowly, 'is there any way we can turn this against them?'

'What? You mean get Gary to feed them false information? No way. He's too scared. I've seen cow pats with more spine than he has.'

'That's not fair, guv,' shouted Martin, his face flushing. 'If these bastards threatened my family, I've no idea what I would do.'

There were murmurs of agreement from the team and Mel scowled furiously at her boss.

'OK. OK.' Chidgey held up his hands. 'I suppose that was insensitive. But Gary really isn't double agent material.

All we can do is protect him and his family until the CPS decides what we should do with him.'

'How about the bug, boss?' asked Addy. 'Could we use that somehow?'

'That's a better idea. The tech guys are looking at it now. If it's not been activated, we could, perhaps, switch it on and have it transmit some false info. Anyone into amateur dramatics?'

'Hold on,' said Jack. 'That's not such a bad idea. We could give the impression that we're doing a warrant somewhere different, when we're actually going for the farmhouse. Like Operation Mincemeat.'

'Wrong time of year for mince pies, isn't it, Jack?' quipped Mel.

'No, Mel. Operation Mincemeat was a plan to make the Germans think the Allies were invading at Calais rather than on the Normandy beaches they really used. They dropped a corpse in the sea, with documents suggesting that Calais was the target, for the Germans to find. A couple of studios made films about it.'

'All right, Mr Pub Quiz Supremo. I knew what you meant.'

'Come on, you two,' reproved Chidgey. 'I think this could work.'

'So how are we going to do this?' asked Mel. 'Presumably, he was supposed to plant it somewhere and switch it on only when it was in place, to save the battery.'

'That makes sense,' replied Jack. 'If we're going to use it, we must activate it before they realise Gary's been arrested.' He thought for a minute. 'All right, we'll put it in the gents somewhere and warn everyone not to say anything that could be useful. When we're ready, we'll get a couple of blokes to memorise a script to mislead the bastards.'

'Excellent idea! I'll run it past the DSup, we'll get it in position and put up some notices.'

The DI phoned DSup Gorman, and within fifteen minutes, the bug was switched on and placed behind a soap dispenser in the male toilets. Shortly after, posters appeared warning users to be careful about what they discussed, one of which reproduced the wartime slogan 'Careless talk costs lives'. It wasn't long before someone crossed out 'talk' and replaced it with 'piss'.

Trevor and Martin, makeshift scripts in their hands, stood in the gents, occasionally running water and flushing the WCs, while reciting their dialogue.

'Looks like we've got a breakthrough on the OCG,' began Trevor.

'Oh yeah? What's that?' replied Martin.

'We've found their base. A cyclist reported some suspicious goings-on late one night. The report's only just reached us.'

'Brilliant! So, when do we nick the bastards? And where is it?'

'Well, the DI says it's going to take a few days to put a team together. Maybe this weekend or early next week. They're holed up in an old office building on Carfax Street, just off the Highchester Road. It was used by a book distributor that went bust during lockdown. It's been empty ever since, but the lights on at night attracted the cyclist's attention.'

'Thank God for the good old British public! I can't wait to have a crack at those shits. Come, on. Let's get some coffee.'

The two detectives barrelled out of the toilets and burst out laughing once they were well clear of the bug.

'The BAFTAs call, gentlemen,' called Jack.

'Don't give up the day job,' joked Mel.

'Honestly,' said Trevor, 'we felt like total twats. Let's hope it bloody well works.'

'What did you get from Chawte's tech, Amira?' asked Chidgey, as the IT expert joined the resumed briefing.

'Not a huge amount,' I'm afraid,' she replied. 'He does seem to have a couple of offshore bank accounts, but I can't get into those. There's an encrypted file marked "Insurance" on his hard drive, and we're working on cracking the password.'

'Probably not details of his no claims bonus,' interjected Mel. The others chuckled.

'I don't think so either,' continued Amira. 'It could be accounts of the work he's been doing for the OCG, to be released if anything happened to him.'

'It didn't do him much good, did it?' said Jack. 'Either they didn't know about it or didn't care.'

Chidgey nodded his head in agreement.

'Getting into that file is our priority job at the moment,' Amira continued. 'Also, there's a folder of some weird photos – shots up women's skirts or down their tops, mainly. I don't know where they came from, but he seems to have been some sort of low-level pervert. The only other thing of interest is the fact that he had Tor installed, which suggests that he's been accessing the dark web. For what, I've no idea.'

'How about his personal phone?' asked Trevor.

'Your guys found two. A normal one, with a contract, which contained personal stuff. The numbers of friends, colleagues, clubs, his doctor and so on. The other was more interesting. It's a burner and he seems to have kept it switched off, with the sim card removed, when he wasn't using it. I'm guessing he received an innocuous text on his other phone, telling him to switch the burner on, when someone needed to talk to him. There was a list of numbers, with code letters rather than names against them, and we've managed to identify some of those. They belong to members of the OCG. We're still working on the rest and trying to retrieve Chawte's call history.

'That's really helpful, Amira. Thanks,' said the DI. 'Any luck with his bank accounts?' he asked, turning to Trevor.

'Nothing unusual, guv. He's healthily in the black, but not massively minted. He pays off his credit cards at the end of the month and puts some money into savings and investments, all above board. There are no obvious extravagances day-to-day, but his house is pretty posh, and he owns a Tesla as well as a top-of-the range BMW. Finding out how he paid for that lot could be useful.'

'I agree, but don't spend too much time on that. It's stuff on the OCG that really interests us.'

'Righto, boss.'

'By the way,' concluded the DI, 'an ARU picked up a couple of OCG members, with pistols and heroin, yesterday evening, after a tip-off. Their car broke down just as they were entering the Eastside.'

'Stroke of luck, guv,' said Martin.

'Yes. Funny about the tip-off, though. Nobody grasses up the OCG as a rule. Still, it's a load of gear and a couple of firearms off the streets, so we can't complain.'

'So, how's Tom doing?' asked Jack, as he and Mel queued at the sandwich machine. 'When's he coming back?'

'Not too bad, I suppose, in the circumstances. He's keeping things to himself, I think, and he usually wakes up at four in the morning after nightmares. Losing his hand has traumatised him, obviously, but his physical recovery is good. He's really keen to get back to work, but Occupational Health have to give him the go-ahead and they're overwhelmed with the aftermath of the bombing. It'll be a while before the hospital can fit a prosthesis, but he's getting very adept at typing one-handed. He even manages to cook, so there's usually something nice waiting for me when I get home.

'Well, give him our best, won't you? Perhaps he'd like to join us in the pub after work one evening?'

'Brilliant idea!' Mel replied. 'He can't drive, though he wouldn't after drinking anyway, but he can get a taxi. I'll suggest it next time we all meet up.'

Chapter Seventy-Seven

Day 30

'Jack,' called the DI, as he entered the incident room, 'there was an arson attack on the new build estate last night. The fire and rescue service found obvious traces of accelerant. Can you get a couple of DCs to attend? It's 23 Boscombe Drive.'

'Oh shit,' said Trevor. 'I know that address.' His face went white. 'It's Gary Bristow's. He's got a partner and a baby. The bastards, they've gone after him.'

'It's OK. Well, not really,' said Jack. 'Gary's in a safe house and his family are staying with his mother. They moved out as soon as he was arrested, without telling anyone apart from us. It could be attempted murder or, if the OCG knew the place was empty, a warning. Can you and Addy go, since you know Gary?'

Addy and Trevor left the incident room, their faces grim, and headed off to the OCG's latest atrocity.

'I can't let you in,' said Peter Dalgliesh, the fire investigator, standing in front of the shell of a modern two-bedroomed house. 'We've not established that the building's safe. But you can see the damage to the floor, inside the door, where a flammable liquid was poured through the letterbox. Also,' he moved across the charred lawn to an empty window frame, 'someone smashed this from the outside. It wasn't blown out by the fire. There's some glass there, on what's left of the floor. I suspect it came from a bottle of accelerant. A petrol bomb, in other words. They wanted to make sure the place burned out. And it did.'

Trevor grimaced.

'Do you know anything about the occupants?' Dalgliesh asked. 'We didn't find anyone in there, living or dead.'

'We can't say too much,' answered Addy, 'but the family moved out for their own safety. Just in time, by the look of it. This may have been an attempt to kill them, to destroy evidence or to frighten them. In any event, they won't be coming back here again. I'll ask for a uniform to guard the place until the SOCOs arrive.'

'Wish them luck,' said Dalgliesh, dryly. 'They might be able to identify the type of accelerant used but not the brand. And there'll be no DNA or fingerprints, I'm sure. OK. We'll hang on until an officer arrives.'

Trevor thanked the fire investigator, and the two detectives returned to their car. As Addy started the engine, Trevor banged his good hand on the dashboard.

'Is there anything these bastards won't stoop to? Trying

to burn a mother and baby to death is just fucking unbelievable. I'm beginning to wish we'd never identified Gary.'

'Yes, but he could have cost the lives of yet more officers,' replied Addy. 'No-one was hurt, and we must hope they were insured. Now, let's knock on a few doors and then get back to the station and write this up.'

'We got nothing much from door-to-door, boss,' reported Addy, when DI Chidgey called them into his office. 'One neighbour, who suffers from insomnia, thought she heard glass breaking and a vehicle driving off quickly at about three o'clock, fifteen minutes before the alarm was raised by the bloke next door, but she didn't see it. No-one else saw or heard anything. I noticed a CCTV camera on a house a few doors down, but the occupants were out. I put a card through their door with a note to call us. If the vehicle went in that direction, we might get something.'

'OK. That's the best we can hope for, I suppose. I spoke to the Crime Scene Manager. He says there are ways of getting fingermarks off some items from fires – something to do with a vacuum – but he's not optimistic.'

'Has anyone told Gary?' asked Trevor.

'Not yet. It's better done face to face rather than over the phone. I'll brief the guys looking after him.'

'Well, give him my number, guv, in case he wants to talk. A sympathetic face and all that.'

'That's thoughtful, Trevor. Will do. Now go and get yourselves some coffee.'

Chapter Seventy-Eight

Three weeks earlier

'I CAN'T DELETE YOUR FILE,' said the NCA officer. 'It would prompt too many questions. There would be a trail. But I can reclassify it so few people can access it. And I can pay you. There will be life insurance. Will that do?'

There was a silence over the secure phone connection and then a young woman, known to law enforcement as Suzy Q, spoke.

'What exactly do you want me to do?'

'I want you to destroy the bastards who killed my wife.'

'Do you know who they are? If so, why don't you arrest them?'

'If you had seen what I was able to view of her, in the mortuary, you would know why a prison sentence is not enough. It's an Albanian organised crime group, working in Mexton. They're into drugs, sex trafficking, extortion and computer scamming. Firstly, I want you to fuck up their activities and get them worried. Then kill them. As many as you can. Whatever it costs, I'll pay.'

'What are the local police doing?'

'They're making progress but they're constantly under attack. Revenge for shutting down the OCG's activities last year. They'll obviously look into any deaths you cause, but they don't have the time to investigate minor attacks. They are competent but overwhelmed.'

'OK. I think I can help. I'll need you to send me as much as you can on the targets. Then I'll be in touch. I'll work out some plans and come up with costings. Exactly what I do to fulfil the agreement is entirely at my discretion, but I will make every effort to avoid harming innocent people. I'm not a terrorist.

'First, a few rules. Some of them should be obvious to you. Don't tell anyone, not even your wife's gravestone. Set up a VPN and buy a cheap laptop to send me the details via secure email. Then destroy it when it's all over. Get a couple of burner phones and give me the numbers. I'll give you some of my numbers, but don't call except in an emergency. If my price is acceptable, I'll require a deposit, and staged payments as I do different things, the balance being payable when it's all done. Any payments are non-refundable. Keep me up-to-date with what the police are doing. I don't want to get in their way, or for them to get in mine. Is this all acceptable?'

'What if the gang captures you?'

'They won't. I rely on technology, not physical confrontation, so most of the time I'll be far away from whatever's happening. I've never been arrested, and I've been doing this work for a good few years, so it's not likely to happen now. If you hear anything worrying, let me know. Now, I'll be in touch in a few days, then we can make an agreement. Is that OK?

'Yes, yes, thank you. I'll send that stuff over tomorrow. Good bye.'

The line went dead and he reached for a bottle of whisky. Christ, how had it come to this? He'd spent his entire career hunting down the most serious of criminals and now he was turning into one himself. If only he hadn't come across Suzy Q's file, which linked an unknown woman to a series of deaths and cases of sabotage. All involved some kind of device, hence the Q suffix, and all were accomplished efficiently, neatly and with minimal collateral damage. It had taken him days to track her down via the dark web and his contacts in the security service. More to the point, if his wife hadn't been cycling past Mexton police station, on her way to her mother's, he would never have been contemplating murder.

Chapter Seventy-Nine

Eight years earlier

EVER SINCE SHE accidentally killed a mobile phone thief in Streatham, with a handful of matches and some sandpaper, she had been fascinated by the power of simple technology. Not so much the giant enterprises, like airliners and nuclear power stations, but smaller things that could achieve their ends with the minimum of fuss. A few wires and switches here, some chemicals there, a handful of abrasive in a tin of lubricant – simple, elegant measures appealed to her. As someone once said, you don't need a chainsaw to cut butter. She couldn't quite remember when she started using her skills to make her mark. Perhaps it was the posh bully that regularly harangued homeless people, congregating in the church doorway, after the pubs were shut. Caustic soda powder, poured into his overcoat pockets while he was drunk and distracted, certainly stopped him from hitting anyone for quite some time.

She studied engineering at university and also developed some computer hacking skills – by no means the best in the country, but sufficient for her needs. A number of false identities followed, and she could move like a ghost when she had to. Her nondescript face and frame wouldn't stand out in CCTV footage. She knew from the start that whatever she decided to use her skills for, it wouldn't involve physical confrontation. She wasn't a fighter. Science and technology would do the work for her. Did that make her a coward? No, she didn't think so. She knew her strengths and her limitations, and all that mattered was that she got the jobs done. But which jobs?

The Streatham incident had skewed her moral compass somewhat. At first, she had been horrified. Someone had died when all she had wanted to do was teach him a lesson. She had dreaded being arrested, her parents finding out, and the prospect of a prison sentence. As the days and weeks went by, she began to feel more confident. There was no official knock on the door, and she was able to start her university course. She regretted the death, of course, but not, perhaps, as much as she should have. The kid concerned was no real loss to humanity, after all, and an overcrowded planet was better off without him.

She would never have thought like this before, but watching the Denzil Washington film *The Equalizer* gave her an idea. Could she be like the character in the film, righting wrongs, sometimes lethally, but using technology rather than physical violence? She couldn't exactly put a card up in the newsagent, offering assassination and sabotage at reasonable rates. But she could keep her eyes open for suitable targets in the community and, perhaps, post a discreet notice on the dark web. Maybe she could even get paid?

Once she graduated and secured a job with an engineering maintenance firm in Cheltenham, she spent a year doing her additional research, reading swathes of material on chemistry, physics and electronics, and tinkering with devices in her garage. She managed to acquire a copy of *The Anarchist's Cookbook*, which she kept carefully hidden, as possession of it was illegal. The neighbours didn't seem to notice the odd smells and noises coming from the premises, and she was careful not to blow anything up onsite. Then she was ready.

She had popped into The Lion's Mane, a pub-cum-wine bar, for an after-work drink with her colleagues, when she overheard a young man in conversation with a group of his friends.

'Look, Nige,' he said, 'I can hold my drink. It doesn't affect my driving. Only a pussy worries about the limits. They're for plebs. I can finish this bottle of Barolo and be perfectly safe.'

'That's what you said the other night, Tristan. Then you hit that dog.'

'Stupid mutt. It was its own fault. Maybe my brakes do need a bit of attention, but it shouldn't have been in the fucking road in the first place. And the bloody owner had the cheek to ask me to cover her vet's bills. I told the old bag where to stick it. Cost me two hundred quid to get the scratches out my paintwork. Now come on, you chaps, let's get a couple more bottles in.'

'He'll do,' she muttered to herself.

She followed Tristan when he finally staggered to the car park and watched him climb into a newish Fiat Abarth. Taking the number, she resolved to watch the pub car park regularly and follow him home. She would also invest in a handy device for copying the signal from electronic car keys. An idea formed in her mind, and she would have to look up some details on the internet. But, one way or another, Tristan would regret driving drunk.

No-one took any notice of the small figure, in the uniform of a well-known motoring organisation, tinkering with a Fiat Abarth at the back of The Lion's Mane car park. Tristan, sinking wine by the pint inside, had no idea what was happening to his pride and joy. It was only when he tried to drive home that he realised something was wrong. The engine didn't sound quite right and became noisier the further he went. A nasty smell developed, but Tristan's attention was focused on the odd noises coming from under the bonnet. He revved the engine hard, cursing, to clear people off a pedestrian crossing. There was a tremendous bang as the engine seized, carborundum powder in the oil system having finally done its work, and the car juddered to a halt. And, as he looked around him, bewildered and furious, the appalling stench from the dog turd placed on his hot engine block hit him with full force and he threw up on the leather upholstery.

Two minutes later, there was a tap on his windscreen.

'Having a bit of trouble, are we, sir?' asked the police officer. 'Would you mind giving me a breath sample, please?'

Tristan broke down and sobbed.

Chapter Eighty

Her success with Tristan thrilled her, and she scanned local newspapers and online media for suitable targets. They soon mounted up – the fraudster who conned pensioners out of their savings and whose expensive ball-point pen, ostensibly from an admirer, blew up in his hand; the wife-beating window cleaner whose ladder mysteriously collapsed and killed him; the neo-Nazi who entered the shed where he assembled petrol bombs, blown to bits when the propane cloud inside was ignited by a Christmas cracker snap, and the drug dealer who hung around the school gates, killed when his car heating system blew a cloud of fentanyl into his face. All these, and several others, were her own idea, and left her out of pocket, so she put a simple message on the dark web: 'Wrongs righted. Reasonable rates,' and waited for customers.

Hundreds of sinister, and frankly insane, people made contact with her, through her VPN, but she was taken by the story of a woman who claimed her husband had forced her into heroin addiction and abused their children. After she blew up his car, with him in it, she realised that she had been tricked by a gangster into killing his rival. She resolved to be more careful in future, but the man who said his wife had been killed in an explosion in Mexton seemed OK. She checked the press reports and confirmed his story, so she responded.

When her client explained that he was a senior police officer, that her activities had not gone unnoticed, and that there was a file on her at the National Crime Agency, she nearly fainted. But, instead of threatening her with arrest, he made her an offer she couldn't refuse. Burying her file and also paying her was too tempting, as long as she could manage to do the job without leaving traces and an electronic trail. She also believed it was morally justified, having read about the bombing. This was why she was taking on the Albanian OCG. Her only reservation was a minor one. She hated being referred to as Suzy Q. She much preferred the epithet she had chosen for herself: The Technician.

Chapter Eighty-One

Day 31, early

THE GREY-EYED MAN glared at the laptop screen as the Zoom session began.

'Give me a full report. Now.'

Twelve hundred miles away, in Musgrave Farmhouse, Fisnik Hasani trembled as he replied to his boss near Tirana.

'Nikolla was killed by the cops while dealing with a policeman. They killed a footsoldier, too. Three others were arrested taxing the shopkeeper. The snooker club was blown up. I don't know whether that was an accident or enemy action. Two operatives were arrested delivering product to that shitty housing estate when their car broke down and a nosy cop came along. Everything else is working fine. The brothels are producing income and the scamming is working well.'

'So that policeman is still alive. What about the others?'

'We shot up the bar the cops drink in and wounded two

of them. I don't know how it happened, but the computer guy got off. His partner escaped our operative's attempt. The drug guy spotted the bomb before he touched it.'

'So that's your idea of things working well, is it? It sounds like fucking incompetence to me.'

'I...I think it's bad luck. The police wouldn't blow up a building, and no-one is challenging us. The cops are harder to kill than we thought.'

'There is no such thing as bad luck. Only stupidity and uselessness. The only thing you've done right is blow up the police station, and that missed the main targets. Do you still have a source and ears there?'

'We did but he was arrested. We burned his house to stop him from talking. He managed to plant a bug, but we've only had one thing of use from it so far. They sweep for devices but they can't have found this one. We don't know much about what the police are doing, but I'm confident they haven't found the houses or the farm, because the bug picked up two cops talking about a disused office building, which they think is our base. They're planning to raid it in a few days' time.'

The grey-eyed man cursed in Albanian, then thought for a moment.

'I am coming to England. You will meet me at the airport and take me to the farmhouse. Make sure the key operatives are there. I will speak to them personally. I do not like travelling, so you realise the significance of my visit. Anyone who does not attend will be killed. Understand?'

'Yes. Yes, boss. Understood.'

The Zoom session ended before he finished speaking.

Fisnik sat quaking in the pool of urine that had collected on his chair. The man he feared most in the world was coming here, clearly to discipline those who had failed. Should he make a run for it? Pointless. He would be hunted down and killed. Should he plead for mercy? No, mercy was not in his boss's vocabulary. Perhaps he could spin things. Shift the blame onto others. He knew Nikolla didn't usually make mistakes, but could the footsoldier who died with him be made a scapegoat? That might work. And the failed attacks on the police? He would shoot someone and claim it was all their fault. Perhaps his boss would appreciate that sort of decisive action. Yes, that's what he would do. But first he needed a large drink, and then a shower.

Chapter Eighty-Two

18.00 hours

'FINAL BRIEFING, GUYS,' began Chief Inspector Gary Callaghan, Tactical Firearms Commander. 'You are Alpha Team and you will be doing a warrant on Musgrave Farmhouse, five miles along the Ryegate road, which, we believe, is the headquarters of the Albanian gang responsible for the bomb at Mexton nick as well as various other serious offences. We believe they have an AK-47 and a number of other firearms, so please be extremely careful. This is the location.'

He put a map up on the whiteboard, along with an aerial image.

'You will approach from the south and breach the security gate here.' He pointed with a laser. 'There's a security cabin just inside the gate, but it doesn't appear to be staffed outside working hours. You will need to cover the front and back entrances and the bird will be flying overhead with lights. The place has changed a bit since last year when, some of you may remember, there were three fatalities at the site, but the house is pretty much the same. Sergeant Carter is OFC and he will do the call out.'

'What vehicles do they have, boss?' asked an AFO.

'A large SUV is the main one, but there are two other, smaller, cars. If, by some mischance, a vehicle manages to leave the site they won't get past you going south. There will be a roadblock, and other area units, three miles up the road to the north. There are no side turnings between the two blockages, and gates and stone walls will stop anyone going cross country.'

'How many suspects are on site?' asked another officer.

'We expect about five or six. That's the usual number. Possibly a couple more. Anything else?'

No-one answered.

'OK. Try and get some rest. Assemble at four a.m.'

'Ladies and gentlemen, you are Beta Team and will be doing the warrant on Jubilee Terrace tomorrow morning.'

DI Chidgey addressed a group of uniformed and plain-clothed officers gathered in the incident room.

'You haven't been given the details before, in case anyone inadvertently lets slip our intentions. Please don't mention this operation to anyone.'

The officers shuffled feet, grinned or scowled, depending on their enthusiasm for the task.

'So, approximately half an hour after dawn, vehicles will block each end of the terrace. At our request, Open Reach will temporarily disconnect the broadband line. Armed officers will take up position in the lane behind the premises, and AFOs, with dogs, will breach the front door. At this point, any mobile phones we have detected on the premises will be rung with a message purporting to come from their service provider, claiming that the bills are unpaid. These messages will, of course, come from us and should prevent the suspects from telephoning their bosses and give us a few seconds advantage. Nobody, I repeat, nobody, is to enter the building until firearms declare it safe.'

'We wouldn't anyway,' muttered one PC.

Chidgey ignored him.

'There are three objectives. One is to apprehend the suspects, obviously. A second is to ensure the safety of the women being kept there. We will have support from the NCA to do this. The third is to seize any electronic devices and documents before the buggers wipe or destroy them. Feel free to unplug any computers you find, pull out leads and shut the lids of any laptops. Don't do anything else, as digital forensics will need to take a look at them.

'Here's an aerial view of the site and a map.' Chidgey pointed to the electronic whiteboard. 'Any questions?'

No-one answered.

'OK. Get some sleep, talk to no-one, and report back here at four o'clock. I'm off to talk to the Tactical Firearms Commander. Thank you.'

Chapter Eighty-Three

22.00 hours

THE GREY-EYED MAN stepped out of the hired limousine, glanced round at the site with obvious disdain and followed his driver/bodyguard into the farmhouse. Its occupants stood as he entered, visibly scared, and waited for him to speak.

'This has been a complete disaster,' he snarled. 'Is there any part of this operation that has worked properly?'

'The online scamming, sir,' ventured Altin Hoxha. 'It is making money. The women are earning too.'

The grey-eyed man glared at him.

'Is that all? For all the resources I have invested? Let me see. We have lost two operatives, a vehicle and a large amount of product because the idiots let their car break down in front of a cop. The Maldon Club blew up because some fool apparently left the gas on. You couldn't even tax a poxy Polish shopkeeper properly, and yet more of you got themselves arrested. None of the cops I particularly wanted dealt with are in jail or dead, and shooting up a bar where they drink was crude and ineffective. Nikolla was killed in an inept attempt to deal with the senior cop, and I hold you responsible for this. Are you stupid bastards fit for anything more complicated than stealing sweets from children?'

No-one in the room could meet his gaze.

'Are all of our operatives here?'

'All but two, boss,' replied Fisnik. 'They're watching the whores.'

'They should be here, but never mind. I will be talking to all of you, individually, to decide what to do next. I strongly advise you not to lie to me or pretend things are other than they are. Is that clear?'

Everyone nodded.

'I need food and drink. Luis,' he indicated the bodyguard, 'will be watching you. No-one is to leave. Put your mobile phones and weapons on the table. Do not attempt to communicate with anyone using computers. Anyone disobeying will be shot.'

Within a few minutes the table was laden with phones and a selection of firearms, as well as knives and a machete. When the grey-eyed man had eaten he summoned the first of his underlings to a side room and closed the door. The fear in those remaining was palpable.

23.30 hours

The Semtex had been the most difficult item to source. Yes, there were offers on the dark web, but some of them were so obviously traps set by one nation or another's security service that they were easily avoided. Eventually, she found the couple of kilos she needed, sent over the bitcoins and collected the explosive from a dog waste bin on Mexton Common. How it got there, she didn't enquire, but it had obviously entered the country undetected, since nobody was watching the bin, a fact she had ascertained by prolonged surveillance herself. After dropping the smelly consignment in a makeshift Faraday cage, in case it was bugged, she cycled back to the garage she had rented, cleaned it off and examined it thoroughly. It was fine.

The detonators she made herself. A forged Home Office licence, and a phoney company name, enabled her to purchase nitric acid, and she found a source of mercury in an antique shop miles from her home. The other materials she bought from a variety of sources, using several different credit cards, all in false names. The transmitters and triggering equipment she made from easily obtained electronic components, again bought from different places, and she was ready to go. The only problem was how, and where, to plant the devices.

Her client had told her that the gang's headquarters was the farmhouse, and she had watched it for several days. She realised that they would be most vulnerable in vehicles, rather than in the building, and decided to plant a device under the SUV that the gang habitually used. The arrival of the limo made her modify her plans, targeting two cars instead of one. It didn't matter. She had plenty of material and duplicate triggers.

She had spotted the CCTV when she first looked at the site, and had little difficulty in hacking into the system, freezing it on short loops depicting night-time tranquillity. As long as there wasn't a fox or a cat repeatedly walking across the same screen, like in *The Matrix,* she should be all right. Cutting through the fence with bolt-cutters was easy, and she crawled along the ground, her rucksack bumping uncomfortably on her back, until she reached the parking area. No-one appeared to be guarding the cars, and there were no security lights to reveal her presence. It took her three minutes, in total, to clamp a device to the underside of each vehicle, put in place the detonators and triggers, and rub some mud on the casings in case anyone caught a glimpse of her handiwork.

By the time she had shimmied back to her entry point, her pulse rate had dropped from 180 to a more acceptable 150 and the pounding in her chest had abated somewhat. She pulled the cut section of fence back into place and walked slowly back to her car with a feeling of exultation. It was the first time she'd done such a dangerous job, and she felt proud of herself. Once back in her car, she unjammed the security cameras and drove back to her garage. All she had to do now was wait for her moment. She poured herself some strong coffee from a flask, bit into a bar of chocolate and glued her eyes to the screen that carried the feed from the drone she had hovering above the farmhouse. As soon as she saw them moving, she would strike.

Chapter Eighty-Four

Day 32, 04.00 hours

THE GREY-EYED MAN summoned everyone into the kitchen.

'Thanks to your gross incompetence, we are withdrawing from this stupid little town for the time being. Most of you will accompany me back to Tirana and I will find something useful for you to do.'

He read out a list of names and ordered those mentioned to wait by the vehicles outside.

'The rest of you, I have no further use for. Luis!'

Before they could register what was happening, Luis shot all three remaining men in the head. He collected the firearms in a large plastic bag, took them out to the limousine and then returned to make preparations for the destruction of the farmhouse. Two hours later, the two vehicles drove out of the gate and headed for the airport, where a private jet was waiting.

05.45 hours

The dawn chorus began as the first police officers arrived at Jubilee Terrace. Two robins, in adjacent scrawny trees, competed vocally for territory, attracting the attention of a crepuscular cat in search of an early morning mouse. None of these took any notice of the vehicles that crept along the road, with their lights off and their engines barely turning over.

Dark shapes in body armour, carrying carbines, emerged from a black van, accompanied by a firearms dog on a lead. On a signal from Sergeant Flora Morris, the Operational Firearms Commander, the lead officer smashed open the door with the Big Door Key and his colleague let the dog loose.

'Armed police,' shouted Morris, through a megaphone. 'Come to the door with your hands on your heads. Leave any weapons behind. Do exactly as you are told by the officers who are waiting.'

There was a silence, and then two bleary-eyed men shuffled out of the house with their hands on their heads. They were quickly cuffed and locked in the back of a police van. When the dog returned, apparently unconcerned about the contents of the house, AFOs went in and, in a short time, pronounced the premises free of weapons.

Mel and Martin entered, accompanied by DS Naomi Wells, from the NCA Modern Slavery and Human Trafficking Unit. The smell of mould and decay was overpowering, and the damp stains and peeling paper on the walls presented a dismal vista. Something unidentified stuck to their feet as they climbed the uncarpeted stairs. Sounds of sobbing led them to an uncarpeted corridor where, it was clear, the original four rooms had been crudely subdivided. All eight doors were padlocked, with the keys left in place, so Mel and Naomi had no trouble in unlocking them and releasing the women held within. Most cowered away, expecting more abuse, until Naomi spoke soothingly. The words might not have mattered, and probably weren't understood anyway, but it was the tone that counted.

Each room contained a cheap bed with filthy sheets, a table with a basin of grey, mucky water, and a waste bin full of used condoms. The latrine buckets stank. One of the women spoke English and explained that they had been locked in all the previous day and night, with no food or water, and no punters had visited since the night before. Everyone, apart from the two minders, had departed, in a hurry, about eight hours ago.

Mel left Martin and Naomi looking after the women and explored the rest of the floor. A narrow stairway led up to an attic room, and there she found the hacker's den. A cable dangled from the broadband router and there were various leads scattered over the floor. Any computers that had been there had obviously been removed.

'Shit,' she muttered, and reached for her phone, dialling the DI.

'They've done a flit, guv. They left the women, with a couple of goons minding them, but there's no IT here. Did they know we were coming?'

'I doubt it, Mel,' Chidgey replied. 'The op was as tight as an otter's fundament. Perhaps they had another reason for leaving. I suppose it makes some sense to keep moving around, but they've made quite a substantial investment in that place. It does seem odd. Mind you, an expensive hired limo arrived at the farm last night. We couldn't identify the buggers getting out, but maybe there's some kind of meeting going on. We'll find out shortly, I expect.'

'If it's all right by you, guv, we'll leave a couple of uniforms guarding the place until SOCOs arrive. Naomi is getting the women into a minibus for a trip to the hospital and a check-up. Then we can talk to them, with interpreters. They're in a pretty poor state. I can't imagine what a squalid tip like this had to offer punters in the form of horizontal refreshment, but I suspect it was pretty nasty.'

'OK, Mel. I'll warn Alpha Team to look out for more suspects than they'd anticipated, and I'll keep the DSup in the loop. We have one bit of intel from Interpol that may be useful. A fifty-year old male, believed to be high up in Okta-pod, was recently spotted at Tirana airport. Albanian police are trying to find out which flight he took, but it's possible he's headed here, given that we've just arrested some of his thugs and killed a couple of others. We're looking out for him, but unfortunately, we don't have a decent picture. He could be at the farmhouse.'

Chapter Eighty-Five

06.00 hours

The Technician jerked into full alertness. She had let her attention drift. Despite the coffee, the aftermath of her commando exploit had left her drowsy and she nearly missed the gate opening and the two vehicles leaving. She reached for her transmitter and did a quick sweep with her drone to check that no other drivers were nearby. She nearly dropped it when she spotted the convoy of police vehicles heading towards the site.

'Fuck!' she shouted. She couldn't abort the mission but she couldn't put the police at risk either. There was only one thing to do, even if it meant breaking her cover. She picked up a burner phone and dialled a direct number for Mexton police.

'Control Room. PCSO McGuire. How can I help?'

'Put me through to the officer running the raid on Musgrave Farmhouse,' she snapped. 'It's life or death.'

'Sorry, madam. I don't know what you're talking about.'

'I don't believe you. Your colleagues are about to stop two vehicles on the Ryegate road. They have bombs attached. Repeat, they have bombs attached. Tell the officers to stand back.'

'And how do you know this, madam?'

'Because I fucking put them there.'

'You do realise that there are serious penalties for uttering a false bomb threat.'

'OK, you bloody idiot. Tell them that the person who blew up the Maldon Club is on the line and trying to save the lives of police officers.'

There was a few seconds silence and the line clicked.

'Chief Inspector Callaghan. Who are you?'

'Someone on your side, believe it or not. Tell your team to stay at least a hundred metres from the two vehicles. They will explode in a few seconds and I don't want innocent lives on my conscience.'

'Are you mad?'

'No, just doing a job. Now do as I say or you'll regret it.'

She hung up, wondering if she'd let too much slip, and removed the sim card from her phone, smashing both objects into tiny pieces. Then she watched the drone images, waiting for a chance to act.

Chapter Eighty-Six

Adrenaline and testosterone permeated the two armed response vehicles approaching Musgrave Farm. The best type of firearms operation was one where no shots were fired and no-one was hurt, but each officer knew that bloodshed was highly possible. And that some of that blood could be theirs. Sergeant Carter, veteran of numerous operations, a few of which had turned nasty, was calmer than the others, but he still felt a degree of apprehension.

Three miles from the target, his radio crackled. It was Callaghan.

'Terry, the surveillance camera's picked up two vehicles leaving the site, heading north. Pull them over when they get close to the roadblock and be prepared for a hard stop if necessary. Leave one of the vans at the farm in case there's anyone still there.'

'Understood, boss.'

Carter relayed the change of plan to his team and the

convoy accelerated. As the target vehicles came in sight they, too, sped up.

'Shit, they've seen us,' swore Carter, increasing his speed and closing the gap to about fifty metres.

Callaghan came on the radio again, his voice panicky.

'Drop back, Terry. Drop back. IEDs on board. Get back, for fuck's sake.'

Carter braked and the ARV behind nearly rear-ended him. He looked in horror as, a hundred and twenty metres down the road, the two vehicles simultaneously turned into fireballs with thunderous explosions. Chunks of metal and windscreen were hurled into the air and various unidentified bits of Albanian gangster followed them. An AK-47 was ejected with such force that its barrel embedded itself in a wooden sign that invited passers-by to pick their own strawberries. Smaller pieces of shrapnel rained down on the police vehicles, scratching the paintwork but doing little damage. And at the site of the explosions there were no signs of life whatsoever.

Back at the farmhouse, the small fire that had been set in the utility room before most of the occupants left met the cloud of Calor gas pouring from the cooker. The explosion, small by most standards, was sufficient to blow out a few windows, but the fire that ensued was quite enough to turn most of the building into a shell, despite the efforts of the fire service, summoned by the AFOs waiting in the drive. It was late in the day before fire investigators were able to enter the premises, and they were shocked to find three bodies, in the pugilist position of the badly burned, in what used to be the lounge. The attending pathologist observed that they appeared to have been shot through the head before the fire reached them.

The Technician recalled the drone, switched off the transmitter and loaded what was left of her equipment into her van. Breaking cover like that was risky, but she couldn't have the deaths of police officers on her conscience. Her client would have been appalled if his colleagues had been harmed. She didn't think she could be identified, but she would have to destroy a good deal of useful equipment. Still, the replacement costs would go on her final bill. She would have to keep things quiet for a while, and certainly take on no more commissions. A pity, but at least this one, her most complex yet, had ended successfully.

Anything that could identify her went in the van, which she would torch somewhere, far from Mexton, after personal essentials had been removed. She contemplated treating the garage with chemicals to remove DNA, but realised that doing so could well attract attention. Instead, she propped the door open when she left, knowing that it would almost inevitably be occupied by some of Mexton's rough sleepers. It would certainly offer more protection from the elements than a shop doorway. Within days, any DNA she might have left would be swamped by that from the garage's new residents and their dogs. By that time, she would be back in Cheltenham, carrying on with her day job and extolling the virtues of camping and walking in the Lake District.

Chapter Eighty-Seven

Day 33

'So WHO DO we think is responsible for this shitshow?' asked DI Chidgey, rhetorically, when he had called the team together, the afternoon after the raids. 'We have six individuals, scattered over the countryside, two from the limo and four from the SUV, a burned-out farmhouse with three shot bodies in it and an almost empty knocking shop. And do we have any suspects in custody? Yes. Two. Low-level thugs who, even if they did know anything about what was going on, are saying nothing. Not a lot for a night's work, is it?'

'Come on, guv,' said Jack, 'it's nobody's fault, least of all ours. We couldn't know gang warfare would break out just as we were going to nick them.'

'I'm not so sure it was another gang, Jack,' said Mel. 'If it was another OCG, they wouldn't give a shit about blowing up a few coppers. Whoever was behind the explosion deliberately warned the AFOs to stand back and told them about the bombs. It was a woman, who also claimed she blew up the Maldon Club.'

'So, what are you thinking?' asked the DI. 'A hit woman? Hired by another gang? Or someone else?'

'I'm not thinking anything at the moment, guv, but maybe a session in the Cat and Cushion would be helpful. We still don't know everything about the farmhouse and why those people were shot. When will we know who they, and the bomb victims, were?'

'You may be right about meeting in the pub, Mel,' smiled Chidgey. 'I always found that a couple of pints of cider lubricate the brain.'

'Perhaps a bit too much,' muttered Martin.

'Anyway,' the DI continued, 'it will be several days before we can identify the OCG members. If their DNA is on record somewhere, we should be able to put names to remains, once the SOCOs and the lab folks have done their jobs. We'll meet up for a briefing on Tuesday, by which time we should know who those bastards were. The DCI should be back, and we'll adjourn to the alehouse when appropriate. Now, I'm sure you've all got plenty to do. Paperwork never sleeps. Off you go.'

Addy caught up with the DI as he returned to his office.

'Can I have a word, please, guv?'

'Of course. What's on your mind?'

'I'd like to go for firearms training and I wondered if you would put in a recommendation for me.'

Chidgey thought for a moment.

'Of course I will. But why do you want this? By all accounts you have the makings of an excellent detective.'

'In the past couple of years, I've been shot at twice. I want to help get armed villains off the streets. I think I'd prefer to be in a position where I can shoot back.'

'I'm not sure that's the best motivation for joining an ARU. What does your wife – Victoria, isn't it – think about the idea?'

'She'll support me. I don't think she'll be any more worried than she is at the moment. At least I'd have protective gear when on duty.'

'OK. I'll talk to Sergeant Carter. He'll arrange for you to spend an hour at the range and get a feel for weapons. If he thinks you'll be OK, I'll recommend you. You'll need a full psychological evaluation and thorough training, of course. Carrying a firearm brings with it an awful responsibility. I know. I did it for a while, though I never actually killed anyone. But if that's what you want, I'm happy to support you.'

'Thanks, guv. Much appreciated.'

Chapter Eighty-Eight

Day 37

Motivation, motivation. That was the key, thought Mel, still racking her brains over the attacks on the OCG. Could another gang be trying to displace the Albanians? Unlikely, as these attacks were so sophisticated. Anyway, the NCA had heard nothing about a rival operation trying to move into the area. She had checked.

If it wasn't a gang behind the explosions, and the Maldon Club attack, who could it be? And what would be their motive for taking out the Albanian OCG? Could there even be a link between the car bombs and the SUV full of drugs that mysteriously stalled on the access road to the Eastside? If so, it looked like a carefully planned campaign to disrupt the OCG's activities.

If it wasn't for financial gain, or territory, it had to be something personal. Hatred. Revenge, perhaps. The OCG had obviously pissed off people during their operations, but surely not to this extent. Unless...People bereaved or injured by the bomb, or the shooting in the pub, would have plenty of motive, but most were law-abiding citizens, unlikely to commission murders. And how would they find out the contact details for whoever did this? How would they pay them? How would they direct them to the targets?

The list of people who hated the gang would run into several pages, but not many of them would have the determination, and disregard for the law, to resort to murder. Maybe they didn't do it themselves. A particular set of skills would be needed, so perhaps they engaged an outside contractor. But this was getting into *Killing Eve* territory. Sheer nonsense. Still, paid assassins did exist, and whoever was involved clearly had excellent technical skills. This wasn't a back-street thug paid to take someone out with a sawn-off. So, who could want the Albanians destroyed so badly that they would engage a hit woman, at considerable expense, conspire to murder and risk exposure and a long prison sentence?

She walked over to the whiteboard that bore the names of those killed in the bombing. Some of the officers she knew. Their families would never have engaged an assassin and wouldn't even have known where to find one. She ran quick checks on the others, and nothing came up to raise her suspicions. She looked at civilian casualties: the man shot in the pub, the pedestrian and the cyclist killed outside the station. And what about those maimed by the blast, rather than killed outright? Then something swam into focus. A name she had seen on a briefing. Oh fuck, she thought. Oh absolute sodding fuck. She knew. And what the hell should she do with that knowledge?

The final briefing for Operation Fieldmouse was held in the afternoon, so that the team could adjourn to the pub as arranged.

'We've had some results from forensics,' began DI Chidgey. 'The fire in the farmhouse was started deliberately, presumably to cover the OCG's tracks. The three men found shot were low-level criminals whose DNA we identified through Interpol and the Albanian police. Of the individuals killed in the vehicles, we have been able to identify four. One was Gezim Kristo, the bomb expert who we suspected was in the country, and almost certainly made the device that killed our colleagues, as well as the others we found. His DNA was recovered from the device planted on DS Palmer's doorstep.'

Quiet cheers and murmurs of satisfaction ran round the room.

'Another was Altin Hoxha, a prolific hacker, and we presume he was behind the computer scams and also the attempt to set up Tom Ferris.'

More satisfied noises.

'A third was a known thug and enforcer, Luis Gjoka. A pistol was found on him and a test round matched the bullets in the corpses in the farmhouse. As to the fourth, Interpol nearly wet their collective knickers when we identified him. Erjon Dervishi. He has long been suspected of being a major figure in Oktapod, if not its leader, but there has never been sufficient evidence, or enough incorruptible officials, to arrest him. Now, I know we don't condone murder, but the planet is certainly better off without the likes of him.'

'Too right,' muttered Trevor, his arm no longer in a sling.

'There is something else,' interjected DCI Farlowe, largely recovered from his injuries, who had just entered the room.

'We have no idea who is behind these killings, and the other stunts that are linked. The NCA reports no knowledge of a hit woman operating in the UK, and it is clearly not the province of MI5. Whoever set them up clearly has specialist knowledge of our operations, or was able to obtain it, as well as contacts and sufficient funds. We will be putting together a small team, in conjunction with other agencies, to find out who the assassin is and who employed them. I will be looking for volunteers. Now, it's been a stressful time for all of you, so please go off to the pub. I've given DI Chidgey some money for drinks and I hope to join you later.'

Murmurs of appreciation greeted this announcement and the team prepared to leave. Mel hung back and asked to speak to the DCI before he returned to his office.

'What is it, Mel? Something worrying you?'

Mel replied, awkwardly, 'Yes, guv. I have a very good idea who commissioned the attacks on the OCG. He had a very strong motive, the necessary sources of information and, I believe, access to funds. He is one of ours, I'm afraid. I've written his name on a piece of paper in this envelope. I will leave it to you to decide what to do with it.'

Mel turned away and headed for the door, leaving a

frowning DCI, whose gaze flicked occasionally towards the shredder as he turned the envelope over and over in his hands. He called to her just before she left.

'What if he gets away with it, Detective Constable?'

'Frankly, sir, I don't give a shit.'

Epilogue

Nicola Fearon was given two life sentences for killing her father and uncle, as well as concurrent, shorter, sentences for her other offences. Grenville Fearon was jailed for life for killing Alan and was also sentenced for perverting the course of justice and burying Alan's body. Davvi Fearon was jailed for five years for perverting the course of justice, concurrent with a two year sentence for the illegal burial.

The Albanians captured while extorting money from Stefan Paweski received jail sentences, as did the two men arrested at the brothel in Jubilee Terrace. The rescued women were helped to return to their native countries, after medical treatment and interviews with NCA specialists. No charges were ever brought relating to the bombing of the police station.

The material found in Vernon Chawte's encrypted files provided a wealth of useful information on the activities of the OCG in Britain and Europe, including the location of bank accounts and other properties. It took Interpol seven months to process it all, and its member police forces made over a hundred arrests.

Abas Sayyid was jailed for life, but subsequently provided information on the people who had brought him to England, linking them to another of Oktapod's tentacles.

The CPS decided it would not be in the public interest to prosecute Gary Bristow.

DI Chidgey stayed with Mexton CID for a few more months until he retired, in a much happier state than when he was first seconded. Emma Thorpe gave birth to a baby girl, Genevieve Lily, and returned to work, part-time, once her maternity leave ended.

Tom returned to work and was eventually fitted with a prosthetic hand. He and Mel were married shortly afterwards.

Sally Erskine passed the detective's course and joined CID permanently.

Martin Rowse left the police and joined Mexton Investigations, who welcomed him with open arms.

Addy was accepted for firearms training and joined an ARU.

The Argus Collective was never traced.

The remains of a young girl, approximately twelve years old, were found buried at Musgrave Farm, along with the bodies of two adult males. She was never identified, but the males were found to be former members of a rival gang.

Attempts to track down whoever launched the attacks on the OCG proved fruitless and the person who commissioned them was never brought to trial.

Glossary of Police Terms

AFO: Authorised Firearms Officer
ANPR: Automatic Number Plate Recognition (camera)
APT: Anatomical Pathology Technologist
ARU: Armed Response Unit
ARV: Armed Response Vehicle
Carbine: Short-barrelled rifle used by AFOs
CEOP: Child Exploitation and Online Protection Centre
CHIS: Covert Human Intelligence Source
CPS: Crown Prosecution Service
DBS: Disclosure and Barring Service
Directed surveillance: planned, covert observation of somebody (*see* RIPA)
DVLA: Driver and Vehicle Licensing Agency
DWP: Department for Work and Pensions
HMRC: His Majesty's Revenue and Customs
HOLMES2: Home Office Large Major Enquiry System – national police IT system for investigating major crimes
IOPC: Independent Office for Police Conduct

Met (the): Metropolitan Police Service
NABIS: National Ballistics Intelligence Service
NCA: National Crime Agency
OCG: Organised Crime Group
OFC: Operational Firearms Commander
PACE: Police and Criminal Evidence Act 1984
PNC: Police National Computer
PSNI: Police Service of Northern Ireland
QGM: Queen's Gallantry Medal
RIPA: Regulation of Investigatory Powers Act
RTC: road traffic collision
SHO: Senior House Officer (doctor)
SOCO: Scene Of Crime Officer (aka CSI)
SO15: Counter-Terrorism Command
TIE: Trace, Interview, Eliminate (possible suspects)
Tor: the onion router – a gateway to the dark web
Twocking: Taking (a vehicle) Without the Owner's Consent
VIN: Vehicle Identification Number
VPN: Virtual Private Network – a means of using the internet with little chance of being traced

Acknowledgments

Firstly, my thanks are due to my wife Jen. If it were not for her, I wouldn't be a crime writer. Her expertise at turning my drafts into submittable manuscripts is beyond price.

I must also thank Rebecca and Adrian, the lovely people at Hobeck, for continuing to publish my books, Sue Davison, for her meticulous editing, and Jayne Mapp for another excellent cover.

As ever, Graham Bartlett (https://policeadvisor.co.uk/) provided essential advice on police procedure. Read his books!

Lisa Cutts, another author and former police officer, explained how the police deal with legal privilege on the death of a solicitor, and fellow Hobeck author Kerena Swan provided insights into social work and the placement of children at risk. Dr Mike Leonard very helpfully explained the effects of acute infection and sepsis.

Any mistakes are, of course, my own.

Finally, my gratitude goes out to all the bloggers and reviewers who have said nice things about my books and those written by my fellow Hobeck authors. You provide an invaluable service to writers published by independent publishers. Thank you!

You can find out more about my books, and subscribe to

my newsletter, via my website www.brianpriceauthor.co.uk. I'm also on Facebook and Instagram.

The Mel Cotton Crime Series

Fatal Trade

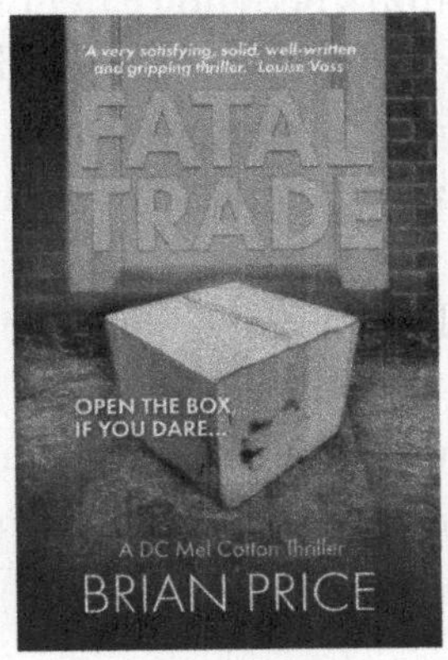

'A very satisfying, solid, well-written and gripping thriller.' LOUISE VOSS

'A fast-paced edge-of-your-seat thriller from a

major new talent. Gripping stuff!'
DAVID MARK

Glasgow, 1999

Reaching the point of no return, Martina is ready to make her move. After years of being the victim, it's now time to turn the tables.

Mexton, 2019

The small grey-haired woman grimaced as she entered the police station, dragging a tartan shopping trolley containing her husband's head.

'What are you useless buggers going to do about this?'

DC Melanie Cotton's fledgling career is about to take an interesting turn. Freshly promoted to CID, Mel is excited by this disturbing and mysterious case – her first murder investigation as a detective.

She's determined to make her mark.

But as she discovers, there's far more to this case than a gruesome killing, and Mel's skills and courage are about to tested to the limit.

Fatal Hate

'This is high quality crime writing. Recommended.' M. W. CRAVEN

'I dare you to try to put it down.' GRAHAM BARTLETT

DC Mel Cotton is back with a brand new case, the murder of Duncan Bennett. But who would want an unassuming warehouse worker dead.

The case soon becomes far more complex and dangerous, with terrorists, a paedophile network and a hitman in town. And against a background of rising hatred and violence, one woman pursues her deadly revenge.

Mel and her colleagues face their greatest challenge yet.

Mel's own courage will be tested to the limits. No-one is safe.

Fatal Dose

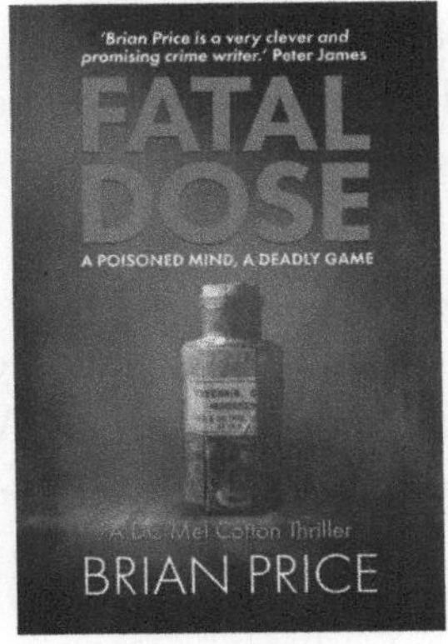

'Brian Price is a very clever and promising crime writer.' PETER JAMES

'Superb!' GRAHAM BARTLETT

'Another highly intelligent cop thriller from Price. Written with huge authority and deeply compelling.' PAUL FINCH

'A true must-read writer.' DAVID MARK

Death stalks Mexton
When a spate of poisonings hits the town of Mexton, DC Mel Cotton and her colleagues are left perplexed. All the deaths seem to be ingeniously planned and the police cannot see anything obvious to connect the victims.

Is a vigilante at work?

Jenny Pike, reporter for the Mexton Messenger, seems to think there's a link and she's not afraid to publish her controversial theories. All the victims seem to have got away with harming people in some way. Is that the connection?

Fear from the East

Already stretched to the limit, Mel and her colleagues also face another huge challenge. A ruthless Albanian gang has launched a crime wave in the area and someone has murdered a notorious blackmailer.

How will the team cope? With a serial poisoner at large, is anyone safe?

Hobeck Books – the home of great stories

We hope you've enjoyed reading this novel by Brian Price. To keep up to date on Brian's fiction writing please subscribe to his website: **www.brianpriceauthor.co.uk**.

Hobeck Books offers a number of short stories and novellas, including *Fatal Beginnings* by Brian Price, free for subscribers in the compilation *Crime Bites*.

- *Echo Rock* by Robert Daws
- *Old Dogs, Old Tricks* by AB Morgan
- *The Silence of the Rabbit* by Wendy Turbin
- *Never Mind the Baubles: An Anthology of Twisted Winter Tales* by the Hobeck Team (including many of the Hobeck authors and Hobeck's two publishers)
- *The Clarice Cliff Vase* by Linda Huber
- *Here She Lies* by Kerena Swan
- *The Macnab Principle* by R.D. Nixon
- *Fatal Beginnings* by Brian Price
- *A Defining Moment* by Lin Le Versha
- *Saviour* by Jennie Ensor
- *You Can't Trust Anyone These Days* by Maureen Myant

Also please visit the Hobeck Books website for details of our other superb authors and their books, and if you would like to get in touch, we would love to hear from you.

Hobeck Books also presents a weekly podcast, the Hobcast, where founders Adrian Hobart and Rebecca Collins discuss all things book related, key issues from each week, including the ups and downs of running a creative business. Each episode includes an interview with one of the people who make Hobeck possible: the editors, the authors, the cover designers. These are the people who help Hobeck bring great stories to life. Without them, Hobeck wouldn't exist. The Hobcast can be listened to from all the usual platforms but it can also be found on the Hobeck website: **www.hobeck.net/hobcast**.

Other Hobeck Books to Explore

I'm Not There by Rob Gittins

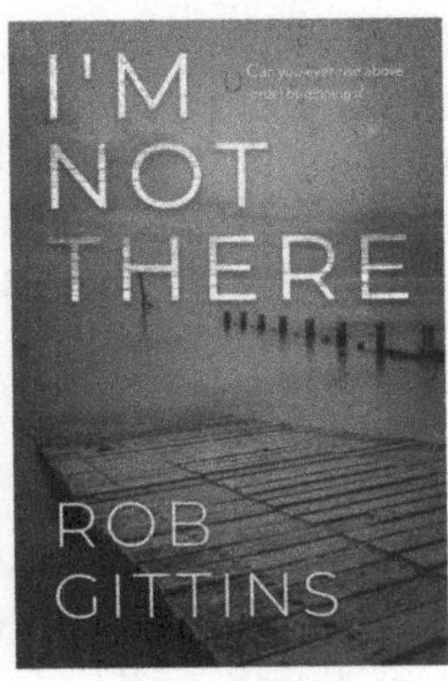

'Everything is cleverly brought together in a thrilling climax.' Sarah Leck

'It has the feel of one of those books that gets a plug and takes off to be a top ten bestseller.' Pete Fleming

'Dark, gritty, well-crafted characters and some gut-punching shocks, first rate crime writing'. Alex Jones

Two sisters abandoned
It was a treat, she said. An adventure. A train journey to the mainland. Six-year-old Lara Arden and her older sister Georgia happily fill in their colouring books as their mum pops to the buffet in search of crisps. She never returns. Two little girls abandoned. Alone.

Present day
Twenty years later, and Lara is now a detective inspector on her native Isle of Wight, still searching for answers to her mother's disappearance.

A call comes in. A small child, a boy, has been left abandoned on a train. Like Lara, he has no relatives to look after him. It feels as if history is being repeated – but surely this is a coincidence?

A series of murders
Before Lara can focus on the boy's plight, she's faced with a series of murders. They feature different victims in very different circumstances, but they all have one thing in common: they all leave children – alone – behind.

So who is targeting Lara? What do these abandoned souls

have in common? And how does this connect to the mystery of Lara's missing mother?

Catch as Catch Can by Malcolm Hollingdrake

'Sucked me right in.' Julia Corri

'I love words and this author is a master of them painting a picture you can fall right into.' Lynda Checkley

'A superb, rollercoaster of an opener. Another must buy series.' Ian Cleverdon

A mutilated body apparently washed up on a windswept beach…

A violent criminal gang preys on moped riders across the area…

A teenage girl is desperate to escape sexual exploitation...

It's a tough introduction to Merseyside for Detective Inspector April Decent, who's just arrived from her native Yorkshire. Together with new colleague Skeeter Warlock, Decent quickly discovers there's a sinister link between them all, one that will bring them face-to-face with some uncomfortable home truths.

Seventh by Lewis Hastings

'This takes thriller to a new meaning.' Handbag Lover

'A very clever novel.' S. Baker Smith

'Excellent read.' D. Scott

Friends and enemies call him the 'Jackdaw'
Alexandru Stefanescu is a man to fear. Known as the Jack-

daw, he's a savage and merciless sociopath, who's become Europe's most powerful criminal. No one who encounters him escapes unscathed.

He's Europe's most-wanted man

Former British cop John 'Jack' Cade still bears the scars of battling the Jackdaw a decade ago. Hopes of a peaceful new life in New Zealand are shattered after an apparently chance meeting with a beautiful young woman. Cade is immediately forced to face an enemy he hoped he'd never have to deal with again.

Now he's ready to unleash the full power of the 'Seventh Wave'

Elena Petrov has all a young woman could want. Beauty. An education. Money. But she's on the run from her past – and her family. Can she find safety in New Zealand? Is Jack Cade the man to protect her?

Milton Keynes UK
Ingram Content Group UK Ltd.
UKHW041911290923
429624UK00004B/110

9 781915 817242

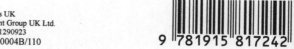